LITTLE MOBILE HOME ON THE TUNDRA

Interrupting Generational Dysfunction

By

T.D. FLENAUGH

WriterTai LLC
Los Angeles, CA

Dedication

This novel is dedicated to my family

Nia Atlas, my beloved daughter. Allen Fowler, my husband.

Nashall Knight, Tanitra Flenaugh Scorza, and Jerry Knight, my siblings.

David Flenaugh, my father. Davida Flenaugh, my mother.

DeAngela Thurman, Gary Fisher, Tamara Fisher, and Johnny Thurman, my cousin-siblings.

Nilotus Alexander, Mahogany Davis, Ahdaecha Mishulette Ross, Ebony Davis, Brandy Alexander, & Rashida Munson, the First Church girls.

This novel is made possible by my gifted writing teachers, talented writing partners, and the wisdom of my advisors throughout my many years of development.

Ruth Nelson, my fourth grade teacher

Ms. Coerr, my third grade teacher

George Beu, my second grade teacher

Natalie Byler, my twelfth grade English teacher

Robin Streichler, my writing advisor

Rita Williams, my thesis advisor

Elizabeth Inglese

Sarah Lowe

Nicole Antonio

Niree Perian

Amy Silverberg

Joy Hartnett

Jemila Pratt

Alice Unger

Vernis Ross

Sara Aiello

Acknowledgements

I want to thank so many people for being a support in my life. The following people have supported this book's publication and bolstered me during different stages of the book's development.

Tanisha Clark

Phillip Cotton

Talia Collier

Marlena Harris

Eno Attah

Maryl Kruger

Sharyn Clark

Wanda Lee Florestine

Marivell Arayasirikul

Chidimma Obioha

Tauanja Kittrell

Jamila Jackson

Charmaine Gilmore

Victoria Chan

Pamela Wright

LaTonja Muhammad

Faiza Makhani

Martin Pratt

Donna English

Jasmine Zapata

Mora Pressley

Chris Liberatori

Laurie Kurnick

Charles Holmes

Jessica Bain

Travonne Dixon

Lauren Moseley

Leon Baker Jr.

Kwame Avery

Sukuma Avery

Ebony Jackson

Tina Ramsay

MarieAlise Recasner de Marco

Dylan Farris

David Berry

Quanetta Hayden

Jeannie Armstrong

Iyaunna Towery

Ayana Boze

Deondra Smith

Table of Contents

Dedication 3

Acknowledgements 4

Prologue 9

PART I: THE BLUEPRINTS

Dreams in the Midnight Sun 11

Belonging 14

Breaking Ground 18

Meeting the Workers 20

Where We Came From 24

Journey to the Midnight Sun.... 30

New Beginnings 32

The First Apartment 34

Reading Lessons..................... 38

Meeting Damon 40

New Daddy 42

The Wedding......................... 44

The Slopes............................. 48

First Church 49

Daddy's Home 55

Our Own Land 61

Soccer Happiness 71

The Shop 75

Normal.................................. 78

Keenan, the Popular Kid 80

Mama's Job 82

Smarter.................................. 84

Sunday Rituals 86

Life on the Tundra.................. 88

When the Water Froze 91

The Bus Incident 96

The Punishment 98

Under a Microscope 100

Mama's Anger...................... 102

Locked Away 104

Family Battle....................... 108

The Hotel 112

PART II: WITHOUT MAMA

The Empty Space 116
Planning the Garden 118
Growth............................ 120
Church Acquaintances 122
Reality Check.................... 125
Cleaning Up 127
The Harvest...................... 130
Children's Church 131
Same Old, Same Old............ 133
The Dogs 135
Tutoring 137
Ticasuk Brown 139
Mrs. Neil's Class................ 142
Not an Adult..................... 146
Helping Mrs. Neil 148
Water Still Freezes 150
Learning More About Racism 153
Promises, Promises 156
The Testimony................... 166

Trying to Be Normal............ 175
Boiling Mad 176
The Bills.......................... 179
The Heater 180
Personal Hygiene................. 183
Holy Water 185
Moose Sighting 188
The Camper 190
Writing About It 193
Weekend at Aunt Denise's 195
The Short Bus 196
The Monstrosity 199
Return to Civilization? 200
Parent Conference with Daddy 203
Asking Aunt Denise 205
Crisis Call 207
The Return 210
Good Again....................... 212

PART III: TEENS

High School Life................. 217
Church Teachings 221
Near Grown 227
Snow and Soccer 232
Honors Classes................... 239

Midway Man 241
Boys Are Bad 243
Another Perspective 247
Pants 251
Late Night Talks 253

A Date? 254

Breaking Point 256

Getting Out 258

New Beginnings 264

A Real Home 266

Watch Night Service 268

Instead of Dating 274

Keenan's Graduation 277

The Job 279

Teenage Realities 281

The Gun 283

Dinner after the Movies 285

Preparation 287

Elimination 289

The Blame 292

Learning to Heal 295

Last Church 296

Brother's Dreams 298

PART IV: RECONCILIATION

Literacy for Healing 300

When the Test is Error Proof .. 304

Killing Myself 306

Another Phone Call 308

Talking to Daddy 314

Finding Peace Together 317

A Promising Future 320

My Graduation 323

Epilogue: The Cycle 325

PROLOGUE

I grew up with this book. At age nineteen, I began writing it while pregnant with my own child. The story needed to be told, but I didn't know how to tell it.

I began writing this story estranged from my parents. Now I am close with both my mother and father because we made a choice to heal together. They opened themselves to listening to a daughter who had cursed them out—each separately—who had moved out, and who couldn't express her feelings coherently.

The accompanying journal, *Breaking the Cycle*, serves as a guide to navigate your own cycles of trauma as you reflect on Tawny and Keenan's journey.

Many people want healing, but they do not know where to start or where to go. We often look outside of ourselves for healing, thinking that someone will deliver the answers. Processing my trauma through therapy and the individual work of self-reflection, reading, prayer, writing, and discipline brought about transformation. Much of the work takes place alone. Healing is born through determination, sweat equity, and time.

I birthed this book for liberation—for my own and yours. This novel summons the ancestors. It resurrects the hurt so that it can bring forth ascension. Read this novel for self-determination, for the legacy of your ancestors, for the glory of your descendants.

PART I:
THE BLUEPRINTS

Dreams in the Midnight Sun

May of 3rd Grade, Age 9

Daddy scooped me into his arms and carried me to the forest behind our mobile home. 'Let's go, you ol' silly girl!' Just me and Daddy: he carried me toward the woods behind our place. Almost seven o'clock, meant four more hours of day. The sun wouldn't set until after eleven. A stand of spindly birch, spruce, and aspen grew over tall weeds and willow bushes on the forest floor. Swallowtails and western white butterflies landed on dandelions momentarily, then flew away.

My father set me on the ground. The mosquitoes flew around me, buzzing into my bare shoulders and the back of my knees. I kept fidgeting to keep the bugs from settling and biting me.

Daddy swept his arms like the wings of a low-flying crow. "We're going to clear the woods from that spruce"—he pointed about a hundred feet to the north—"to that tangle of aspen." Speaking simply, so I'd understand, he said, "Since our mobile home doesn't have a foundation, that's the first thing."

He explained that a foundation is the bottom of a house. The green tin siding matched its constant smell of mildew. Instead of a foundation, tin surrounded the bottom of the house, called a skirt, that hid the wheels and the crawlspace under our home.

Daddy dragged his foot to mark a line in the dirt where the humongous hole had to be dug and the cement poured. Details about the insulation and the plywood, I couldn't follow. "Once it's in, it will protect the water pipes so they'll never freeze again. Won't that be nice?"

I nodded, remembering the blueprints rolled up in the corner of the kitchen. I pictured the neat boxes and the careful letters marking *Tawny's room*.

I squeezed Daddy's rough fingers, feeling the raised scars from years of picking cotton, welding, and engine repair. I knew those giant, sturdy fingers could do anything.

"When will it be finished, Daddy? When can we be living in a new house?"

Daddy sighed and looked into the forest, his gaze traveling beyond the limits of our land. I could almost see him adding up the costs, measuring the time and space between dream and reality.

"Oh, I'd say six months. Maybe more time, or it could be less."

I focused on that last phrase: it could be less, it could be less. It *had* to be less. A year would be too long because the pipes would freeze in the winter again. They would break ground tomorrow: May, June, July, August, September, October, and November. By Thanksgiving, we would be living in our brand new house. It was going to be better than *Little House on the Prairie*, better than any TV show. I'd have a canopy bed with a ruffled pink comforter like the ones in the JCPenney catalog, a bay window with a cushioned bench where I could read and watch the seasons change. Most importantly, I'd have a library with floor-to-ceiling bookshelves filled with books: a set of encyclopedias, novels, poetry books, scientific books, and dictionaries as thick as telephone books.

The Alaska wilderness taught me to dream without limits. Out here, where the summer sun never set, regular rules didn't apply.

Last year, we moved to the mobile home—our temporary home that would soon be replaced by something magnificent. I mentally arranged my future library. *The Little House* books would go on the shelf by the window so I could compare Laura's prairie life to the wonders of life on the tundra. The science books would go near my desk where I could study to become the smartest person in the world, just like I'd promised myself.

I hugged Daddy and kissed his stubbled cheek as he carried me back inside our old, mildewed mobile home.

Belonging

May of 3rd Grade, Age 9

On the Tuesday after Memorial Day, Keenan and I waited for the bus on the side of the frontage road. As we boarded the bus at 7:07 a.m., the sun already shone brightly in the sky, having been up for over three hours. By this time of year, we had nearly nineteen hours of day, with sunrise before 4 a.m. and sunset not until after II p.m. Everything felt possible.

Badger Road Elementary was named for the main street in the middle of the forest town. The bus drove us over gravel-paved trails and dirt-packed roads to the site of our powder-blue school. The building stood surrounded by willow bush, spruce, and evergreens.

Mama had combed my hair into five neatly braided ponytails with knockers on the ends so that the ponytails could swing when I walked and weighed down my plaits. I wore a white button-up sweater just in case I got cold. Other girls wore their hair parted into one or two ponytails; some let their hair hang down around their shoulders or down their backs. This school made me aware of my thin body, my kinky hair, of how small I existed in the world. In our school of three hundred kids, there were only five black kids. This year, I would be the only black child in the class.

Everything turned out all right because of my teacher. For the first time, I had a man teacher named Mr. Beu. He looked like the guy on *Magnum P.I.*, with thick eyebrows and a thicker mustache and dark hair. At the beginning of class every day, he wrote out the same word, then spelled it out to us. "P-o-t-e-n-t-i-a-l. Potential means you have the power inside of you to become whatever you want to become in your life. You have the ability to reach the goals that you set forth for yourself. No matter who you are, you can be anything you want to be."

When he repeated this, I sat up straighter at my desk. Keenan told me before that scientists were the smartest people in the world. Mr. Beu told us, told me, that I could be a scientist if I just set my mind to do it. Something about his calm authority made me believe him completely.

Soon, we'd have a brand new home and a separate library of my own to help me get there.

"Today we're going to explore the concept of potential energy versus kinetic energy," Mr. Beu continued. "Can anyone tell me what that means?"

Several of us raised our hands. I had read about energy in one of the encyclopedias at home.

"Tawny," he called, and I felt that familiar thrill of being chosen, of being someone with answers.

"Potential energy is stored energy," I said, thinking of a rock sitting on a hill, full of possibilities. "Like energy that is waiting to happen. And kinetic energy is when that energy is moving, like when a rock rolls down the hill."

"Excellent," Mr. Beu said, and he smiled.

"That's easy," one of the other kids said.

I glanced over at S.A.—the orange-haired boy who insisted that we call him by his initials instead of Shane. He scowled as his pale eyebrows drew together in a frown—his normal expression.

At mid-morning, we rotated for reading groups: individuals would work independently or meet in leveled reading groups with the teacher. At the beginning of the year, I tested into the highest reading group with the advanced kids who were known as G.T. for being gifted and talented. If you're G.T., you're a white boy and your mom or dad works at the school. At least that's how it worked at Badger Road Elementary. At first, I felt out of place. Now I sat up straight at the kidney table with the G.T. boys and confidently completed my end-of-year reading assessment.

Shane's round mother taught 5th grade. Blonde-haired Troy's slender mother taught 1st grade. Peter's shape mimicked a bean pole, and his older mother worked in the main office. Morgan had black hair and blue eyes. His dad served as the school's music teacher.

In the afternoon, Mr. Beu announced the reading scores.

"Shane got three wrong. Todd got two wrong. And Tawny got only one wrong."

"What?" Shane and I said it together.

I felt frustrated getting even one wrong. Surely I had done better than that.

But Shane continued, "How did *she* get that score?"

He rose up from his desk and met Mr. Beu in the back, reaching out for Mr. Beu to hand him his paper.

"Let me see," he demanded. I watched him; his red face nearly matched his orange hair. His translucent eyebrows knit, trying to figure it out. He tucked his lips into a thin, straight line. His eyes continued to search his paper. Shane sat down finally and hit the heels of his hands against his forehead.

At first, I laughed a little. Mr. Beu's eyes locked on Shane and his lips curved downward, genuinely concerned.

He sat down finally and hit himself against his forehead again. "But she..." he trailed off, burying his head in his folded arms.

For me, his statement needed no more explanation. Everyone continued working quietly, but I couldn't work any longer. Shane had called me *she* with such contempt that it conjured up pride and disturbance simultaneously. To him, my status made me an unworthy intellectual opponent. Besides being a poor black girl, I did not get whisked away twice a week to a special Gifted and Talented session—a place where the smart kids were challenged —so that they wouldn't get bored with the work given to normal ungifted and untalented kids—like me.

All this time I hadn't realized that he hated me. Before he pointed me out, marked me with the twisted pronunciation of *she*, I didn't have any particular feelings about him. I noted his thin, lanky build and high water pants. When he spoke, I noticed that he tried to mimic adults by using big words. While I regarded him as smart and a little quirky, he regarded me as an enemy and a threat.

I decided to be, not just as smart, but smarter than them. Then I'd belong here—not because of what my parents did, but because of who I am.

Breaking Ground

May of 3rd Grade, Age 9

The next morning, I awakened to the electric whirring of a saw. I ran to the window that overlooked the woods. Right where we'd been the day before, two men with goggles and gloves snapped branches and cracked trunks of the aspen, spruce, and birch. Bright morning rays blazed through the trees. At 7:30 a.m.in late May, the sun rose before 4 a.m, casting long shadows across the clearing. We had nearly twenty hours of daylight now, the days stretching longer every day as we approached summer solstice.

I ran down the hall to wake Keenan. When I told him about the construction, he came to look out my bedroom window. We squealed together and started talking about the new house. My new bedroom would have a bay window with a cushioned bench nestled against it. A deep brown chest of drawers and a vanity table, chair, and mirror would match the wood on my bed. My brother imagined a grassy backyard on which to play soccer. I longed for a study with flawless lines of floor-to-ceiling bookshelves: an updated set of the World Book Encyclopedia, a huge dictionary containing all of the words in the English language, rows of novels, and non-fiction books. I wanted to have time to read every book and be the smartest kid in the world. We both envisioned the stairs that we would trot down to breakfast like the kids did on TV. We were so wrapped up in our fantasy that we jumped at the banging against my room wall.

"Get ready for school!" Mama yelled from the other room. Her bedroom shared a wall with mine. Instead of getting up and telling us to get ready for school, Mama pounded on the wall from her bed. Keenan and I scurried out of the room to make sure we wouldn't miss our school bus.

Meeting the Workers

May of 3rd Grade, Age 9

A few days later, Keenan and I walked from the bus stop. The afternoon sun blazed high in the sky, still hours from setting. The sun wouldn't dip toward the horizon until after 9 p.m. The bright light cast sharp shadows across the construction site where Daddy and his workers continued pouring concrete for the foundation. I watched a thick gray mixture churn inside of a machine.

One man had an afro and black inky skin that glistened through his sweat. The other worker had dark skin with a short cut, almost bald. His defined muscles had veins that poked out like wires when he picked up the large bags of thick dust.

When Daddy saw us, he put down one of the bags.

"Hey, Keenan and Tawny. I want you to come say hello to my friends, Mark—you know him—and his brother John."

I shook their rough, dusty hands first and told them "Good evening," like Daddy had taught us. Then Keenan took his turn greeting them. Keenan became shy around new adults. My brother headed to the porch. I lingered, watching them work.

We had already met Mark—the one with the afro—when Daddy had fixed his car after he slid on some black ice into a ditch during the winter.

"Yeah, I owe your Daddy. That is why we're working on your new house now."

At the time, Mark had no money to repair the dented car, but Daddy fixed it anyway. Since only a small number of black people lived out here, my father impressed upon us the importance of black folks sticking together.

"Naw, we always do stuff for each other. We're always gonna help each other out no matter what," Daddy said.

That's right," Mark said, nodding his head and reaching out to slap hands with Daddy.

Daddy had known Mark for ten years, as long as he'd worked on the slopes. They were among the few black men working the pipeline. Daddy said that he and Mark, with the afro, were like brothers.

"These guys are gonna get me into the Laborer's Union so I can work on the slopes with them," John said as he rubbed his hands together, flexing his biceps.

He lived in Texas, but he couldn't find work there. Daddy, Mark, and John nodded their heads.

John turned to me, "I've got a little girl about your age back in Texas. She wears her hair in braids like that, too. Really pretty."

"Thank you." I pressed my lips together, and I smiled so he wouldn't see my bucked teeth. John smiled with his whole face, extra white teeth and glowing cheeks. Even the bones at the base of his neck formed an arc with his shoulders curved upward. I'm sure his daughter missed him. I thought I had it bad when Daddy worked on the slopes. I couldn't imagine my father living in a whole other state.

"What's your daughter's name, John?" I asked.

Daddy cleared his throat, "Mr. John to you."

"Sorry—Mr. John, what's your daughter's name?" I said.

John shook his head, "That's all right. Her name is Carrie." I nodded my head and felt sorry for Carrie way in Texas without her dad. I used to have a missing father, too.

"Tawny, go on into the house like your brother. Get started with your homework."

I pouted and walked toward my father. "Daddy, why can't I help you guys?"

Mark, who hadn't spoken, laughed a little. "Let her help, Flint," he said, stuttering. Some people called Daddy Flint because of his strength—like a rock.

"All right, move that bag right there next to the concrete mixer," Daddy said, pointing to the stack of large bags that reminded me of dog food bags.

I skipped to the bags. I tried to pick one up, but it didn't budge. I moved to the back of the pile. The bags had words printed on them, and I attempted to read them despite the smudges. I could only make out the words "concrete mix". Taking another breath, the dust filled my nose and itched the back of my throat. I blew the air back out, but the dust remained. Deep inside, I began to heave and applied the pressure into my hands as I leaned my feet at an angle and pushed with all my might. Still, no movement. I stopped for a moment to rest. If they could move it, so could I.

Searching around, I found a thick branch a couple yards away. I pried it between the bags. The top bag shifted forward—a little. I knew I could do it. Mustering up more strength, I twisted the stick in deeper. The wood pinched my palms as my skin gathered against the wood. I began lifting with all my might. Grunting as sweat collected along my hairline, the bag lifted about one inch. Then someone grabbed the stick from me. I looked up in surprise into Daddy's irritated expression. "Tawny, what are you doing?"

I shook the strain out of my arms and hands. "You said I could help!" I frowned back at him. What did he think? My dad shifted his expression to a smile. I looked around and saw that they were all trying to hold in laughter. Mark held his breath. John's shoulders moved up and down slightly.

"What's so funny?" I asked.

Mark cleared his throat and walked toward me. He easily grabbed the bag I had been trying to move, put it on his shoulder, and walked to the concrete mixer. I folded my arms over my chest and hung my head.

Daddy rubbed me on the back. "Look, this is hard work. In a few weeks, you can help us nail the planks into the bricks. But right now we can't use you out here."

I looked up at Daddy and crossed my arms. "I just wanted to help."

"I know, baby. This is hard work," he said softly. "You're going to have to help another time."

For dinner that night, Mama made cornbread, green beans, and fish cakes from the nets set in the Tanana River. By 6:30 p.m. bright evening light still poured through the kitchen window with over four hours of daylight left.

My mother sampled the food as she smacked loudly, chewing on a piece of salmon. Keenan and I gathered at the stove to make our plates. Brother stacked his plate with three fish cakes, a huge helping of green beans, and a hunk of cornbread. I only got one salmon cake with small servings of beans and a chunky piece of cornbread. Mama made Daddy's plate heaped with even more food than Keenan's. We ate together around the kitchen table, discussing the next phase of the house building on our own land—our own corner of Alaska. I wanted that house to be more than wood and concrete. I wanted it to be the place where everything would finally feel steady.

Our first couple of years in Alaska passed in a blur of new experiences. I learned how to navigate frozen playgrounds and classrooms where there were only a few other black kids.

Where We Came From

Five Years Earlier - Age 4

Over the next few weeks, I thought about Grandma a lot while watching Daddy and his friends build the foundation. We used to live in California at Grandma and Grandpa's house. Mama wanted us to leave California to have a better life. Grandma told Mama to find us a daddy, and Mama had done exactly that. As I watched my new father pour concrete for our new house, I finally understood.

***

The plum weighed heavily in my hands as I sat on the couch next to my brother. Grandma handed him a peach. From behind the couch, sunlight spilled through the floor-to-ceiling windows—warming my neck and back. Grandma wanted us to take a picture with the fruit, the last one in her living room. Wearing my favorite yellow tank top and Toughskin jeans, I tried a few poses. Like the fruit we held, we were California grown. But we were leaving that evening on a flight to Fairbanks, Alaska.

"Say cheese," Grandma said, in the high pitch she used when she spoke to her grandbabies. While trying to hold up the plum and smile and say "cheese",

I forgot to pose. From a thin slit at the base of the camera, the film slid out.

Grandma shook it. She loved pictures. One living room wall displayed photographs of me, Keenan, Mama, my eight aunts and uncles, and their kids. Grandma, petite with pole-thin legs, wore a burgundy pencil skirt and a silky buttoned blouse. Only fifty years old, she didn't look like she had eleven grandkids. Like her mother and mine, she had started having children as a teenager.

Mama stood at the threshold between the living room and kitchen, watching us with her head cocked to the side. Her eyes burned bright brown under the sunlit windows.

"Can I shake it, Grandma?"

"Tawny, you are too little to shake the Polaroid. You might mess it up."

"I won't mess up the polar bear. I promise," I said, grabbing for the picture.

Mama laughed at me and Keenan sucked his lips. "It ain't polar bear. It's the type of camera, Tawny."

"So what," I said, still reaching for the picture.

Grandma held it out of my reach and handed it to Mama. She blew on it and shook it while she leaned against the wall. I ran to Mama and reached up for the picture. She lowered it so that I could see. "Look at it. Done."

I grasped Mama's wrist and moved the photo toward me.

"Tawny, let go of my wrist. Stop being so forceful," Mama said. I didn't let go of her hand until after I got a good look. In the photo, I noticed how tall Keenan looked beside me. It always seemed we were the same age. He was six; I was four; Mama was twenty-two.

Grandma walked across the room and turned on the television, a floor model as tall as me.

"You little ones come over here and watch TV," she said, pointing to the space on the carpet in front of the TV.

My brother and I ran to sit right in front of the television. "Yeah, it's Roadrunner," Keenan said. We both laughed at how fast the bird traveled around the desert.

Grandma stood a short distance away from the television. She motioned to Mama. I turned around to see her still leaning against the wall. I knew from her sad face that our mother would miss Pomona. Grandma disappeared down the long hallway and moments later Mama followed. They were about to talk about something, and I wanted to hear.

A few minutes later, I walked down the shaded hallway where more picture frames lined the walls. I found them in Grandma's bedroom with the door cracked so I could see inside. Mama and Grandma sat on the bed beside each other. They held hands as Mama slumped her head on Grandma's shoulder.

Instead of going inside, I stayed in the hallway. I knew they would stop talking if they saw me.

A tear rolled diagonally across Mama's reddened nose before she wiped it away. I got really scared when Mama cried. My fear helped me stay quiet and listen.

"You may have your doubts about leaving, but I don't. You got to get out of this place, girl," Grandma said.

In the distance, a siren wailed. Mama sat up straight and sniffed. The two focused on each other, face to face.

"You're too much like me. When I met your daddy, I was nineteen. I already had Raynell and Ryan. Neither one of them daddies was helping. I had to move on. It's like your kids' daddy, Pete—"

Pete is the name of my father, but I didn't remember what he looked like. Keenan remembered him. He said Pete used to come around when we were real small. But then Pete stopped coming. Mama told Keenan to stop asking about him.

"Mabel, don't. I don't want to talk about him. He don't help. He got those other kids and a wife now," Mama said. My mother had always called my grandmother by her first name. She put a hand to her head like she did whenever she got headaches.

"I know, but we've got to. I don't want this happening anymore."

Mama lifted her head. She and Grandma stared at one another. Grandma finally patted Mama's hand.

"It'll be all right. Keep that house clean and stay cute."

"Mabel, you keep talking about a husband, but…" Mama said, smiling.

"Now you know if your crazy sister Denise got married, you can go up there and find a daddy for those kids. They need one."

"They do, but I just need my own place and a safe neighborhood for my kids to grow up in."

Grandma pointed her finger in the air and narrowed her eyes. "But make sure that man loves those kids and accepts them. Your daddy never could accept Raynell and now——" Her strong voice broke and weakened. A muffled cry came from deep inside of her.

Grandma had been crying a lot since Uncle Raynell had been shot and killed a few months earlier. I held my breath. Mama and Grandma were both crying. Now I felt even more scared, but I wanted to hear everything they had to say.

"Mabel," Mama said, stroking Grandma's back. My grandmother shook the tears away and put a hand against her heart.

"We're not going to let that happen to Keenan, right?"

Mama sat up straight and shook her head. "No, Mabel, I'm going to take care of him."

"These years will go by fast. If he doesn't have what he needs when he leaves you, he'll be lost. The world out there will get him. A gun claimed my Raynell. But there are a lot of other things that can get hold of a man-child, especially a black one."

Uncle Ryan couldn't even go to Uncle Raynell's funeral because of being in jail.

"I'm getting them ready for life. I read to them every night. I make sure I talk to them and use longer words. I hug them and kiss them," Mama said.

Grandma took both of her hands and held them inside of her large, rough ones.

From the living room, I heard Keenan laughing at Roadrunner. I never got to hear Mama and Grandma talk like this before. They always whispered and went to a back room, or they'd make us leave the room while they talked.

"I know, but it's still hard no matter what you do," Grandma continued. "For girls, it's giving birth too early that takes away their hope. I don't have to tell you that. You're still my baby, and you got those two in that living room."

"Yeah, Mabel. I know, but——"

Grandma put a hand on her hip. "You know now don't you? Well I couldn't tell you nothing a few years ago. Watch that baby girl, Damita. Keep her close. Keep her away from those boys."

"You got that right. She needs to know that boys are bad," she said, shaking a fist.

Like Keenan? What did Brother do to be bad?

"She's already cute," Grandma said, smiling. I smiled, too.

"Shit, the cute girls are more trouble than the funny-looking ones. She going to look just like her pretty mama," Grandma said, nudging her daughter. Mama smiled and wiped a tear.

I didn't want to be bad like Keenan. I would be good. The bedroom window rattled as a car on the street outside pounded music.

"I'm on her, Mabel. She's so strong-willed, though."

Grandma nodded and turned her head so that she looked sideways at Mama. "I wonder who she get that from?"

Mama threw up her hands. "Well I guess she got it honest."

"Get a husband with a good job and a heart for loving my two babies in there," Grandma said, shifting and wrapping an arm around her daughter's shoulders.

"If I find someone, I'll make sure of it."

"When you meet someone, figure out who he is first."

Grandma and Mama stood and embraced; they both let out a huge breath.

"Let's go finish getting you ready to get on that plane, girl. New and better things are ahead."

Journey to the Midnight Sun

Five Years Earlier - Age 4

I had never flown on an airplane before. Keenan and I held hands, and I squeezed tight when the airplane left the ground. As the plane climbed into the air, I felt awestruck by it all: the way that the cars shrunk into toy sizes and buildings became as small as matchboxes. The grass fields transformed into oddly shaped green rugs. All the people on the streets and sidewalks disappeared. The airplane cut into the clouds as smooth as cotton balls. Looking below and above, white fluff surrounded us.

My voice sounded far away. As the sun set, the white fluffiness turned into gray and gray changed to blue. As I munched on salty peanuts and played with the window shade, the blue sky bled into midnight ink. I could only see a few dots of lights from the wings of the plane.

When I woke up—I didn't think I had been asleep that long—the light had brightened again. The clouds glowed white and gold. Again the daylight white of the clouds enveloped the plane.

"Mama, what time is it?"

"It's still nighttime, almost midnight. We're in Alaska now. It is daylight all the time during the summer."

I felt my eyes widen, and I turned toward my brother. His eyes matched my excitement.

The pilot came over the loudspeaker, "Welcome to the land of the midnight sun. We will be landing soon."

The sun seemed close enough to touch, much closer than in California. It brightened up the sky over the empty, long brown stretches of earth with only a few patches of green. The mountains looked as if they could reach out toward the plane, but we floated above them.

New Beginnings

Summer before Kindergarten, Age 4

When we arrived at Aunt Denise's house in Fairbanks after midnight, the sun still blazed like midday. We moved to Alaska in the heart of the midnight sun season. The sun wouldn't set at all tonight. Everything felt backwards and strange. The air smelled different—cleaner, sharper, like cold metal. The endless light—made it impossible to know the time without looking at a clock.

Aunt Denise looked like Mama but rounder, softer around the edges, with lighter brown eyes and quick smile. She had two kids — cousins I didn't remember. Her husband worked out of town, so we did not get a chance to meet him. Their apartment had two bedrooms. It smelled like fried chicken, Pine-Sol, and something sweet baking in the oven.

"Y'all can stay as long as you need," Aunt Denise said, leading us down narrow stairs to the basement. "We're family."

She showed us the room where Keenan and I would sleep—each of us would share a bed with one of our cousins. Two twin beds sat against opposite walls. A small window near the ceiling let in a rectangle of that strange midnight sunlight.

That first week passed quickly. Keenan played with our cousin, Lamar, in the backyard. My cousin Angel and I played with barbies in her bedroom.

Aunt Denise spent her days cleaning the house, and a lot of time in the kitchen. She fried salmon the way they did in Alaska—crispy on the outside, tender and flaky inside. Salmon quickly became my favorite fish. Mama looked for work every day, coming home with the newspaper circled in red ink.

The First Apartment
Summer before 1st Grade, Age 5

***

"Lalala," I sang. With my mouth stretched out, I screeched in my highest register. Twirling on the hill behind our apartment building, I imagined myself in front of an audience like the opera singers on PBS. After Sesame Street and Electric Company had gone off, I had kept watching and became enthralled by operatic voices filling the empty stage, conquering large auditoriums with the force of enormous notes.

Keenan played with boys from the apartments across the street. I played with Hyacinth, the next-door neighbor, and Nia, the girl downstairs, in the front yard. Hyacinth had brown-hair. She wore her hair short in a bob like that other white girl from the book titled Ramona by Beverly Cleary. Nia had thick ponytails and smooth brown skin. We looked like stair steps standing beside one another, Hyacinth, then me, then Nia - from the shortest to the tallest. My friends and I created our own opera for the bees and flies darting in and out of the grass.

During a break in our performance, I came inside for water. As Mama swept, she sang off-key to the radio playing "Rock With You" by Michael Jackson. Putting the broom aside, she danced. Unconcerned with real moves like the snake and the cabbage patch, she made up her own. A mixture of steps creating a unique flow: she pranced, bit her bottom lip, and snapped to the music. Still balancing my water cup, I tapped the beat with my foot. I jigged with my lanky mother before rejoining my playmates.

In the late afternoon, Keenan and I had to go inside for a nap. We would awaken to lunch, salmon salad sandwiches and green leaf lettuce with boiled eggs, diced tomato, and chunks of avocado. After lunch, Little House on the Prairie played on TV while we helped her fold loads of clothes.

I loved the rolling plains that Laura ran through as the wind played with the blades of grass. They built their house from the trees that surrounded them. Instead of working at a job, the family sold their carrots and cabbage to the store in town and their father sold horses and cows that they all helped raise.

Mama reminded me of Ma Ingalls, cooking tasty meals and keeping the house clean. She even sewed. Using McCall's patterns, she made me rompers and short sets. I got to choose the printed fabric from the rolls of cloth at the fabric store. Sometimes she'd make herself a dress or a shirt out of the same pattern, and we'd match.

After doing laundry, she sat between Keenan and me. She curled an arm around me until her hand caressed my chin. Using her fingertips, she traced the edge of my face, my lips, my eyes, and finally slid her finger down the ridge of my nose. My whole face prickled under the gentle love strokes. Then she did the same for Keenan.

That night, Mama called me musty. I needed to check for myself by lifting up my right arm and sniffing. Then lifting up my other arm, I tucked my head toward the accordion-like skin to sniff again: a little damp and a faint scent of dirt had lingered until the scent sharpened.

Mama made Brother and me get in the bathtub. We weren't even that dirty. This time, Mama made sure I lathered up and scrubbed my armpits with the bar of Ivory Soap. I hated feeling so cold when we got out of the bath water. After Mama lotioned me down, I put on my nightgown. Keenan put on his foot-in Spiderman pajamas. We posed in the mirror behind the bedroom door.

While sleeping, I dreamed of an opera with wailing and screaming singers. When I opened my eyes, I could still hear the racket. The sun burned bright in the middle of the night. Downstairs in Nia's apartment, a woman wailed and a man's voice cut the cry short. A door slammed before heavy feet stomped up the main hallway stairs and outside the apartment building. I lay in my bed afraid to move.

Keenan lay still on the top bunk, so I know he had not awakened. Minutes later, someone knocked on our door. Who knocked? I tiptoed to the edge of the hallway where the carpet met the kitchen floor. Mama held the door open. Holding hands, Nia and her mother stood in the building hallway at our doorstep. Her mother, Cynthia, covered one eye. Mama let them in. Some of Cynthia's hair wrapped into pink rollers, part of it straight. One roller hung by a strand about to drop.

"Mama," I said, stepping out into the kitchen.

"Nia, you can go into Tawny's room and go to sleep."

In my bed, Nia laid on her back and spit angry curses toward the ceiling. "I hate him."

Cynthia cried in the kitchen, three huffs at a time. My friend paused to listen to her mother, staring at me with blank eyes. "I should kill him," Nia growled.

"Why would you want to kill your daddy?" I asked, concerned.

I hadn't thought of hating a parent or of killing anyone. When my mother wouldn't allow me to walk to kindergarten by myself like a big girl, I felt disappointed with her treating me like a baby.

"Please, that idiot is not my dad."

We heard the refrigerator door open and close; an ice tray cracked. Mama knew what to do with hurts and pains; she had once put an ice pack on my head after I ran into a wall while playing with Brother.

"My Papa died in a car accident when I was a baby," Nia said. "I bet you he didn't hit Mommy."

"Oh."

I couldn't think of what to say. I just concentrated on her words. I thought all black kids called their mothers mama. Why did some men hit women? I didn't know that parents fought like kids.

Firm knocking, the whine of the door, the static of walkie-talkies, and heavy voices: the police had arrived.

"Where did he go?" I asked.

"He ran away before the police came," Nia whispered.

I patted her shoulder, "The police will take care of everything."

Sitting up to rest on an elbow, Nia spoke to me unblinking with wise and sad eyes, "No, he'll be back tomorrow when the police are gone."

Neither of us spoke again. Maybe a new daddy would be too much trouble. We lay listening to the police talk to her mother. I fell asleep grateful that we remained a family of three.

That's how we lived in those early Alaska days—me and Keenan and Mama, building something new from broken pieces.

Reading Lessons

September of 1st Grade, Age 5

I learned how to read when my brother learned. After school, Mama taught him at the kitchen table. Brother sat in front of his book while Mama stood above him, watching closely.

"Boy, what is that word?" my mother yelled at him.

My brother sat loosely holding the pencil, but the rest of his thin frame trembled. As his sister, I could see it—Brother rocked inside his core.

"Huh?" She got closer to his face.

He looked at the word and squinted.

"What is the damn word?" She came even closer.

Still, he did not answer.

"Boy, you better say something," she said in a low voice.

"The, she sat—," He sputtered over the words as he read.

She interrupted him with a slap on the back of the head. Though I couldn't feel my brother's physical pain, I felt something else—something being broken, could feel the air thick around us as his thinking scattered into shards.

"NO! I told you it is *then*, not *the*! See the letter N at the end of it?" she yelled.

My brother's suffering taught me the difference between the words 'the' and 'then'. He took those ass whippings so I didn't have to. I learned how to read through the potent mix of fear-motivation. Mama had shown me the importance of reading, and I didn't want to let her down.

Meeting Damon

July before 2nd Grade, Age 7

This is how it happened—how Grandma's prediction came true. How a baseball game on a summer night that never ended brought us a father. How Mama found someone who would stay.

***

Trees, willows, and bushes with wild raspberries filled every open space without a house or an apartment. Over the baseball diamond, the sun stationed high in the sky made the green grass look almost golden. On Hunter Field, Fairbanks southside showed up: young men, old men, a few children darting in and out of the metal bleachers, and a couple of women.

The two teams of men wore tight pants and baseball jerseys. One side wore black and white, while the other team dressed in red and white jerseys.

Since Mama didn't talk to many people, she sat in the stands by herself while Keenan and I played tag with another child. At some point, I noticed a tall man with a blue team uniform talking to our mother. He had broad shoulders and muscled arms. He smiled wide with a gap like Mama's.

The next moment, a kid asked to join our game of tag. We ran away from him and left Mama with the man. After some time had passed, we saw the man holding a glass bowl - so out of place. At first I thought it might be cereal and milk. I stared at the man with his spoon and bowl, standing next to Mama. As I walked closer, she leaned in to eat from his spoon. What a surprise! I got even closer to find out what made Mama risk the threat of germs. The bowl contained sliced peaches and ice cream - an odd combination. Our mother had never been so familiar with a stranger before.

After the game, we headed home around ten o'clock at night, and it still looked like early afternoon.

I forgot about the man until we saw him inside of KFC a few weeks later in mid-July. He followed Mama out to the car and leaned into the window of our yellow Chevelle. The box of chicken warmed my lap. Speaking in a friendly tone, I listened while he urged her to talk with him a little longer. Keenan and I smiled uncomfortably. As we drove away, I watched his figure through the rear window. He remained in the parking lot staring at our car, the evening sun still persistent behind him.

The following week, he visited our home and brought flowers for Mama. We learned his name when Mama introduced us. Damon's name matched Mama's. They had matching names and matching gap teeth.

Mama and Damon spent a lot of time together. On many nights over the passing months, Aunt Denise watched us as the two dated.

New Daddy

April of 2nd Grade, Age 8

On a Saturday afternoon in late April, Mama and Aunt Denise sat around the table. With two large bowls and a pot filled with greens, Mama and Aunt Denise were preparing a family dinner. All six of us would be together: Denise and her two kids with Mama and her two kids. After tearing the leaves from the stem, they plunged the greens into a second bowl of water. The sun held its dominant place in the sky at three o'clock. The sun shined for over sixteen hours in late April. Its rays soaked into the bowl of water through the kitchen windows, making everything glow.

I read a book in the living room, and got up now and then to watch the process. The rest of the kids played outside. We had to decide whether to stay in or get out—no back and forth. I settled onto the couch and read my book while the music from Luther Vandross's latest album floated around us.

My cousin, Angel, rushed into the house. Her tank top looked stretched out of shape, and her shorts twisted unevenly on her legs. She huffed a few times and looked around the room before making her announcement. "Damon is here! Just saw his car outside!"

"Your man is here, Damita!" Denise said, pushing Mama on the shoulder. Mama rolled her eyes and smiled.

"OK, girl! Now go on back outside," Mama told her. My mother took a moment to dry her hands on a towel. She waved off her sister before pulling up her tube top a bit higher. She rolled her eyes at Denise before grabbing another handful of greens.

I set my book aside and walked over to get a closer look at Mama's reaction. Damon would be joining us for family dinner! Aunt Denise pulled me close to whisper, "Damon is going to be your Daddy!"

I bounced and nodded in agreement. I didn't remember my real father—what he looked like or how he acted. Sometimes, I couldn't even remember Pete's name. But I knew Keenan and I should have a father.

"My daddy is here!" I yelled. I ran to get my shoes.

"What? Wait!" Mama hollered, suddenly out of breath with surprise.

I stopped running, and looked at my mother. "What?"

"Who told you that was your Daddy?"

I stared at my only parent for a moment. I didn't dare tell on my aunt—didn't even look at her. So I gave the question right back to her.

"Well who is supposed to be my daddy, then?" I let the question hang in the air.

Mama shook her head, looked at Denise, and let out a long breath of discomfort. "Well... How embarrassing..." I heard her say as I ran out the door.

I didn't know why she felt embarrassed. I knew who would make a good Daddy, and I went outside to greet him.

The Wedding

April of 2nd Grade, Age 8

"Let me show you," Aunt Denise took the basket and took large steps across the room, dropping petals on each side of her after each step. Yesterday, my aunt showed me how to pull the petals from the bud of the rose. Separating each part, I piled the petals into the white basket.

My aunt helped plan every detail of Mama and Daddy's wedding, including my white shiny shoes with a criss-crossed set of buckles. I knew that being a flower girl held a lot of importance, so we had to practice.

On the wedding day, I put on my white dress with a lacy bodice and layers of ruffles at the bottom that moved around me when I twirled. At two o'clock in the afternoon, the sun soared high and strong in the sky. Sunlight poured through the church windows, making the fabric of my dress shimmer.

The organ started up to cue my turn. A long series of yawned notes filled the room. As I began down the aisle, a fat lady called out. "Oh Jesus, thank you." Later, Damon told me that she was his sister, my new Aunt Mary.

From the basket, I pulled out a petal with my gloved hand. Dropping it, I stepped forward. Repeating the same procedure with another petal, I stepped forward. Careful to alternate sides, evenly sprinkling petals on the floor of the aisle and moving forward. In the middle of it all, I decided one side would be much easier. Continuing, I decorated with petals only on the right side. Some petals on the same side, and more petals on the same side until I reached the front. Someone led me to a seat on the front row pew.

"Thank you, Lord," the fat lady's voice again floated above everyone else's. Keenan served as ring bearer, but he only got to do a quick dash to the front. His little job really did not have the importance of a flower girl. He joined me on the pew.

Daddy stood beside the altar smiling as Mama made her way down the aisle. Light streamed through the stained glass windows, painting colored patterns across her white dress until they stood beside one another in front of the preacher, smiling. I can't remember what the preacher said, but it took a long time before they kissed.

Finally, we filed down the aisle to the outside of the church, where we squinted in the bright sunlight. People threw rice and more flowers. Around three o'clock, the sun warmed to about sixty degrees. The light felt like a blessing, like the world celebrated with us. Damon became my Daddy. We had a whole family: two parents and two kids.

In our apartment, family, friends, aunts and new uncles gathered for the reception. On the stereo system, "We are Family" played as Daddy took Keenan and me around to introduce us to his brothers and sister. For Aunt Mary, I held out my hand but she pulled me toward her, smushing my cheek against her bosom. A whiff of rose-scented powder puffed out of her chest and affected my nose. After a moment, she held me out to look at me from my hair all the way to my shiny shoes.

"How you doing, girl? Ain't you happy yo' Mama found you a new daddy?" I nodded and snorted the powder out of my nose. "I'm going to take y'all to church with me. Every Sunday I load up my car with kids and take them to church. All right?"

I looked up at Daddy.

"Are y'all saved?" she said to us.

I looked at Keenan to see if he knew what she meant. He shrugged.

"What do you mean?" I asked. "Saved from what?"

Aunt Mary turned to Daddy. "Damon, you know Ma'Dear would have a fit if she were alive. Imagine if she'd knew you were keeping these here kids from the Word."

Aunt Mary and Daddy called their mother Ma'Dear, short for Mother Dear. Keenan and I laughed at how country they were.

"Have you accepted Jesus into your heart? If you ain't, you can't get into heaven."

"What will happen?" I asked.

"You'll go to hell. That means you'll be burning forever."

A hard ball of worry knotted up inside me. I didn't want to go to hell.

Daddy pulled us away to meet his brother, Jessie.

Uncle Jessie wore his hair in an oval-shape afro, thinning at the top. His white wife Cyndy stood with her hip jutted forward and her butt sloped inward. Uncle Jessie gripped my hand too hard when we shook.

"Hello. Such a pretty girl," he said to me. But to Keenan he said, "What's going on you little rascal? You play sports?" Keenan shook his head, no. "Well we gotta do something about that, Damon."

"Yeah, we'll worry about that later," Daddy answered.

Then we met Daddy's older brother Uncle Jeff. He walked with his legs far apart, looking around the room with bucked eyes. "How you? I'm yo' Uncle Jeff. Townie? That your name?" After practicing my name a few times, he got it right.

Aunt Denise brought in a tall cake, three layers with two black people kissing at the top, their once beige faces painted brown to match my parents. Damon, I mean Daddy, and Mama stood in front of the kitchen table grinning. I got shuffled into the back of the crowd and could no longer see Mama's face.

Instead of dancing in our tiny apartment, everyone rocked and swayed to the music. Stevie Wonder sang "Superstitious." Uncle Jeff did a two-step, slow and methodical with arms locked stiffly in the air. I nudged Keenan, and he threw back his head to laugh. That made me laugh, but I tried to hold it in. It came out in a spurt, and it stopped Jeff for a moment. Then he smiled, waving us off and kept up his stiffened old man dance. Keenan pushed me forward, and we sauntered next to Uncle Jeff so that we could watch and laugh.

"Hey! There they are: Keenan and Lil Bit," Having forgotten my name, he had given me a nickname already. "You" He pointed to Keenan, "And you, you just a little old thing. Who you guys laughing at?" We kept laughing and pretended to dance all stiff like him with our arms locked in the air. Then he looked around as if he had lost something. "Where is that flower basket? I'll show you how to do it right," he said laughing at me.

With that dancing, I knew he couldn't show me how to do anything right. But whatever he wanted to show, I knew it would be funny.

In all the excitement, I ran into our bedroom and swung the door with so much force that the door mirror fell off and broke. I thought of telling Mama, but I decided not to bother her with problems on her wedding day. I stepped over the shattered pieces and grabbed the flower basket. I'd tell her later. Uncle Jeff waited to show me more laughter.

The Slopes

April of 2nd Grade, Age 8

Daddy returned to the slopes the weekend after the wedding. For work, he traveled to Barrow, Alaska—the northernmost tip of the state. He'd be there for eight weeks at a time and return for two weeks of vacation.

Every night at 7:00 p.m., Mama set Keenan and me on routine. When Mama put us to bed, bright daylight still poured through our windows, soaking through our curtains. I had to pull the covers over my head. Even still, I always stayed awake for at least an hour or more before sleeping. I listened to what Mama watched on television. The endless light made Daddy's absence feel even stranger, like time had stopped moving forward.

Mama would call Daddy. "Damon, when you coming back?" I could not hear everything, but I could hear that same question. She'd start to cry while speaking on the phone with him. From our room—closest to the living room—I heard her tear-soaked voice.

After she got off the phone, she would cry more, long sobs that curved, ranging from low and muffled to high pitched and muffled. She tried to hide it from us, but I could hear it all.

First Church

April of 2nd Grade, Age 8

As I walked towards the building, I remembered the white structure and the double doors that opened to the sanctuary. It made sense that Mama and Daddy had their wedding at Aunt Mary's church. We entered the foyer a little after twelve o'clock.

A group of people with maroon robes gathered in the golden light. They organized into a line as the drums and an organ began to play.

My new aunt convinced our parents to allow her to take us to church, but Keenan decided to stay home.

"The choir is about to enter. We're late," Aunt Mary explained in a hushed voice.

In unison, the choir began to sway left and right. Two ladies wearing white gloves opened another set of doors. Inside the sanctuary, two columns of black people sat on gray and crimson benches. Surprisingly, all black people attended the church.

At first, I felt frightened by the number of people. But the audience turned to welcome the choir by standing. In keeping to the beat of the drums, the audience clapped along with the choir. The long sleeves of their robes puffed and deflated with the force of the clapping.

One of the ladies in white gloves held up a hand as I tried to walk behind the choir. She also wore white shoes and a white dress.

Aunt Mary pulled me back. "Girl, the ushers are going to have us wait 'til the choir finish entering."

I wanted to get inside and sit down, but I stayed put. Aunt Mary and I watched the choir from the foyer.

The row of twelve singers floated down the aisle, mouths fully open singing "When the Saints Go Marching In." I admired the uniformity. Rocking, singing, and clapping, the choir snaked their way to the front of the church, turned on the side of the pulpit stage, and up to the choir stand.

Once they had reached the choir stand, the ushers finally allowed us to sit down. One of them walked stiffly down the aisle. We followed her to a pew near the front. She stretched out a white-gloved hand to signal where to sit.

The choir sang two more verses while standing in front of their benches. Remaining in front of the pulpit with her back to the audience, one lady moved her hands to direct the rest of the chorus. They followed her, singing lower when her hand moved down or higher when her hand moved up.

After the first song, the choir led the church in other spirituals: "I Don't Know What You Come to Do," "What a Mighty God we Serve," and "This is a Holy Church." Each song mimicked the same organ playing, foot stomping, body rocking, hand-clapping rhythm. Together, a whole church of black folks that looked like me sang together. Their voices resounded beautifully in a spectrum that ranged from high soprano to a deep bass. Each voice found its place in the melody and my insides warmed until all of my inhibitions fell away. Rocking my shoulders and snapping, I stood up and swayed along with the music. Unexpectedly, I felt a sharp finger tap me. When I looked back, Aunt Mary had leaned in close to me.

"Don't be finger-popping in here. This isn't the night club. This the Lord's house," she said in a hiss. My aunt sat back down on the edge of the pew.

Forgetting about me a moment later, she moved her head back and forth enjoying the music.

I didn't know anything about night clubs. Finger-popping? Why did she get mad at me for snapping? I frowned and looked around to see if anyone else had caught me. Old ladies sat in the first few rows of the church. Mothers and their children sat together. Three young women had babies in their arms wrapped in blankets. Everyone continued moving around me. No one seemed to have noticed. I sat down, unable to delight in the music any longer.

A series of orange plastic windows punctuated the side walls of the sanctuary, casting amber light across the pews. Behind the choir stand featured a huge painting of a white man with stringy brown hair hanging to his shoulders, eyes directed upward.

After the singing, the choir sat down, cooling themselves with flat paper fans.

The Mistress of Ceremonies, named Sister Barner, explained that the next portion of the service allowed for testimonies. During this period, church members stood up and waited for their turn to share about how the Lord helped them. A woman and a man stood up. The woman spoke first.

"Praise the Lord saints," she called with a strong voice.

The church members responded: "Praise the Lord."

She waved a hand in the air. "I just want to stand up and testify about how sweet Jesus is to me. I been praying for a raise and I go over to the boss man this week and axe for it. The Lord said 'Ye have not 'cuz you axe not.'" She jumped a few times and let her head fall back so that she faced the ceiling. Waving her hand again she said, "Hallelujah!"

She also sounded like she used to live in the South.

Aunt Mary said, "Amen. Go on, Sister Charles."

"Hallelujah," said a lean pole of a woman with perfectly coiffed hair.

"Look at God!" said a man with square glasses and an afro.

When she sat down, the man spoke. I couldn't follow everything, but Aunt Mary and the other adults yelled out to him like they had for the woman.

After the testimonies, the choir stood up and began to sing "Give and it shall be given unto you. Give and it shall be given unto you, pressed down, shaken together, and running over."

The man with the square glasses and afro came up to the front of the church. The choir continued to sing, but softly to allow him to speak. He introduced himself as Deacon Wilson.

"I collect offerings. For some people, this is their least favorite portion of the service, but it is my favorite. I give happily, freely."

The choir continued to harmonize softly and the piano played timidly as he spoke.

"The choir is singing so beautiful on this Sunday, a day that the Lord hath made. Listen to the choir. They're quoting the Word. The Bible says 'Give and it shall be given unto you.' If you need a blessing, giving is the way to get it. Open your heart and your pocketbooks, your wallets. Give."

The ushers came forward and stretched out their hands to indicate when the people on each pew should stand. Aunt Mary placed a dollar into my hands before I followed her into the outside aisle, and to the offering table to drop my dollar into a golden collection pan. We circulated through the center aisle and back to our pew.

After the singing, testimonies, and offering, the pastor got up to speak. As he approached the podium, he seemed surprised that his time to preach had come so soon. The congregation quieted themselves. Parents quieted their babies with pacifiers and fresh bottles of milk. I couldn't hear what he said at first. He spoke quietly—softly even. He wore a collar that folded in so that just a rectangular piece of pale gray could be seen at the collar of his blinding white shirt. It looked like his tie had been stolen.

Aunt Mary sunk her back against the pew and crossed her legs at the ankle. She reached for her Bible, and I scooted in close to her so I could read along. I felt the warm fat of her arms underneath my ear. Carrying the microphone in his pancake shaped hands, Pastor put it close to his mouth as if he were kissing it. Still, I could barely understand him.

"Let's get to the Word, starting in Matthew chapter 5, verse 3. Blessed are the poor."

His charcoal hands scratched at his silver slick of hair. "Will someone read?"

The long skinny lady stood up. Her voice rang out loud, reaching every corner of the sanctuary without a microphone.

"Go ahead Sister Jolene, read. I'm feeling good this afternoon, saints. 'For God so loved the world that he gave his Son that *who-so-never* believe in him should not perish but have everlasting life.'"

Pastor repeated that same verse at different times during the sermon. It seemed to be stuck in his head like a line from a song, bouncing around, coming back up unexpectedly from time to time. It resurfaced without reason.

A couple of the church members agreed with a hearty, "Amen."

"Sorry, Sister Jolene. Now you can read."

She read, "Blessed are the poor in spirit: for theirs is the kingdom of heaven."

"That's right, the poor shall rule the earth," Pastor said.

He confused me. Pastor walked to the left of the podium where we could see his entire body.

"That's what the world don't want you to know, saints. Some of us is working two, three jobs to try to get ahead, trying to get rich. But I got news for you: you need to be storing your treasures in heaven!" Pastor pointed a finger toward the ceiling. "When you're poor, you're right where you need to be."

The saints were quiet. I thought about it. Maybe everyone couldn't be rich. It sounded fair if people had a poor life, to have a wonderful life after death. The pastor paced the pulpit stage, reading the eyes of the congregation members.

"Aw, y'all don't believe me. Y'all don't want to hear the Word." He stamped his foot and hit the podium.

A few children jumped. A couple of men cleared their throats. One sister in the back called out, "Ain't that the truth."

Pastor turned to Sister Jolene, still standing ready to read. "Now skip down to Matthew chapter 6:20. The Lord knows how to show you what will happen if you get off the mark and spend too long focusing on the outside world," Pastor Thurman cocked his head to the side watching the congregation's reaction, "Read Jolene."

Jolene turned a page in her Bible and began reading again. "But lay up for yourselves treasures in heaven, where neither moth nor rust doth corrupt, and where thieves do not break through nor steal."

"I know you see those rich folk, those celebrities who got a lot. Some of you might want what they got. But God says that this stuff on the earth is temporary. It ain't going to last. You can't focus your energy on a financial planner and the Stock Market. Get right with God. The Word says stay poor and you'll inherit the earth. Store up treasures in heaven. Don't worry about this old troubled world."

One of the brothers stood up and hollered, "Thank you Jesus."

Aunt Mary jumped up and yelled, "Praise the Lord." She eased herself back down on the squeaking pew. I rested my head against her arm again. Her body heat made me more comfortable, and my eyelids started to feel heavy. My drowsy head snapped back and forth until it settled on Aunt Mary's meaty arm.

Then I fell asleep.

Daddy's Home

June of 2nd Grade, Age 8

I came into the kitchen holding my Muppets bedroom trashcan. Mama had hung newly sewn yellow kitchen curtains to cover the windows over the sink. At 7:30 a.m., the sun poured through the translucent curtains and made the room glimmer. We had nearly twenty-four hours of daylight now.

On her knees, Mama scrubbed a spot on the kitchen linoleum with Pine Sol. I dumped my trash into the large garbage can in the corner of the kitchen. The white and black linoleum shone like the floors in television commercials. The muscles in Mama's shoulders and arms pulsed while she worked. My mother straightened her back and threw her head toward the ceiling and wiped her sweaty forehead, "Woo!"

Mama always kept our home neat, but today the house had to be especially clean. Daddy would be home soon.

Our mother had been cleaning before Keenan and I had awakened this morning. I watched as her eyes lingered on the stovetop, the sink, and counters. Concentrating on the floor, she stepped back to look at it from a different angle. The floor shone.

"Another spot," she said, bending down with the old, ragged t-shirt she used for cleaning. She began wiping the floor in a circular motion again, even though I couldn't see any spots. When she finished, she stood up straight again and scanned the kitchen once more. "Perfect."

Keenan had vacuumed our bedroom floor. I put all of the clothes in the dirty hamper, all of our toys in the toy box, and folded up the clothes inside our drawers.

We finished dumping out all of the trash. Keenan entered the kitchen with an armful of wadded paper.

"Mama, when is he coming?" he asked. That's what Keenan always called Daddy—he.

"In a few hours, he'll be here."

"Is he driving a car or taking a cab?"

"I don't know," she said without looking at him. She reached for a pan out of the cabinet.

"Well, why didn't we pick him up anyway?"

Mama's head whipped around toward him. "Boy, leave me alone. It's just question after question with you nowadays."

For truth, Keenan and questions... Lately more and more Keenan questions. Mama got so annoyed with him for it.

Keenan dropped the load of wadded paper into the large trashcan and walked out of the kitchen holding his head down.

The living room carpet had been vacuumed twice. Mama had scrubbed down the countertops with bleach; all the clothes were washed.

After we finished cleaning, our mother told us to get dressed. A pink jumper lay on the bed that she had sewn for me. Mama creased Keenan's jeans so stiff that the pants could stand on their own.

Mama had a delicious lunch waiting: fried catfish, black-eyed peas, cornbread, and yams. The house burst with sweet and peppery scents. We couldn't eat until Damon arrived. The cornbread came out of the oven; she swiped a knife with a chunk of butter over the bread's surface. About fifteen minutes after that, I heard the service door open. Keys jingled. Damon came through the door, large and jolly, like a muscular, black Santa Claus. He held a light blue suitcase in each hand. He stood so tall, I worried he might hit his head on the doorframe.

I ran past Mama and leapt into his arms.

"Daddy, Daddy!" I said it twice on purpose. The word burst out of my mouth happily, and I liked the way it sounded floating in the air.

He scooped me up, and I sat up against his forearm. I guessed that's the way fathers carry their kids. Mama always carried me on her hip, although she didn't pick me up much anymore. I had grown too big for her thin and short build. I would have to think of more reasons for him to carry me around like this. I wrapped my arms as far around him as I could and squeezed. His rough, stubbled cheek scratched me. I jerked my face away from his.

"Wow, your face is itchy," I squeaked from the back of my throat so that I sounded like a baby. As I rubbed my palm against his face, he moved around so that I could feel short rows of stubble growing on his chin and the other cheek.

"Yep, that's because I shave my beard every day. I have to, or I'll get really hairy."

"Oh, will you grow it out? It'll be like Santa Claus," I said, smiling big and nodding my head with exaggerated enthusiasm the way I had seen toddlers do. Swaying in his arms as he laughed, I felt his strong grip tighten around me. "I don't know about that. Sounds like you want me to look like an old man."

I laughed and put a finger in my mouth, continuing the baby act. He put me down, and I ran to stand beside Keenan. While I knew that I found a new daddy, Keenan still didn't feel sure about the new relationship. Standing by one of the kitchen chairs, my brother watched Mama and Damon hug. He waited for an opportunity to speak, until Daddy noticed him standing there.

"Hey Keenan, how are you doing?" Then Brother could address Damon without calling him by his proper name.

"All right."

"Well why don't you come over here and shake my hand or something?"

Keenan let go of the chair and when he got close to Damon, he held out his hand. His hand swallowed Keenan's bony hand. After a moment, Keenan walked back to the chair, gripping the edge again.

Daddy walked into the back room with his suitcases. He had a strong walk; with each stride, the floor quietly groaned beneath the carpeting. To travel from the front to the back of the hallway I usually took ten or fifteen paces; Daddy took only three or four strides. He closed the door behind him.

I set the table, placing forks and spoons on napkins. Mama poured red Kool-aid into cups for Keenan and me, while she set out glasses for herself and my dad. As we worked, Keenan continued standing beside the chair dazed. I didn't even tell him to move out of the way when I bumped into him while setting the table. Instead I spoke politely, using a voice that I imagined sounded like an English person, "Excuse me young chap."

Keenan stopped staring into an invisible scene and tried to glare at me before he started laughing. "What kind of voice is that supposed to be?" he asked.

"It's my British accent."

He sniffed and smiled. "That sounds nothing like a British accent."

I laughed, "Who cares."

"Go wash your dirty hands," Mama said.

Daddy came from the back room with a small soccer ball in one hand and the other hand closed in a loose fist, hiding something colorful. When he saw us, he quickly put both hands behind his back to draw our attention. Keenan and I exchanged looks. He had brought gifts. I rushed over to Daddy and started prying his fist open. After a moment, he allowed me to spread his rough, gigantic fingers. Inside, he held a toy hat that rolled and made static noises when I wound it up. Brother put the ball to his nose and smelled it with his eyes closed.

Mama came up and hugged Daddy. My brother and I went to our room to play.

Inside of our room, the sunlight had heated the carpeting and our bed comforters. We squatted on the warm carpets and started playing with the new gifts.

"Isn't Daddy really nice?" I asked, looking at Keenan. He let the smile melt off his face and shrugged.

I knew Keenan wanted Damon to be his father, but he didn't know if he could forget about our real daddy, the one who had forgotten him. It might have been fear that held back his smile. If Keenan tried to speak to Mama about Pete, she cut him off and told him to shut up.

Keenan attempted to spin the soccer ball on one finger.

"He's your daddy, too," I told him.

Letting the ball fall, he stretched out on our bedroom floor. He balanced his head against his elbow and forearm.

"How do you know? How did he become your daddy anyway?"

"He's always been my dad. I don't know why," I told him.

I clasped one of his warm hands.

"Daddy is nice. Let's go talk to him."

"What if he's just nice to you?"

I shook my head and squeezed his hand.

"No he's both of ours. He's our new Daddy."

I pulled Keenan's hand, and I waited for him to stand. After that, he kept up with me. In the kitchen, Daddy and Mama hugged. Both of them had their eyes closed. When we came out of the room, they kept hugging for a moment before opening their eyes.

"Daddy," I said, pulling his hand from around our mother.

"Yes," he said, backing away from Mama to follow my pull.

"We have to talk to you about something," I said pointing at Keenan and me with a shaky thumb. Suddenly, I felt awkward. Keenan dropped his head and backed up, ready to forget the whole thing.

"Alright," Damon said.

"Keenan wants to know if it's o.k. to call you Daddy, too," I said.

Keenan kept his head down. Damon looked from me to Keenan and let out a large breath and stood up straight. I realized that Damon felt nervous, too.

"Well, of course you can, Keenan. You don't even have to ask. I'm already your father. I love you," he said. His eyes held steady, looking straight at Keenan. I felt this truth inside of me. My eyes moved toward Mama who stood in the same place in the middle of the kitchen. She smiled at me as a tear dropped on her cheek.

Keenan looked up and gave a little smile, afraid to show major relief and happiness. Keenan spoke softly, "All right," he said. "Can I ask you a question?"

Daddy nodded, "Go ahead."

"Why is the sky blue?"

Damon put his hand to his chin, pausing for a moment. "Well, son, I'm not sure. We'll have to look that up. I think it has something to do with the water vapors in the air and the sunlight."

Keenan nodded, "Oh, ok."

I smiled at Mama. She winked at me.

"What is water vapor?"

Damon paused again, considering the question seriously.

"Water vapor is little bits of water in the air. They're so small you can't see it."

Keenan furrowed his brows and folded in his lips. "Daddy, why does it look like the earth is flat if scientists say it is really round?"

Our Own Land

June before 3rd Grade, Age 8

Daddy bought three acres of land with a double-wide mobile home and an auto body shop on a plot of wild land with chunky brown soil that spread out until a thick forest of evergreens grew along the border. On the other side of the forest, sand stretched out to the banks of the Tanana River. There weren't any neighbors for at least a mile and no other buildings.

Our family's Chevrolet Riviera rolled onto the property around eight o'clock on a late June morning. Although the sun had been shining for hours, my legs tingled as the cool air seeped from the driver-side window at barely fifty degrees. I hopped on my bottom and rumbled my legs against the seats, trying to contain the giddiness pent inside. We stopped in the parking lot of the auto shop with pale yellow siding. A large painted wooden sign proclaimed Midway Auto Body Shop.

Daddy told us that living on the outskirts of town would be peaceful. I thought of the apartment downstairs from us, and its revolving door of fighting couples who argued in the middle of the night.

"It's going to be like that show you like where the people live out in the country," Daddy said.

In the front seat, Mama shook her head. "No, are you serious? This is the boonies. Way out here?" she asked.

"What do you mean the boonies? This is our land. This here place is called Midway Industrial Park," Daddy slowed down his words as he pronounced the name of the property.

Then I remembered, "You mean *Little House on the Prairie*?"

"That's right, Tawny! You got the right idea!" Daddy said. He reached out for Mama's hand. "You'll see, Damita!"

The car stopped, and Keenan opened his back door and scooted along the cushioned seats to the outside. As soon as I landed on the tiny sea of rocks that made up the shop parking lot, I spun in a series of clumsy pirouettes, letting the chill of the morning air whip through the holes of my old tight jeans. The barrettes at the end of my ponytails flew into my face. I stopped and caught my balance before I ran after my brother, trying to keep up with his long, knobby legs.

Keenan grabbed my hands and started to swing me by my arms. I yelped so loudly that the tolling of my voice echoed through my throat and inside my head. His spindly fingers were holding me tight as I picked up speed. Mama intervened just before my feet flew off the ground.

"What are y'all doing playing around on these hard gravel rocks?" Mama shook her finger at us as her shoulder length jheri curl vibrated. Her nostrils flared wide. Keenan twirled me around one more time.

Then Daddy's voice boomed, "Stop that shucking and jiving!" Keenan slowed down and let go of my hands. We both began to skip beside Mama whose narrow hips swayed from side to side as she strutted forward to explore the property.

Our father strode past us. His muscular arms swung beside him like ebony branches swaying in the wind.

"Where's the house, Daddy?" I said, looking up into his thick-mustached face.

"It's still gotta be built. Come on, I'll show you."

Daddy led the three of us to the backside of the shop. A rusted blue old-fashioned style car and a formerly red Camaro were propped up on cinder blocks soldered into the sod by time.

"This is all our land."

Daddy pointed to a thick forest of evergreens growing far on one side. His hand swept over the land until it reached the New Richardson Highway on the opposite side.

About two hundred yards from the shop, Daddy led us to a dull green double-wide mobile home surrounded by shrubbery and bushes. As we continued on the path, I noticed scattered garbage everywhere. The trash had been there so long, I could only identify white bits of paper and plastic, Barbie heads, flattened KFC buckets, and bright blue plastic bits from a demolished toy bucket. I couldn't understand where all of the garbage came from.

I thought this place would be full of bushes and trees, but only a few patches of willows and forget-me-nots sprouted through the gravel rocks. Keenan frowned and kicked the head off a dandelion as he walked behind Daddy.

A gray weathered porch with four short steps led us up to the front door. As soon as we opened the door, we were shocked by the stench of mildew, dust, and sewage. The warm air felt clammy against my skin. Mama, Keenan, and I held our noses as we walked inside the mobile home.

In the living room, the light from the window spilling onto the shaggy green carpeting matched the outside aluminum siding. Sprinklings of glass and dirt littered the floor.

"This is disgusting." I waved my hands and scrunched up my face at Keenan, who nodded in agreement.

"Don't touch nothing! This place is full of germs!" Mama crossed her arms in front of her to make the message clear.

"Oh, it's not that bad. We got to clean up a bit, that's all," Daddy said walking ahead of us.

I started biting my nails as we followed Daddy into the kitchen. With the floors creaking, I worried about what else we'd see. As we continued walking, the pungent scent of fungus overpowered the air. Mama put her hands on her hips and raised an eyebrow. She scanned the filthy sink, filled with broken cups and food splattered plates. I knew she wanted to say something, but she kept quiet. As newlyweds, Mama and Daddy didn't argue in front of us.

Keenan sneezed, and we all blessed him. Then he turned and batted his watering eyes at Daddy. "We gonna live here, Daddy?"

I quickly answered, "No, Daddy is going to build us a house." I couldn't believe the questions he asked sometimes, especially as the oldest.

"Well… let me show you something," Daddy said, leading us to the kitchen. Near a sliding glass door on the opposite wall, he pulled a long brown canister from a corner. After removing a couple of foam cups from the stained kitchen table and brushing off the crumbs, he popped the top of the cylinder and pulled out a set of rolled up sheets of paper. "It's all planned out. These are blueprints. These are the drawings for the house we're going to build."

Daddy tried to smooth out the huge papers, but they still curled up. Mama sat forward and held down part of the papers, while Keenan and I each held down a part.

Using my teeth, I bit off a piece of skin hanging on my pinky. With rumpled eyebrows, Mama swatted my hand out of my mouth. "Mama, why'd you do that?" I said, frowning at her.

"I told you to keep your hands out your mouth. It's nasty in here!" she said without looking at me.

Keenan sneezed and once again we blessed him.

She focused on the black boxes drawn on the paper. Since my father had called them blueprints, I thought the paper or the writing would be blue, but it wasn't. Keenan and I grinned when we read our names on the boxes: Keenan's room, Tawny's room.

Mama squinted. I could read her face as she decided how to react: delight, suspicion, anger. We all knew that if Mama didn't like it there, our father wouldn't build the new beautiful home. Daddy would have to continue working up north in Barrow, four hundred miles away, on the oil pipelines.

"See if we put this place together and live here for a little while—just until I get our new house built—I won't have to go back on the Slopes to work any more."

Daddy delivered these last words especially for Mama, searching her eyes as he spoke. I had heard Aunt Denise say he earned up to $70 per hour working on the North Slopes. Despite the money, Mama got too sad when he wasn't around.

Our father put his hand on top of Mama's hands, rubbing them while looking into her eyes. They stayed that way as he explained that we had to move into this mildewed double-wide before we could build the house.

My eyes went back to the plans. "Can we have an upstairs and downstairs like on TV?" I asked, beginning to imagine my own brand new room and the playroom that he pointed out on the drawings. Daddy answered in a weird high pitch and his voice cracked as he said, "Sure we can."

We all watched Mama search the drawings once more, still waiting for her approval.

Daddy squeezed her hand. "We will only have to live in this mobile home for a few months, just long enough to build the house."

Finally Mama spoke.

"So I guess we have some cleaning to do," Mama sat up straight and pushed out her heavy bosom.

"I want to help!" I said, jumping up and down.

"I'm going to help, too!" said Keenan.

"Alright. That's what I want to hear. With everybody cooperating, we will be ready to move in after a few days."

"What?" Mama spoke in a shrill, high-pitch. "It's gonna take longer than that. We probably won't be ready for a few weeks or a month."

Keenan agreed with Daddy, and hit his chest with his toothpick arms as he said. "I'm not no sorry little kid. I can get a lot of work done. It won't take us long."

Keenan looked up at Daddy, and he patted him on the back. While I bit my nails, I stared at my dad and Keenan. I wanted to believe them, but I couldn't see this dump being ready in a few days.

He rolled up the blueprints and put them back in the corner. Mama stood up and crossed her arms tightly across her chest again. Daddy grunted playfully at her and kissed her on the forehead. She smiled a little and dropped her arms. As he walked out the front door, he called Keenan to follow him.

Mama went outside to get some cleaning supplies from the Chevrolet Riviera. When she returned, she came back wearing an old 1983 Hughes Family Reunion shirt and carried a plastic grocery bag. She tied up my ponytails and covered my hair with a bandana. Then she tied her own hair into a bun and covered it with a black bandana. From the bag, she took out yellow rubber gloves for herself and me. Keenan and I were already wearing play clothes: tight holey jeans and tank tops.

Mama, Keenan, Daddy, and I started working around 9 o'clock. We girls cleaned inside of the mobile home while Daddy and Keenan worked outside.

I worked alongside Mama with her strong arms and broad shoulders. We scrubbed the grime from the gray linoleum floors until the faded lemon colored pattern revealed itself.

My tiny hands could only endure about a minute of scrubbing at a time. The aching forced me to give up scrubbing, and I started picking up the trash. Beside a knocked over tan sofa with dark brown stains, a hairbrush filled with wooly black hair lay in the middle of the floor. A matted, blonde-haired, blue-eyed baby doll head lay crushed beside the wood-paneled wall. I picked up a crumbled McDonald's bag lying beside the doll head. Underneath a coffee table with a shattered glass top, I found a waterlogged book that had Kim McCallister's name written on the inside. I knew the McCallisters from church. Just like our parents, Kim's mama dropped her off at Sunday school.

The McCallister kids came to church smelling like spoiled black-eyed peas. Why were we cleaning up after the dirtiest people I had ever known? Were we lower than the McCallisters?

I thought the point of moving would be to improve our situation, but the condition of this junkyard even made the McCallisters relocate.

"Mama? Did Kim McCallister and them live here?" I asked.

"Yeah, the whole family."

I tried to imagine all of those people: seven loud adults, each one with at least three children. All of them jammed into this three-bedroom home.

"That's a lot of people."

"They're poor. Sometimes you have to do what you gotta do."

"Are we poor too, Mama?"

"No, your daddy is setting up a new business and we're going to tear this place down soon."

"Why didn't they clean their crap up before they left? And why did we have to move here? Our apartment is better than this," I said, whining.

Mama stopped scrubbing for a moment and brought her chin towards her chest, pushing her gaze into mine. "Look girl, your Daddy has a plan. So we're going to make sure we work together so it happens."

I couldn't get the moldy funk out of my nose. Still, I wanted the house more than anything. I had seen people live in houses on television. In Pomona, we had lived in Grandma and Grandpa's house, but I wanted us to have a house of our own.

As I cleaned, I had to keep reminding myself that Daddy said we only had to live here until we built our new house. Just like Laura's family, we had our own land now. We just needed to clear the land like Laura and her family had cleared the trees.

Standing side by side with my mother, I watched her determination to get that last speck of dirt from the linoleum. It made me proud to work with Mama. I wanted to work as hard as I could so that she could be proud of me, too.

Around 10 o'clock, Daddy brought in our silver and blue Hoover vacuum cleaner, and I vacuumed the shaggy green carpeting five times. It still needed to be shampooed. By noon, the heat seeped in from the sunlit windows as the rays focused on part of my back not covered by my red tank top. Dust in the air floated in the wide sunrays.

From the master bedroom, we hauled out dozens of bags of old clothes and rotten smelling towels. In the kitchen, we found old boxes and filled them with cracked and food-crusted plates, cups and bowls. The bathroom counters held more used up hairbrushes, half-used bottles of Carefree Snapback, and an assortment of black, clear, and yellow dried-up jars of hair gel.

Now we would have two bathrooms, but both toilet bowls smelled like decaying skunks. Even after Mama scrubbed them with ammonia and a brush, a yellowish-brown tint remained. Mama broke her nails scrubbing the kitchen and bathroom countertops. She tore through four pairs of yellow rubber work gloves, and we hadn't even finished the cabinets.

My face got dirtier than my hands from the flying dust. Even though I wore gloves most of the time, every part of me felt grimy, and I didn't have any more urges to bite my nails.

When my throat got dry, I drank water from the kitchen sink. The dirty penny taste wrinkled my nose, and I spit out the water. "Mama, this water tastes funny."

"Oh my goodness! Girl what are you doing drinking the water out here? You can't drink water out here. It's not clean!" Mama spoke with her face scrunched into a grimace.

"I didn't know. What's the difference Mama?"

"This water comes from a well."

"A well?"

I smiled with my lips wide open. This place had even more similarities to *Little House on the Prairie* than I thought. I ran through the kitchen to search for the well through the dining room window.

"Where is it? I can't see it, Mama."

"It's not that kind of well. An underground tank holds the water."

I dropped my head as I let go of another bit of my prairie fantasy.

Around two o'clock, I sat on the kitchen floor to rest.

"What do you call yourself doing, Laura Ingalls Wilder? Get up off that floor," Mama said.

"I'm not Laura Ingalls Wilder. I'm Tawny." I stood up and poked out my lips.

"I don't care about your pouting. Get the window cleaner, some paper towels, and hit up the mirrors and windows all around the house."

I closed my eyes and puffed up my cheeks before I grabbed the window cleaning supplies.

As I wiped the dining room windows, I saw Daddy and Keenan dragging an old mattress to a huge pile of trash. When I saw Keenan and Daddy working outside, I opened the window and yelled to them. I wanted to try out my country accent since we lived out in the country now.

"How y'all doing out there-there!" My voice echoed across the land. I shouted again. "Daddy! Daddy! Keenan! Keenan!" I looked back inside the kitchen at Mama.

She thrust the wobbly kitchen table into a corner, scraping the ragged linoleum as it moved. "There aren't any buildings to absorb the sound, so your voice echoes."

A few hours later, Mama and I walked back to the shop where Daddy and Keenan dragged stuffed trash bags to a steel barrel. Using lighter fluid, Daddy set the trash on fire. I put my hands in my pockets and surveyed my clothes. My tank-top had transformed from a deep jaded rose color to a dingy reddish brown and my jeans, once bluish-white, now were solid gray. As the flames leaped into the air, I realized that it would take a long time for the mobile home to be ready. Still, I felt a rush inside my chest down to my stomach flowing to my toes. We had made progress. Daddy would stay in town and work close to home.

In the land of the midnight sun, we didn't have to worry about losing daylight. Around eight o'clock in the evening—after nearly twelve hours of work—we were too exhausted to continue. We loaded into our car and headed back to our apartment in town. The evening sun remained high in the sky, refusing to set.

Daddy squeezed Mama's hand resting on the back of the seat. "Remember this is just temporary. We only have to live in this mobile home for a few months, just long enough to build the house."

Soccer Happiness

August before 3rd Grade, Age 8

Soccer finals began on a cool August morning, barely 50 degrees though the sun had been up before 5 AM. Players dotted the fields at Ladd Park. Beyond the parking lot, grass met the sky as far as I could see. I rode with Mama to drop Keenan off around ten o'clock to warm up with his team, the Snow Tigers, for their first play-off game. The cloudy sky tinted the fields, the soccer balls, and the boys in a muted gray. We still had over seventeen hours of daylight in mid-August, though we were losing six minutes every day now, the summer dying even at its height.

Returning a few minutes before the kick-off, we searched for a group of boys wearing Keenan's yellow and green uniform. On a perfectly even terrain with eight soccer goals, I spotted the Snow Tigers colors on field #3. White chalk outlines separated the four different fields. I easily spotted Keenan, one of only two black boys at Ladd Field.

Mama and I made our way to the sidelines. Around the field, a dozen mothers sat in lawn chairs. Without a chair, Mama found a place to stand and crossed her arms, waiting.

The Snow Tigers shared a field with a white and black uniform team with Ice Knights printed on the jerseys. Keenan's face wrinkled with concentration. Bent over with his hands on his thighs, his long yellow shorts and long green socks combined as though he wore tights underneath his shorts.

Even though Daddy wouldn't leave the shop to watch the games, he had thought that soccer would be a perfect way for Keenan and me to form friendships before we started at our new school in the fall.

During the regular season, I had played soccer, but my team—known only as the Red Team—had not been able to win one game. Now that my season had ended, I would finally be able to see my brother play.

Readying for the kick-off at the centerline, Keenan and two other forwards from the Snow Tigers faced three players from Ice Knights. All six boys focused on the ball, waiting for the bald referee. He sounded the whistle; the Ice Knights got in the first kick. The Snow Tigers's center with shoulder length brown hair responded quickly, jumping up and stopping the ball with a thump against his chest. He then gained possession and gingerly passed to Keenan. My brother dribbled the ball down the field in zig-zags as the other team attempted to steal. Black and white cleats trampled the grass. I paced the sidelines, running back and forth a few times only resting when I felt the pulse of exhaustion under my tongue. The enthusiasm he brought to the game caused me to run up and down the field. I couldn't believe how fast he got to their goal. A blonde defender set his jaw and kicked the ball, and it flew through the air and out of bounds.

During the regular season, Keenan's games had always eclipsed mine. To further Mama's annoyance, our games were never at the same park. She'd have to pick him up after my games at University Field, or he'd be already stinking up the car by the time she came to get me.

He played soccer all the time around our home. From the beginning of the season, he had started carrying his soccer ball around with him, bumping it from his forehead, patting it on the inner curve of his foot, to his knee, and to his chest.

As they played, Keenan and his teammates signaled one another by nodding and passed the ball around in syncopated glides, knowing when to bunt gently and when to kick hard.

Right before the end of the half, Keenan kicked the ball over the goal and it rolled a hundred feet away from the field.

I cheered for him. "Go Keenan. Go!"

Despite their efforts, the Ice Knights goalie had blocked all the attempts in the first half. The challenge of the sport rapidly expanded and collapsed all of the boys' chests.

During half-time, the team revived themselves with refreshments. The players' eyes remained on the coach, nodding, as they stuffed their mouths with quartered oranges. The tangy liquid drizzled on their chins and leaked on their jerseys. Their coach spoke to his team passionately with veins stretched taut on either side of his neck. "Luke, we have to score. Dribble it down the field and pass it to Keenan. I know he can score a goal."

I didn't realize his level of skill, his importance to the team. Keenan only nodded as he devoured a handful of oranges and deflated a Hi-C juice box in one suck.

Their brand of soccer appeared to be more real than mine. While I had enjoyed playing with the girls on my team, the constant running to and fro on the long fields and dribbling with the slippery ball were not challenges I wanted to overcome. I had found it unbelievable that the coach expected me to bounce a ball off my head.

The Snow Tigers had gone beyond play and the game had taken on a higher level of importance. At that moment, Keenan was more of a Snow Tiger than my brother.

After the coach gave them the plan, the Snow Tigers switched to the other side of the field for half-time. They gathered in a circle formation and practiced kicking the ball to one another.

Once the playing restarted, Keenan dribbled down the field, controlling the ball with his feet. He kicked the ball off his foot and hit it on his knee, outrunning everybody as he chased the ball toward the goal.

Finally, he made it to the other team's goal. Feigning a kick to the left, he bunted it to the right. All those pats and pops from his hand to his arm had paid off in a goal. He smiled and jumped up and down. His teammates patted him on the back as they passed the ball to one another after the game.

Mama hooted, "All right, Keenan. All right," she said smiling.

By the second half, the clouds had broken apart. The sun burst through like floodlights from above the field, transforming everything. The green grass sharpened into golden points. The temperature had climbed into the 60s.

Parents yelled from the sidelines. With the ball crouching at his feet, Keenan was right where he should be: wearing a silky green jersey with the Snow Tigers on a soccer field chasing a ball. A bright expression lit up his face, and he stood with erect posture. The passion streamed through his flared nostrils.

The team won that game—had won every game.

After the game, each team lined up to face one another. Then they slapped hands with the boys from the opposing team.

I enjoyed the last ritual best: all of the parents formed a bridge of arms, lacing their fingers together at the crest. The Snow Tigers ran through as they yelled "good job" and "way to go."

The Shop

August before 3rd Grade, Age 8

As the eternal summer days spun into fall, we began to have moonlit nights again. Almost time for us to return to school, Keenan and I only had seven days left of vacation. We finally moved into the mobile home at the end of August. Mama was taking us into town to buy new school clothes.

Around four o'clock, Keenan, Mama, and I stopped by the shop before we headed to the stores for the back-to-school deals. The sun streamed through the open garage door while Mama and Daddy talked near the opening of the garage.

My brother and I had to wait in the car, and the weather felt just right - not too hot or cold. Late August gave us over fifteen hours of daylight, but we lost six minutes every day.

Straining to hear what they were saying, I turned down the radio in the car.

Mama leaned in close to Daddy. "Good thing we've got some savings since nobody coming to the shop."

Even though Midway Auto Body Shop could easily be seen from the New Richardson Highway, hundreds of cars passed every day without stopping. Out here, no one really cared about the body of their car - just making sure that their vehicle drove smoothly. Daddy had only two customers since he opened for business in July. My best friend Day-ja's mother had been my father's first customer when she needed a new transmission. Mark, Daddy's sole black friend from the North Slopes, had needed the dent in his bumper repaired after an accident.

"Don't worry," Daddy said, wiping his brow.

"My mama didn't raise no fool. I know that new businesses take some time to turn a profit. I'll help out if I need to," My mother spoke confidently.

"I still might have to go back to the Slopes."

My mother clasped his hands and brought them to her chest. "You know how I feel about you being away, especially during the winter. I could barely handle it when we lived in town. Now that we're out here…"

"If I have to go back, that's what I gotta do. We're eating up the money I have saved for the new house."

As they spoke, a beige station wagon pulled up. Mama lifted her arms and wiggled her fingers.

"All right, Mary. You're number three," Mama said.

Aunt Mary opened the door and stuck out a thick leg. "Y'all do oil changes around here?" she said with a quick smile. My aunt spoke with a much stronger Southern accent than Daddy's. She always said words like y'all and pronounced words in a funny way.

Daddy stepped up to her car. "You know it. I know it says Midway Auto Body, but we do it all: oil changes, new engines, whatever you need, ma'am."

Aunt Mary watched his face for a minute.

"I'll say," she said, "All's I need is an oil change."

He winked at her. "We will definitely take care of that for you."

She grinned at him. I could tell Aunt Mary tried to hide her concern by the way she sat partly inside and halfway out of her car.

"How much is it?"

"That will be fifty dollars," he said.

Aunt Mary withdrew inside of her vehicle. "This must be a luxury car place.

I ain't never paid that much for no old oil change."

"You know I'm just pulling your leg. It's on the house."

She shook her head. "Damon, you can't be giving no free services away. I am here to support you. That's what families do. Besides, the Lawd laid it on my heart to come out here and help you out."

Daddy nodded. "What do you usually pay?"

"'Bout fifteen dollars, but you're my brother and I know you need support, so I'm going to pay you $25 today."

"Well all right. Sounds good."

As September arrived, I started third grade. The darkness returned quickly—by mid-September, we were down to twelve hours of daylight, and by the end of the month, barely ten. The sun set before dinner now. Every morning when we woke for school, it got darker than the morning before. We lost six minutes of daylight every single day, the autumn dissolved light faster than seemed possible.

By the time October arrived, the eternal summer had become a memory. We had ten hours of daylight, sunrise at 8:30 a.m. with sunset at 6:30 p.m. The darkness that had vanished in June returned to claim us for another winter.

Normal

October of 4th Grade, Age 9

By October of fourth Grade, Keenan (now a 5th grader), and I had just started our second year at Badger Road Elementary.

The kitchen dimmed by the shadowed outdoors around 5 p.m. Losing six minutes of daylight everyday, left us with ten hour days. In the evenings, the gale force winds whined around the corners of the doublewide mobile home where tiny cracks in the structure leaked in air.

Mama transformed the mobile home from filthy to clean. The carpeted and linoleum surfaces had been scrubbed regularly until they held a permanent cleanliness. Flowery contact paper decorated the once stained and scratched bottoms of the bathroom drawers and kitchen cabinet cupboards. The pale shag carpeting had been shampooed and vacuumed until only a faint scent of mildew could be sniffed when lying on the floor.

The kitchen, long and wide, had a new rectangular table with six high-backed wooden chairs. On the opposite wall from the sliding glass door, Mama placed the Kenmore deep freezer.

Mama furnished the dining area with a single cushiony rocking chair and a three bookshelves stocked with a full set of encyclopedias and dozens of reading books. I'm sure Mama designed the library area for me, but Keenan had access to my library whenever he wanted.

A new midnight blue L-shaped sectional couch dominated the living room. Its design also worked as a wall, guarding us from the cool winter air. The stereo system took up the remaining space in the living room with its record stands and a cassette tape storage unit. She had a pair of speakers taller than me in the living room. She stored another pair of speakers in the master bedroom so that our home would be filled with Rick James, Cameo, and Evelyn Champagne King from the front to the back.

Near the threshold of the living room and the kitchen, three empty long neck Riunite wine bottles lined up along the wall. I wondered why every week another wine bottle lengthened the collection.

Keenan, the Popular Kid

October of 4th Grade, Age 9

One afternoon, I walked over to the field to watch my brother play soccer during recess. One of the kids at Badger Road, named Tim, had played soccer with Keenan during the summers. Tim stood on the sidelines and cheered Keenan on while he played.

The afternoon sunlight focused on the field as Brother kicked the ball into the goal. Tim turned to me with excited eyes. "See, that's my buddy. Your brother is the best soccer player in the school," he said proudly. I raised my eyebrows at Tim's enthusiasm. I hadn't seen anyone display this level of admiration for another kid.

Keenan really played—all out. He stumbled on a tuft of grass and stained his new blue and black flower-print Bermuda shorts, which fell below his knees.

"He's already scored five goals," Tim pointed it out to everyone watching. Tim's enthusiasm made other kids want to watch. About fifteen kids gathered along the edge of the soccer field.

John, a player on the opposing team, yelled at Tim. "Shut up Tubby!"

Tim blushed and stopped speaking. On the soccer field, Keenan tripped John. The boy fell on his chest and rolled over. My brother stood over him and pointed down at him, "Don't make fun of Tim because you can't play. You're a sorry player so you want to make fun of him. You're sorry. It's not his fault." Keenan held out his hand to help him up. "Now do you want to play or what, Sorry Soccer Boy?" The other players laughed and snorted. John refused Keenan's hand and pushed off the ground on his own. He walked away from the field. The other kids repeated it, "Sorry Soccer Boy". All over school John became known as Sorry Soccer Boy. Brother had also become the most powerful boy on the playground.

Everyone gave Keenan attention. At school assemblies, the girls waved at him. Other boys whispered, "That's Keenan" when they saw him in the hallways.

Tim became his best friend. When Keenan got upset about something, I saw Tim with his arm around my brother's shoulder. Keenan took deep breaths and nodded his head while Tim spoke to him calmly. My brother had a blow up at least once a week, and Tim helped calm him down.

Mama's Job

October of 4th Grade, Age 9

Mama had been working at University of Alaska Fairbanks for nearly two months. Even though she'd get off work after we got home, Mama had prepared beef stew before she left for work. The stew simmered on low in the Crock Pot all day. We reached home around four, its comforting aroma wafted over us when we entered the front door. We ladled the chunky soup into bowls and sat down in front of the television to eat.

By the time the outdoors dimmed the kitchen around 5:30 p.m., Mama came through the door. She went straight to the refrigerator to take out the pitcher of vodka and orange juice. I had accidentally swallowed a bitter swig last week, thinking that I'd enjoy a sip of Tang.

Unbuttoning her blouse and skirt, Mama signaled that she felt tired. As I leaned in to kiss her, she turned her head so that it landed on her cheekbone. Keenan came up and hugged her. She pushed him away.

"Boy don't be jumping all over me."

Keenan let go of her and slumped. "I'm sorry Mama."

Walking into the kitchen, she scanned the room and dropped her purse on the floor.

"Why isn't this kitchen clean?"

"It's Tawny's turn," said Keenan.

She glared at me.

"Get this damn kitchen clean, Tawny," she said, stomping at me. I jumped into action. I washed the dishes hurriedly.

Afterwards, I went to my room and cried as I read *Where the Red Fern Grows*. Crying about Lil' Ann and Old Dan felt easier than facing the change in Mama.

Work stressed her too much. Daddy worked long hours at the shop for six days of the week. Even though he toiled only a couple of hundred yards away, we barely saw him.

Back when we lived in our cozy Fairbanks apartment, Mama had been neat, organized, and calm. She used to dance out her stress, shifting the blue moods with movement. Other times, she sang away moodiness in an off-key.

Smarter

October of 4th Grade, Age 9

Later that week, we went to Fred Meyer's for groceries and household cleaner. As we wandered the aisles, I strayed from my mother when we got to the magazine and book aisle. I found books to make me smarter there. All kinds of books. Some that I knew would make me smart. I found a writing book, a grammar book, and a math book. I wanted all three, but I decided to choose just one. Just one, the lowest price without being too easy. I found a three-dollar book that focused on math. I loved to read. I loved to write, but math was a problem for me. It took me a long time to add and subtract. I still used my fingers. Mr. Beu drilled us during Around the World, but I always got beat. I never asked Mama for nothing at the store because I knew that we had a tight budget.

"I need this book Mama."

"What is that?"

"A book so that I could get better with math," I said. I tried to look at Mama with the most serious face I could. So she could see that this wasn't me asking for ice cream or a sweet treat.

"Another book Tawny?"

"I have to be smart. I'm really slow with my math facts. I need to practice. I am going into the fifth grade next year and Mr. Beu says school gets harder. I have to make sure I'm ready."

"How much is it?" Mama asked.

"Two dollars and ninety-nine cents," I said.

"Alright, Tawny," she said, rolling her eyes and smiling.

She turned to Keenan, "You want a book to work on your math Keenan?"

"No!" Keenan said, cutting off Mama and holding up his hand. "Tawny is a nerd. I'm going to be practicing on my handling techniques so we can make it to the state championships this year."

I shrugged. "I'm going to be the smartest person in the world," I said.

He waved his hand, dismissing me.

I was going to be, not just as smart, but smarter than them. The next time I beat them on a test and Shane got upset, I would be smiling.

Sunday Rituals

November of 4th Grade, Age 9

On Sunday afternoons, I read in the dining room. Soft afternoon light filtered through the windows. Outside, eight feet tall snow banks surrounding the house tucked us into our home.

I stood up, stretched, and yawned before picking up my book again. A brown comfort chair had been placed in the center of the room. Instead of using the dining room for an eating area, Mama furnished it with a single cushiony rocking chair and three bookcases—two that reached the ceiling and a short one with three shelves. The room served as a library study stocked with a full set of encyclopedias and dozens of reading books for everyone to enjoy. My next literary adventure entitled *Little House in the Big Woods* demanded my full attention. I had only been willing to put it down to eat, use the restroom, and occasionally stretch. Even more than the television series *Little House on the Prairie*, the *Big Woods* captured the prairie life, its scents, recipes, and the close-knit family. Laura Ingalls Wilder wrote this book first.

Through the dining room window, I gazed over the property with all the trash hidden by the snow. Every time I looked through the window, I grew a little more satisfied. I began to see the parallels between Midway Industrial Park and the Ingalls family in so many ways.

"Come here, girl. Let me take care of that hair," my mother said.

She was in the living room. I only had to swivel the chair to the left to see her sitting on the couch with a comb in her hand, she motioned for me to sit down between her legs. Beside her, she had placed a rattail comb, a jar of Blue Magic, and a wide toothed comb. Every Sunday she braided my hair into a new style. I touched the soft cumulonimbus wave of hair that stretched from my scalp. Yesterday, she had taken down last week's braids. I wished I could wear it out, that it wouldn't dry out and knot up without the braids.

"Just a couple more pages, Mama. Please," I said pointing to my book.

Her eyes emitted an immovable gaze, and her head dropped to a solid forty-five degree angle. Negotiation wouldn't work right now.

She parted my hair, her index finger slid along the lip of the Blue Magic grease, coconut scented. Next, her finger glided over a part in my hair, stroking my scalp while dragging its way down to the nape. Finally, she braided my hair.

As she combed my hair into neat cornrows, I had to hold my head still. Forced to stare at the wall across from the couch, I learned to love the painting above the television. The African Ashante woman with black skin featured with hair in natural kinks cropped close to her scalp. Her arrow thin arm helped balance a gourd atop her head. Mama explained her beauty—ebony skin glowing under her crown of short hair and scarlet lips, round and full. This image created a feeling of pride and connection to Africa within me. I thought of myself as a beautiful African, likening her hair to my own. Mama finished my braids in the late afternoon, and I felt beautiful and loved.

Life on the Tundra

November of 4th Grade, Age 9

On Sunday evenings, the four of us were all home together. In the darkness, we sat on the couch in front of the wooden entertainment stand to watch our 19" color television. Each end of the L-shaped couch had a recliner. Daddy sat in the reclining part closest to the front door, Mama sat right next to him, Keenan scooted in next to Mama, and I sat beside Keenan.

One Sunday night, Daddy cleared his throat. "Look, we need to be well informed around here. We all should know what is going on in the world. That's why I think we should watch *60 Minutes*."

"The A-Team is about to come on," I said, frowning at Daddy.

"And Dukes of Hazard," Keenan added.

Mama waved an arm loosely in the air. "I don't care what we watch." She sat with her legs crossed at the knees and looked towards the television before she tipped a fiery red plastic cup to her lips. Ice cubes knocked dully against the inside of the cup. Since Mama started working, it had become her habit. Did her cup contain wine or vodka? I wasn't sure.

"*60 Minutes* is boring," I said.

"Well that's what we're watching." Daddy said.

I folded my arms across my chest. Keenan stood up, stretching out his thin arms above his head.

"Where are you going?" I asked him.

"Going back to my room. Andy Rooney is boring. We watched that last Sunday."

"Suit yourself. That's your problem," Mama said before she dipped her head again towards her cup.

Daddy used his muscular arms to heave himself off the couch. "I need something to snack on." Walking into the kitchen, he flicked on the light. He opened a cabinet and rustled with something plastic. Something heavy thudded against the countertop. I ran into the kitchen to see.

"Stop running in here girl. I got my drink on the ground here. Don't knock it over," Mama called after me.

I rounded the corner to the kitchen. Daddy had already poured in the canola oil and the sunshine bits of kernels began plopping onto the metal bottom of the popper as the metal wand began to rotate around, spreading the oil and corn seeds evenly.

"You're making popcorn!" Keenan yelled out excitedly.

"Well, don't you worry about it. You're going to your room remember? Go on in your room. This is for those of us who are watching TV."

As thin as he was, Keenan never turned down food. He ate like he was racing somebody. Daddy gave him a slight smile.

"One, two. It's already popping." I said, moving my face as close to the popper as possible.

"Three, four," counted Keenan.

"Five, six, seven, eight," I said.

Then the two of us tried to see how long we could keep up the count before the popping got too fast.

Daddy cut a chunk of butter to put on top of the popper dome. The butter dripped into the popper, coating the popcorn.

"All right, you all go sit down," Daddy said.

Keenan and I ran to the living room and sat in our place. After a few minutes, he came into the living room with a huge bowl of popcorn.

First Daddy took a handful and passed the bowl to Mama. She took a moment to place her cup on the floor. She filled her hand and half of the kernels slipped through her fingers back into the bowl. Then Keenan filled his bony hands with popcorn, gripping every piece. I took it out of his lap and grabbed a handful. Keenan pushed his face into his hand and a few seconds later his hands were empty. Mama smacked her lips and dropped a couple kernels into her mouth one at one time. Daddy looked down at me and screwed his voice into a high-pitched playful tone.

"Hey what you doing down there with the bowl?"

I grinned at Daddy, smiling back at me. Mama gave me a loose-lipped smirk with glassy eyes.

"Hey," he continued, "Send that bowl down here."

I passed it to Keenan so that he could hand it down to Daddy. But Keenan took another handful, more this time. I looked in the bowl and could see that there wasn't much left, and I only had a little. I took the bowl from Keenan and got up to run just beyond the television. I plunged my hand into the bowl and stuffed my face.

Daddy jumped up, taking two big steps.

Mama shifted and reached for her cup, "Uh, be careful. Don't spill my drink, Damon."

With Daddy close enough to reach out and grab me, I raced away from him into the dining room and into the kitchen. The cool linoleum floor slid against my loose tube socks. When I came back around to the living room, Keenan met me there. I squealed as a soft thud knocked over one of the Riunite bottles as I tried to back away. He took the bowl. A chuckle bubbled out of me, Mama screamed a high-pitched guffaw.

When the Water Froze

November of 4th Grade, Age 9

Getting out of bed, I felt a spidery cold against my toes creeping to the tip of my nose. The temperatures had been getting colder, but this morning the air spun my breath into clouds. The darkness remained until after 9 a.m. From the pale moonlight outside my window, I could make out a new layer of snow covering the wild grasses, weeds, and tips of tree branches.

My Disney princess nightgown and flowery thermal pants kept me warm last night. But as my bare feet slapped at the slab of linoleum on the bathroom floor this morning, I couldn't help shivering.

As usual, I flicked on the bathroom light to brush my teeth and wash my face. I turned the faucet handle—but instead of water—a brown liquid sputtered out, smelling like rotten boiled eggs and dappling the brown liquid all over the sink. Then a trickle came out. I couldn't believe the water wouldn't come on. Stunned, I turned the knob on and off again and again, which brought less and less water each time until nothing came out.

I looked under the sink. Maybe I could tell that something had broken. The scent of mildew and dampness met my nostrils, but everything looked the same.

As I used the bathroom, I thought of knocking on Mama and Daddy's room door to let them know. When I flushed, no whoosh of new water filled the commode. Out of habit, I turned the sink handle again. Not even a drop.

From the bathroom, I heard Mama. "Damon!" Mama yelled to my father at the top of her lungs as the vibration of her feet stomped down the hallway. "You better take care of this."

I walked out of the bathroom and followed Mama who wore a zipped up robe and gray thermal socks with worn light blue house slippers.

She stood over Daddy, looking so peaceful in his palazzo p.j. pants and a dingy wife beater as he sat in the living room listening to "Time in a Bottle." He wore brown house shoes with the backs folded under his feet.

"Only a little water is coming out, what's going on?" she said, yelling with hands on her hips.

Daddy closed his eyes calmly before opening them again. "I know. The pipes froze over night. There is still a little water coming out because the tank for the water heater isn't quite empty."

"Well what are you going to do about it?" Mama said, swinging her arms widely. She couldn't stand it when Daddy matched her anger with calm.

Daddy answered with a high-pitched defensive voice. He glanced at me and gave me a smile that failed to spread to his eyes. "Look, I'm going to get it fixed."

I wondered about the well water. Was it frozen solid underground, too? But I knew not to interrupt. I shivered. "You cold, Tawny?" Daddy said.

I nodded. "Daddy, will you turn on the heater?" I said.

"I already turned on the heat, Tawny. It's warming up, but you have to put on some more clothes."

Obediently, I rushed back to my room and pulled on the socks I had on the day before. Finding my flowered thermal shirt in one of my drawers, I pulled it on over my gown. The bottom section of my gown still hung down below my knees.

The heat in our home came through floor vents. I waved my hands over the one in my room, nearest to my bed. Cool air still blew through the vent. A few minutes later, I waved my hand over it again, and this time the warm air compelled me to stand over the vent. When the air became hot, I kneeled on top of the vent, pulling my gown around my folded legs. All the air flowed up into my gown and over my shivering body. I stayed there a few more minutes until it got so hot that I couldn't stand it.

Not sure what to do next, I walked into the kitchen. Daddy and Mama were still in the living room discussing the water. I drifted toward their voices.

"I'm going to take care of it," Daddy said, "Don't worry. When I was a little kid we never had running water." Then he added, "You know, this kind of thing is a good experience for them."

Mama's hands slipped from her hips at that notion and her mouth opened into a smile. Surprisingly, she nodded and turned to me. "You hear that, Tawny? Good experience for you."

Daddy explained that as a little boy in Arkansas, he and his family had to relieve themselves in the woods and find whatever they could to wipe their behinds. According to him, the best find was a corncob. Most of the time, they had to use a stick. I cringed in disgust.

Mama completely agreed with him, trying out the new phrase a few more times, "Good experience for you. That's right, good experience for you." She laughed in a high piercing pitch. I glared at them. Wouldn't they want things to be better for their children?

The urge of my bladder caused a dull pain in my abdomen. Mama's laughter stung in my ears. "I need to go to the bathroom again," I said.

"Go on and use the bathroom if you need to. Just don't flush," Daddy said. As he walked into the kitchen, his house shoes popped and scraped under his flat feet.

In the bathroom, the sink had dried. Spatters of the rusted water flecked the sink. Once I used the bathroom again, my hands felt dirty. I shook away the image of Daddy using the bathroom with a stick.

Back in the kitchen, Mama began cooking things that didn't require water. She cut a pat of butter and scraped the block against the side of the pan, watching it as it melted. My mother cracked five eggs into a skillet. She scrambled the eggs and slathered toast with butter.

Keenan groaned as he entered the kitchen, dragging his slippered feet along the kitchen floor. In all the excitement, no one woke up Keenan. He wore his same Spiderman pajamas, once foot-ins. As he grew taller, Mama cut off the footed bottoms. Now the cut-off legs stopped at least an inch above his ankle. Since he grew taller and not any wider, he could still fit into them. His nose, eyes, and mouth scrunched together as he stretched out his arms.

"What's wrong with the water?" Keenan said.

Daddy answered, "The water's out because the pipes froze last night."

"Good thing we have a jug of drinking water in the fridge," Mama said. "Tawny, we're going to boil some water so you and Keenan can wash up this morning. Then you'll have to take your toothbrush and your toothpaste with you to school so you can brush in the bathroom before class. You can't go through the school day with stanky breath."

"Good, I have to keep my teeth clean," Keenan said, nodding. He went to the bathroom right away to pack up the materials.

"Mama, why can't we brush here?" I whined.

"No, you going to use up all the water. Do it when you get to school!" Her pointed finger informed me of the final decision.

One morning without brushing didn't matter. I decided that I would not brush my teeth at home or school. If anyone at school saw me, it would be too embarrassing to explain. My teeth were already bucked. That would be drawing attention to my messed up teeth. On the other hand, my brother was very proud of his straight white teeth. He flossed every night and brushed three times a day instead of just twice a day like I did.

Fortunately, the water began flowing again in a few days. Once the water flowed again, it made me really appreciate it.

Every so often, the water would freeze and Daddy would have to go down below our home to use a blowtorch to thaw out the pipes. When necessary, Daddy hired someone to thaw it out.

With only six and a half hours of daylight, November descended with its relentless darkness. Then December arrived, the darkest month. We had barely three and a half hours of daylight. I went to school in the dark, and came home at dusk.

During the winter break, the winter solstice gave us the longest nights. During those few hours of weak light, the sun hung low on the horizon but never climbed. The darkness pressed down on everything, making the cold feel colder, and the isolation more complete.

The Bus Incident

April of 4th Grade, Age 10

Most of the year, the school bus picked us up before the sun penetrated the darkness. In April, morning light streamed through the windows with nearly sixteen hours of daylight. The kids stayed awake, turned around, played hand games, and had conversations over the rumbling of the engine.

I sat in the middle of the bus, right in front of Victoria, a tall fifth grader. A few minutes after I got on the bus, the tall girl glared at me and pointed, "Your hair is so weird. You have a whole bunch of parts. Weird." Sarah, her seat partner, nodded in agreement. They both snickered.

"What is that African or something?" she said using air quotes. I glanced at their reddening faces, teasing me. "Leave me alone," I said, putting my hand on one hip and speaking as strongly as I could.

"*Leave me alone*," Victoria said, mocking me. She snapped her fingers in a sloppy z-formation and moved her neck in a clumsy circle. The taunting laughs spread further down the aisles as more kids leaned in to listen.

Keenan sat in the back of the bus, but I didn't want to call for him. That would make me look like a baby. So I propped myself up using my leg. That way I could see over the back of the seat. I yelled out loud enough for him to hear me, "Leave me alone!" It seemed that a wall of kids rose up against me, taunting me, laughing even louder now. My brother heard me shout. He looked around. Over the noise, I heard his voice. "They're making fun of Tawny?"

We were not allowed to get out of our seats while the bus was moving, but Keenan moved up next to me anyway. His body shielded me from the others. Lifting his chin he started in on them. "Who you laughing at? Look at you with your flat butt, your stringy, straw hair. You're ugly. I'll whup all your asses if you say something else, if you laugh at her, if you try to do anything to my baby sister."

All the kids stopped laughing. Victoria and Sarah froze, their eyes bulged. Victoria's reddened face went white with embarrassment. I was so glad to have a brother like Keenan. I could have hugged him.

The bus swerved suddenly, and we all jerked sideways. The driver pulled over on the side of the highway. I had never known a driver to stop the bus like this. We would be late for school. All of the talking ceased as he clicked his seatbelt off. His pudgy body shuffled down the aisle. He stuck his meaty finger into Keenan's face. "You are not to get out of your seat on the bus. Do you understand?"

Keenan's eyes turned glossy as a few kids stepped closer, crowding around to see. He focused his eyes on the driver's and trembled with anger. Through gritted teeth he spoke, "They were bothering my sister."

Everyone stood, watching. Then as if a spout had opened, Victoria let out a pink-faced wail. Her face wriggled out of shape, her lips stretched out with her eyes squeezed tight. I couldn't figure out what caused her to cry. She started it all and hurt my feelings. The driver turned his head and a few oily strands shook from his feathered bangs. His voice softened, "What happened Victoria?"

She didn't speak, but Sarah spoke up for her crying friend. She explained to the driver with a tear-stained face that my brother had threatened her friend and how Keenan terrified both of them.

The driver made Keenan sit in the seat right behind him. I got Keenan in trouble; I wished I knew how to defend myself.

The Punishment

April of 4th Grade, Age 10

After the bus ride home, Keenan and I cracked up about how Victoria's face had turned from red to white after Keenan made her shut up. She and her friend did not even ride the bus home.

When we entered the house at 3:30, afternoon sunlight poured through the kitchen windows. The sun hung high and bright, and it wouldn't set until after 9 p.m. Daddy and Mama stood in the middle of the kitchen, silhouetted against the bright window. Why would both parents be home after school? We knew then to expect punishment.

Daddy spoke first, "The school called. The principal told us that you had harassed some white girls on the bus this morning. You threatened her."

Keenan moved his eyes nervously from my parents to me and to the ceiling.

I tried to explain. "Daddy, they didn't tell you what those girls said—" Daddy shifted, revealing a long belt with a buckle at the end of his arm. It scraped against the faded linoleum.

"It doesn't matter, Tawny." Daddy said, keeping his eyes on Keenan.

"Daddy —," Keenan faltered.

Daddy snapped the belt with one hand and thrust his finger into Keenan's face. The skin below one of our father's eyes twitched. "Be quiet. Didn't I tell you not to be going to school acting a fool? Now you're suspended from the bus for three days."

While Daddy spoke, Mama stared at Keenan. Her chest puffed out more with each detail and she sat down erect with both feet planted on either side of her as if she were ready to pounce.

"I'm supposed to take him to school? Shit!" Mama shook her head and lingered on the word shit for a few seconds. "I'll be god damned." Then Mama got up and poked a sharp finger into Keenan's face. "He wants to cut the fool at school, he going to have to miss a few days. I'm not taking him no damn where."

Mama worked from 7:30 to 5. She had to leave right before our bus came at seven o'clock. Daddy started work in the shop around seven in the morning. Neither one of them could take Keenan to school without missing work.

He stammered, "They were talking about my —"

Mama grabbed him by the neck. Her face was so close to his, I thought she might bite him. "I don't give a damn what happened. I don't give a damn!"

Keenan's eyes welled and Mama's eyes cinched into evil slits. Keenan's chin lifted like it had earlier and his chest began to swell under the pressure. He could do nothing with his anger this time, no one to tell off. He'd never win against Mama.

"Damita!" Daddy said finally. "Damita, let him go."

She released her clutch on him. When she stepped back, she saw Keenan's clenched fists. She lunged back at him, grabbing his shirt. Beside the refrigerator, I screamed. This time, it seemed Mama didn't hear me or Daddy calling her name.

"Oh you mad? You mad? You think you can whup me?" she shouted.

Keenan unclenched and she grabbed his face. Mama hit him on the back of his head. He stomped out of the room, grabbed his ball, and ran outside.

Under a Microscope

April of 4th Grade, Age 10

A week later, we came into class and a group of microscopes were set up on the back table. Morning sunrays flooded the classroom windows, making the metal instruments gleam. We had over seventeen hours of daylight, so morning felt like midday.

I couldn't wait to pretend to be a scientist.

"You can use these instruments to take a closer look at things," Ms. Coerr said, "For example, let's try putting a strand of hair on a lens so that we can view it magnified."

I looked around, worried that my "weird" hair would be in danger of curious peers.

Shane came up to me, greeting me in an unexpected friendly way.

"Hey, Tawny! I really like your hair!" I took a few steps away from him. He was definitely acting strange.

"Can I have…" He leaned closer with his hand already poised.

"No!" I said, but he had already grabbed a loose strand from one of my fuzzy braids. I yelped as he yanked it from my scalp. I rubbed my head.

"Hey!" I said.

But Shane ignored me. He placed my hair on the slide, positioning it under the lens. I could only stare in shock—transfixed to the place where I stood. I wanted to see what they would say!

Shane, Peter, and Morgan were leaning over the tables. "Don't you notice her hair is shinier than other people's?" Shane said.

"Wait, let me see," Peter said, nudging Shane away from the microscope.

"Yeah. You know why don't you?" Morgan asked.

I heard a low whisper say, "She uses Crisco grease in her hair."

Right then, I felt a welling up inside, a churning of sadness and shame. This must be what the African people on National Geographic feel as they are analyzed and studied without anyone speaking to them about their own life and their own bodies. I did not see much of Shane after that year, but his behavior toward me stayed with me longer than the memory of his face.

Mama's Anger

April of 4th Grade, Age 10

Mama banged through the door. She had just returned from work late to make up time lost for attending a mandatory parent conference. After Keenan's three-day bus suspension, the school required that a parent, student, and the principal meet before a child could return to riding the bus. At home, she could curse Keenan out for his transgression - again.

"Keenan! Where you at? Come on in here!"

I sat in the living room, watching t.v. and completing my homework.

My brother came out of the room.

"There you are! Come in here and sit down!"

Keenan walked slowly to the table.

"Let me tell you something, boy! They think it's my fault. My fault," Mama said, hitting her chest. The kitchen fixture cast harsh shadows across her face. "I've stayed up late typing your papers. I've read to you when you were a little snot-nose. I made damn sure you learned how to read. I made sure you were cleaned and fed. But you go to school and act a fool. Act like you ain't had no damn home training. Those white mother fuckers think that you don't care. And since you don't care, neither do I. That's what they think.

"You gonna take your ass to school and act like you give a damn. Act like you got some mother fucking sense or Imma whip yo' ass everyday until you graduate. Every. Damn. Day. Do you hear me? Every. Damn. Day.

"I can't believe that bitch. I went up into that office and that bitch crossed her arms and crossed one of her pale legs over the other and sat back in that easy chair. Sat back and judged me. I'm not no sorry ass mama. I've given every damn thing I could. Then gave some damn more, but apparently that's not damn good enough. It's never fucking enough. Never!"

Mama provided warmth and shelter, but I could not hold her, and she couldn't hold me. So from her I developed this godly fear of her fire, a treacherous balance between not getting close enough to get burned and not being too far away to miss her attention.

Locked Away

April of 4th Grade, Age 10

When the spring break-up hit, the mud puddles and the last bits of dirty snow made me want to forget homework and play outside all evening. The days stretched later into the night hours with sunset coming around 11 p.m. The shining sun hypnotized me. The light from our mobile home windows glared on my white multiplication worksheets and the glossy pages of my reading textbook. But I knew that if I fell into the mood of the weather, I'd spoil my grades. So I did my homework every night no matter what.

Even when Keenan kicked the ball against the side of our mobile home, I learned to concentrate beyond the ball's beat. With Daddy working at the shop and Mama at work until six, no one interrupted him.

About an hour after we got home, I heard Mama coming up the front steps. Ready to embrace her, I opened my arms. Ignoring me, she opened the refrigerator and quickly poured herself a drink. She yelled at us about the dirty bowls in the sink and headed to her room. The lock clicked on her door.

To be considerate, I waited about thirty minutes before knocking on Mama's door. She answered with a roar. "What you want?"

In a timid voice, I asked, "Um, can we have some ice cream?"

"No."

"Why not, we already ate dinner, plus we haven't had no ice cream in a long time." I said, slightly fearful of pushing too much. While I waited, I did a shuffle outside the door before I realized she had given me her final answer.

Back in the kitchen, I surveyed the dishes piled up in the sink and the crumbs collected on the linoleum. Since my brother and I had neglected our chores, I understood how we had upset Mama. I needed to remind Keenan to wash the dishes.

In his room, I stepped over Keenan's wrinkled English folder and a Hulk Hogan wrestling figure so that I could face him as he lay on the top bunk.

"It's your turn to wash the dishes."

"No, it's not. I looked at the calendar."

"It says my name, but those dishes are from yesterday when you didn't wash them."

"The calendar says it's your turn," He said without looking at me.

Brother wasn't about to make me do his work. If I told Mama, I knew she would make sure he did his job. Instead of knocking, I just spoke loudly outside of the door. "Keenan won't wash the dishes from yesterday."

The familiar bittersweet scent of marijuana leaked from the other side of her door. "If I come out there..." Mama spoke as if controlling an eruption building up inside. She started getting high a few weeks ago. I must've interrupted her inhaling. Aunt Denise sold weed and grew it under halogen light bulbs in her coat closet. We had seen Auntie smoke it many times. Mama acted like we didn't know that she smoked, too. After hanging around Denise's house, we recognized the unmistakable aroma of a weed joint.

I hurried away from the door and decided to handle the situation. Back in Keenan's room, I put my hands on my hips. "Mama told you to wash the dishes, I said.

If the house got clean, she would come out of her room and spend some time with us.

Keenan rolled his eyes and dragged himself into the kitchen to wash the dishes.

Minutes later, when Mama emerged from her room, I already wiped off the table and was in the middle of sweeping. Swinging her cup as she drifted into the kitchen, she approached the refrigerator. Her eyes, tinted like pale pink roses, slid over my face without focusing.

"See, Mama, we're cleaning up."

I reached out to her, but she swatted me away. Setting down her cup, she went into the refrigerator. I shrugged like I didn't care, a defense that I had taught myself. Shrugging worked better than crying. Tears only made her more irritated. Rounding the corner into the living room, she turned up the music on her bedroom speakers and sealed herself back inside of her room. I went into the living room and worked on homework while watching television.

Aunt Denise called for Mama. She cracked the door enough to reach for the phone, a thin stream of weed exhaust escaped from the room.

"Cut down that music," she demanded, closing the door again. I heard her drop her voice and shoot out loose words the way she always did with Auntie.

"I'm still out in the boonies slaving for The Man."

A few moments later, her cackle rang out shrilly.

"No! We might not ever have the money to get this raggedy trailer together! Dammit!"

I dragged my feet back through the kitchen and into the living room where *The Cosby Show* theme music played. The parents on Cosby always talked to their kids. Cliff, the dad, rarely worked during the night and Claire, the Mama, was there after school.

After *The Cosby Show* ended, I remembered my history test. I knocked on Mama's bedroom door, and she yelled from the other side. "What do you want?"

I had already tattled on Keenan and asked for a snack. Now I thought of earning her attention.

"Mama, I want you to see my history test."

"Let me guess — an A?"

"Yeah — 100%!" I said smiling.

With a deflated voice, she said, "Great, I'll look at it later."

I threw a silent tantrum outside the door, flailing my arms and punching at the air.

Family Battle

May of 4th Grade, Age 10

A few nights later, my sleep had been interrupted by a splintering voice. It must have been after midnight. In May, true darkness never came. The sky stayed that strange blue-gray color all night, what passed for darkness this time of year. A stream of light leaked beneath the door from the hallway, brighter than the twilight outside my window. I remained silent and still and listened petrified.

The sounds sharpened. Daddy's voice growled angrily, like a jolt of thunder, "You hate yourself. You hate yourself."

My grogginess evaporated and slid into an unanchored spectrum of emotions off-balanced and sinking. Their voices crashed into each other.

Mama yelled, "I hate you. I hate you." Their words jabbed like swords.

Daddy roared back at her, "You can't treat these kids like you don't want 'em."

Their voices continued as colliding waves, "I told them no! You got a problem saying no! They're *my* damn kids!"

Their angry tones continued to claw. "Whatever—*our* kids," Daddy corrected her.

Why were they arguing about us? Why wouldn't they be fussing at us about it? Maybe Mama had been in her room so much lately because we were always acting up and fighting.

Someone turned on the stereo and the pounding beats of Cameo's "Word Up" blasted, but my mother's voice screeched above the singing, "I hate you!"

I waited underneath my covers until I didn't hear any voices. Sliding out of the covers, I sat on the edge of my bed and decided to go out. When I put my bare feet on the cold carpet, I contemplated returning to the warmth of my quilt. I heard footsteps coming up the hallway. When I reached the bedroom door, someone went into the bathroom and locked it. A sob echoed through the wall, and I recognized my mother's voice. I knocked.

"Go away!" Mama yelled, still in her fighting voice.

"Mama, it's Tawny," I said in my softest audible voice, "I have to go to the bathroom." Hopefully this excuse would allow me to see if she was all right. I thought of Nia's mommy with her black eye.

"Use the other bathroom," her voice wilted with tears and a strong tone.

I felt that familiar sting of Mama's continual rejection as if I wasn't enough. I still tried to reach her through the closed door. "Alright," I said. But I couldn't leave. After a moment, I knocked again.

"Who is it?" Mama asked. I had her on the verge of losing her patience.

"Mama, what is the matter?" She might be mad at me, but what if she needed my help?

"Please don't cry. It is going to be alright," I said, speaking to her as if she were my little girl.

She told me to go to bed. Then the weak sobs melted into the air.

I did not have the words for what I felt, but something in me shifted every time she broke open like this.

Where was Daddy? No light in their bedroom meant he must be in the front.

I found my dad listening to music in the living room. The music had changed from loud and upbeat to the slow Glen Campbell song "By the Time I Get to Phoenix." His eyes were closed. I touched his hand, and he opened them.

"What are you doing up, girl?"

I told him I couldn't go to sleep.

"All you have to do is close your eyes and keep them closed," Daddy gently touched my eyes, and I closed my eyelids. After he removed his fingers, my eyes opened again.

"We woke you up? You heard us arguing?"

Even though he appeared to be calm, he had pronounced arguing in a funny way. He had slipped into his native Arkansas lilt the way he always did when he got upset.

"Tawny, you need to get some sleep. You have school tomorrow."

I reminded him that he had to go to work. We would both be sleepy.

"Naw, grown-ups don't need a lot of sleep like kids. *You* are still growing."

"Why are you and Mama fighting?" I watched his eyes, expecting a flash of guilt, but his eyes held steady.

"Sometimes adults have disagreements and they have to work them out."

I frowned at my father. "Are you guys getting a divorce?" Down the hallway, the bathroom door opened, and I heard Mama close her own bedroom door.

"No," he answered quickly. I believed him.

"Why is Mama crying?" I kept my eyes on him.

He blinked and rubbed hands over his bristled face, "Well she is upset about our disagreement."

I crossed my arms and stood there for a minute, "Will you get mad if I ask you something?" I thought about Nia's mom and the ice needed for her swollen face.

Daddy answered in a deep, solid tone, "No, whatever you need to ask — go ahead."

I uncrossed my arms. "Did you hit Mama?"

Daddy held me around my waist and gently lifted me up on his knees so that my legs dangled to the side. Our faces and eyes aligned.

"Tawny, I would never hit your mother."

I felt my body relax, and I swung my legs, "I just thought I would ask."

"Don't ever be scared to ask anything, ok?"

"All right Daddy." We hugged. He held me for a few minutes before he carried me to bed.

In the blackness, I heard Daddy knock on their bedroom door. The lock clicked, and the door creaked open and shut again. A few moments later, the doorknob turned again and Mama's steps faded down the hallway. I listened for more sounds, certain I would never go to sleep. The bed springs squeaked as I adjusted my body a few more times.

The next thing I remembered, I heard rustling in the kitchen hours before anyone would be making breakfast. Under the veil of pale gray light, my room felt drafty. The front door opened and closed. When I got up, I realized Mama had left.

The Hotel

May of 4th Grade, Age 10

We found out that Mama stayed in the Regency Hotel in Fairbanks. Daddy dropped us off to visit her for the weekend. The hotel had calligraphy style lettering on the marquee. Many times, we drove past it on the way to church on New Richardson Highway. Its long, white rectangular structure spanned twenty windows with royal blue shutters.

I felt a leap in my stomach as we approached the smooth white door. Maybe Mama and Daddy breaking up wouldn't be too bad if we got to live in a hotel room, like rich people.

We entered a neat room with beige carpeting and even white walls. The room had two beds and a large bathroom. It also had a kitchenette with a tiny refrigerator, a sink, and a few cabinets. The white linoleum featured curly decorative black lines. Beside the kitchenette, we sat at a miniature table and four chairs. Mama gave us vanilla ice cream and turned up the heat so that we could burrow into the hotel covers. We sealed in the heat except for frosty tongues.

The next morning I woke up to Keenan and Mama's voices. Sunlight streamed through the windows, making everything look bright and hopeful. They sat in the dining area. Both of their heads bent. Brother's jaws clenched against the sides of his face. His hands gathered together like fists. I walked over and stood beside him, looking at Mama.

My mother's eyes edged with tears and her nose appeared bright, reddish pink.

"What happened?" I asked.

"Why is Keenan upset?" I asked again.

"She's leaving!" He shoved the words out of his mouth.

"Well sometimes people break up," I informed him matter-of-factly, "like in Judy Blume's novel *Are You There God It's Me Margaret*, or in —"

"Shut up! I don't want to hear about your dumb white people books!"

"What?" I yelled at him.

"Tawny! I'm moving away from Alaska."

"Oh," I said.

We wouldn't have a mother anymore. I just stared at the blank walls in the beautiful hotel room. Brother couldn't accept her leaving; his wet stone face streamed with tears. From an unknown place, a column of cold air blew on my bare legs. "Oh Mama, we have to go with you. Why are you going to leave us?" I felt my eyes sting with salt water. Tears turned my nose pink and my eyes puffy.

"Your dad said y'all can't go," she said.

"But why? You are our mother?"

"I know but you can still take us," Keenan said urgently.

"He can stop me," she said, avoiding our eyes. My eyes cleared the water, and I crossed my arms.

"How Mama?" I challenged.

"I'm going with you," My brother announced.

"I don't have the money," she said, putting up her hands and moving away from us.

How could she afford this fancy hotel room? She had been here for days.

"But Mama, when are you coming back?" I asked her.

I watched Keenan's jaw push forward, and he rubbed the tears out of his face.

"I am going to live there."

"But will you send for us when you get the money?" I asked.

"Yes," She answered, but I didn't believe her. That hollow 'yes' bounced off the walls of the room.

"But who will comb my hair?"

It took her a moment to answer, like she hadn't thought about it before.

"Your Aunt Denise will braid it. You'll keep it braided."

In Judy Blume's book the father left the children and the mother. Where was my mama going? Margaret's dad just moved to another place around the corner. Mothers were not supposed to leave their children. I didn't believe her about Daddy. How could he keep her from her own children? She didn't want to take us with her. She decided to leave us because she didn't want us. Daddy didn't have the power to make that decision. Our mother gave up on us.

PART II:
WITHOUT MAMA

The Empty Space

June before 5th Grade, Age 10

I watched the time click by mercilessly on the VCR digital clock. Another moment, a minute more without Mama while summertime spun around me. At 6 p.m., the stubborn sun burned into the dining room window as bright as noon. The relentless light amplified Mama's absence.

The vacant parts of our home crept upon me: the now hollow space where Mama used to stand above the stove, mixing greens soaked in neck bone juice. The lingering scent of perfume in the master bedroom dissolved. Now the stench of my father's musty boots and his soiled clothes replaced it. The stereo sat unused. I yearned for her fingers to draw fresh cornbraids in my hair.

But Mama left, and Daddy worked all the time. Mama used to budget the money and mail the checks. Without Mama's income, Daddy could barely pay bills.

We got used to eating twice a day since grocery money became scarce. The Food Bank donated boxes of food to needy families. Our first box contained generic cans of creamed corn and green beans. I looked at the dinged up cans and turned them over to check the expiration date—all expired. The lettuce smelled rotten and appeared to have the limpness of death. At the bottom of the container, two moldy blocks of American cheese remained. The Washington Braeburn apples were bruised and mushy on the inside. Only the oranges, rice cereal, and boxes of Jiffy mix were edible.

After receiving the donations from the Food Bank, I knew we had to come up with a better plan. Living in the wilderness reminded me of the Midwestern prairie lands I had read about in *The Little House on the Prairie* and *Little House in the Big Woods*. Our land should be useful. What good was having three acres at Midway Industrial Park if we needed donated food boxes?

Planning the Garden

June before 5th Grade, Age 10

We could grow a garden. I read about how the Ingalls family built a life out of the raw earth. At school we learned about how the Eskimo and Inuit people led a subsistence lifestyle by picking berries and hunting. Daddy had been raised on a farm outside of Little Rock, Arkansas. So why couldn't we make a garden to grow and live off the land as well? When I made my case to Daddy, he agreed.

On a warm day in June, Daddy and I planted the garden. At church we learned that we would reap what we sowed. When we did good deeds, Aunt Mary called it sowing good seeds. Later we would reap good things.

Daddy explained that when we plant, we are sowing seeds. According to the information on the packets of seeds, I'd be able to reap heads of lettuce, cabbage, broccoli, and collard greens after ninety days or so.

Bending down, like Daddy taught me, I pointed my index finger and poked it into the soil. The moist dirt hugged my finger and when I removed it a hole remained. Noticing the tiny slivers of sticks and miniscule rocks that made up the soil, I dropped in two tiny broccoli seeds. I felt a bubbling in my chest rising up through my throat and tickling my fingertips. I let out a squeal and let my fingers wiggle around for a couple of seconds. It would be magic for broccoli to grow from these little dots.

I stood up straight and looked around. Before gardening, I heard people speak about the beauty of Alaska. I even witnessed it as I landed the first time in the midst of a midnight sunlit sky. As we flew, I took in the landscape as a museum patron. I couldn't accept its beauty when I scarcely slept in the season of summer sun. Gardening changed that for me.

At school, all the kids called me weird because of my hair. I also hid the neck bones, chittlins, and the collard greens we ate. In Alaska, I couldn't even tell my classmates that I washed my hair once a week (instead of daily) and that I added synthetic hair to my braids. The white kids at school couldn't understand that my scalp required hair grease to shield from the skin chafing winter. In the garden, I didn't have to explain myself.

Moving the hair out of my face, I didn't care if I was pretty right now or not. In the garden with the dirt, I was enough. I kept moving down the row; every few inches I poked another hole in the soil. I dropped a few more seeds. As I planted seeds, I began humming. Into the belly of the earth, I cultivated a new crop of vegetation: greens, broccoli, onions, carrots, and cabbage.

With Mama here or not, I had my hands in the ground pushing and the earth began to move ahead for me. My mornings became consumed with tending to the manifestations of sun and soil and water. With the garden occupying me, I formed new memories at home in the places where Mama had left pain. As I worked, I opened myself up for more possibilities—an improved reality.

Growth

June before 5th Grade, Age 10

On the next Saturday, I walked up and down the rows to look for sprouts, like I had every day for the past week. At high noon the sun held a position in the sky that spotlighted the earth with full strength. I could feel the sting of its rays on my bony shoulders and wrinkly neck. As I rounded the row of broccoli, I noticed a nick of green, out of place in the solid row of raw brown earth. I paused in mid-stride and covered my mouth with my hands. Maybe I had imagined it. I walked closer, and I could see a loop emerging from the soil, a bright lime color interrupting. I got on my knees and looked real close, so close that I could smell the faint damp of the soil. I felt a smile coming, and I pressed my lips together. I watched it for a moment, enraptured.

I moved a lump of soil so that the sprout wouldn't have to work so hard to stand upright. Looking around, I noticed more sprouts coming.

The collards emerged as two tiny leaf sprouts, almost identical to the weeds. I started removing the weeds, uprooting white-haired dandelions and clover leaves that I once adored.

Every day from then on, I woke up and nursed the garden. I watered the garden every other day like Daddy had told me and pulled the weeds faithfully.

The growth each day reminded me of myself, that each day I was getting closer to fulfillment. Sometimes, I had to remember that my gifts, my talents, my contribution to the world were sometimes buried, but if I took time to dig them up, I might find them in my roots like the potatoes or onions.

Daddy added a potato hill for planting pieces of potatoes with sprouts that he called eyes. He also raked up a hill to plant a bunch of strawberry sprouts.

Gardening taught me to treasure natural space and tranquility. It taught me to recognize my strength and power. I dreamed of the day that I would become the fully mature person that I wanted to be. I discovered that strength lay in growth. If I focused on changing and improving, my life had a chance to be empowered.

Church Acquaintances

June before 5th Grade, Age 10

With Mama gone, Aunt Mary picked us up every Sunday to attend church. Now I could sit with whoever I wanted. I chose to sit beside Mayleen, Eve, and Day-ja. We sat in Sunday school together while Mother Avery taught us our Bible lesson.

Around noon, the sun glared high and hot through the colored windows. Outside, the temperature climbed into the 70s, rare warmth for Fairbanks.

Mama left a month ago. Thirty-one days, but I wasn't counting anymore. Well, maybe I was. Every time the phone didn't ring, I counted.

During afternoon church service, the four of us inspected each other's palms, tracing the creases with our fingers like they were maps.

"You have one long line right in the middle," Day-ja would say, holding up my hand to the sunrays.

Day-ja moved from North Carolina when she was eight. Her biological mama had died from Sickle Cell Anemia, and she lived with Sister Barner, her aunt. Even though her mama died, she consistently beamed a bright smile and wore colorful dresses. She had brown skin and wore her hair in a jheri curl. With her unusually long neck, she had an air of grace that made her endearing to us all.

"Look! What about my palm," Eve asked, pushing her hand forward. Eve had impenetrable skin of a medium complexion, smooth and shiny as obsidian.

She had soft doe eyes that made me want to tell her secrets, but her mouth always talked too much and laughed too loud. She loved everyone big and close, hugging and grabbing even when we didn't want it.

Mayleen was Eve's older sister. She had dark skin, with a black splotch of a birthmark over her right eye. This made her look exceptionally beautiful—a kiss from God. She smiled with perfect, straight teeth and a dimple in her left cheek that made everyone love her.

Mayleen and Eve lived with their grandmother. Their mama had been gone for years — "off somewhere addicted to some substance". I had heard some of the saints whispering about it after service.

During Praise and Worship, we'd sit near the front and bang on tambourines and play with the saints' fidgety babies.

On Sunday evenings, we loitered in the restroom and passed notes while the services continued through the night.

We acted in church plays together, read the Bible, and even got saved together. Sunday after Sunday together.

I tried to have faith. I really did, praying before bed, reading my Bible—the children's version and the King James Version. I sang the songs in church and meant most of the words. But underneath it all was a question I couldn't ask out loud: What if I'm doing all this and God still doesn't fix things?

Caught up in my own loathing of the world, I focused on reading books. I thought so much about Edison's repeated failings. He kept trying. I told myself I could be like that. I told myself I was strong. But really, I stayed angry. Anger and sadness and confusion churned inside me about why Mama left us. Why did Daddy keep giving money to the church when we barely had enough for food?

I used to think about all these things while messing with my hair in the church bathroom, and the other church girls would just stare. Mayleen would always ask me what was wrong.

"Nothing is wrong, why do you keep asking me?" I asked, annoyed. I always said "Nothing" even with heated eyes and a tight throat. I was the mean one in the group. I snapped at them when they asked too many questions. Mayleen would always return my lemon with sugar. "Sorry, it just looks like you're about to cry."

And I was—always teetering on the hurt of the present and past.

When Eve laughed too loud at my sarcastic comments during Children's Church, I'd blame her for getting me in trouble. I didn't know how to be a friend.

We sang in the junior choir together. Eve could hit the high notes in a way that made people's eyes water. Day-ja harmonized without even trying. Mayleen sang loud and off-key. I sang, too. Singing solos and harmonies lifted to the sky made me forget my anger and sadness.

I learned a lot since Mama had left – about gardening, about reading, and singing. And contemplating the confusing parts about God. How could God be good and still let bad things happen? How could He be "making a way" while our house still fell apart? How prayer worked—or didn't work, depending on what you prayed for.

And I learned that I had friends. They were closer than friends. We were church sisters.

Reality Check

July before 5th Grade, Age 10

We sat in Aunt Denise's cloudy living room choked with marijuana clouds. The late afternoon sun held its station in the sky and a quiet settled in the room as we watched MTV videos. I sat on the loveseat next to Angel. Keenan and Lamar laid across the floor.

Auntie toked a joint. Then she threw back her head and started busting up, laughing so loudly that we all stared. Her gut jiggling and her bosom vibrating. "Know what I just thought about? I'm gonna take some pictures of that three acres of land Damon got out there in the boonies."

"What?" I asked her, twisting my face defensively.

"He got people who ain't never been out there believe he livin' high on the hog. They don't know it's a junkyard. I can't blame yah Mama for leaving that sorry motherfucker. Your Mama couldn't live like that. No real woman would."

I frowned at my aunt. I knew she was high and her words were loose, but I didn't want to hear her analysis of my crappy life and confounding parents.

"What you getting all puff-faced for, Tawny? You like living out there?"

Keenan spoke up. "No. You're telling the truth. We don't like it." His head rocked in agreement. "Shoot. There ain't no way I like livin' out there."

I folded my hands on my lap. He was right.

By early July, the darkness I'd known all winter had completely vanished. With covers over my face, I could sleep for half the night. The endless days made everything feel unreal, like we were living in a dream—or a nightmare—that never ended.

Mama had been gone for over two months. In the midnight sun, I couldn't even count the days properly anymore. Every day felt like one long, continuous day. Time had broken apart.

Cleaning Up

Summer before 5th Grade, Age 10

Back at home, I stared out the dining room window overlooking the junkyard where we lived. Evening light cast long shadows across the scattered trash on the spacious land for which I used to feel proud. My mind spun, forming pictures of what it could be like in the future. Sharing these imaginings with my parents, I'd be so hopeful. Since Mama had gone, the trash had increased around our home. The trash piled up for weeks. Some of the bags tore open and paper and tissue blew on the ground. Trash lined the path from the mobile home to Daddy's shop. More abandoned cars arrived on the lot and now blended into the scenery.

I turned to my brother who was watching TV in the living room. "I'm tired of living with all this trash around us everywhere."

"I know," said Keenan.

"This don't make no sense."

"Yeah," Keenan agreed with a stiff nod of his head.

"If we get together and pick up the trash, Daddy could plow up the rocks and gravel and we could plant some grass. We could have a nice yard."

"Yeah, probably so…" Keenan agreed haltingly.

"Well, let's do it!" I said, pushing my voice forward.

I smiled and looked at my older brother, nodding my head, urging him.

"Let's tell Daddy. Okay?" I said.

"Alright," Keenan gave his final word of agreement with shielded enthusiasm.

The next day, I took a bandana and wrapped it around my head like I had seen Mama do. We both put on old t-shirts and cut-off jeans. Among the boulders, pebbles, and gravel, we squatted down and picked up odd bits of paper and plastic, crushed Barbie heads, flattened KFC buckets, and bright blue plastic bits from a demolished toy. A few boards of plywood with sharp rusted nails jutting out were strewn along the path. Sometimes we'd pick up pieces of trash, and find more trash underneath that piece of trash. Other times, we freed a flattened willow branch. We stuffed our first bags until we could not drag them any further. I ran to get Daddy.

"Daddy, Keenan and I have been picking up trash. Our bags are so full, we can't move them anymore."

"Wow. Good job," he said, following us to where we left the bags.

"Whoa. You're right. From now on, you need to only fill it half way."

Keenan and I nodded. He lifted both bags and threw the trash into the rusted truck. The bags banged against the floor of the truck bed. He had just emptied it the day before.

"Thanks, Daddy."

As our father walked away from us, we ran upstairs to get another plastic bag. An hour later, we dragged our new half-full bags to Daddy to show off.

"Look, Daddy. I got a whole bunch of trash!" Keenan boasted.

"You should've saw how hard we were working," I added.

"You should have *seen*," Daddy corrected as the sweat dripped off his nose.

"You should have seen how hard we were working," I repeated correctly this time.

"I saw you guys. You guys are really something!" He said smiling.

"Keenan, make sure you all are throwing those bags in the back of that yellow truck right there," Daddy said pointing. "When I get a chance, I'll take the trash to the dump."

Every day we added more bags to the trash truck from our household and bags filled with the litter that we collected. Soon white bags peeked over the truck bed walls. We started having to balance each bag added, or it would roll back onto the ground.

That evening, I cleaned out the refrigerator and dumped a canister of used cooking oil that had been there before Mama had left. The kitchen bag was too full. Lard and pickle juice dripped as he carried it. The lard container must have opened under the weight of the other trash. I had to mop the kitchen floor and rinse the line of juice and oil that had leaked.

Daddy said, "Tomorrow I'm going to have to take that trash to the dump."

The Harvest

August before 5th Grade, Age 10

A full meal lay before us of roasted red russet potatoes, broccoli, baked chicken with onions, and a salad with tomatoes, red and green lettuce, onion, and pickle cucumbers.

Aunt Mary joined us, she had helped cook. More than half the food came from the garden. The tomatoes were hearty on the inside, vibrant, not mushy like the ones from the grocery store. The broccoli felt more solid, less rubbery. The fresh lettuce crunched when I ate it.

I thought of tomorrow's meal—pork chops with onions from the garden, salad with carrots from the garden, green leaf lettuce from the garden, and tomatoes from the garden. We could even have baked Yukon gold potatoes. Maybe we could use the strawberries from the strawberry hill to make strawberry shortcake, a dessert of sponge cake with whipped cream and strawberries. In my imagination, I planned meal after meal including vegetables and fruit grown in the garden.

Growing food made me believe in my strength and the power of hard work. This food came from specks, and it fed our hunger. The garden grew, and it healed a piece of me that I didn't know how to mend.

My aunt stayed late, talking and laughing with us. She left soon after sunset around 10 p.m. We'd lost over an hour of daylight since summer solstice, and autumn announced itself with lengthening shadows.

Children's Church

August before 5th Grade, Age 10

Aunt Mary heeded the calling from the Lord to work with children, so she gathered school-aged kids in the church basement almost every Sunday for her Children's Church program.

While the adults engaged in the traditional afternoon worship and listened to preaching, we got a snack right after Sunday School. Instead of sitting on pews, we sat in folded chairs around foldable tables. Like the adults, we got the opportunities to share a testimony. Sometimes we made art for a Bible story. We even got to discuss Bible stories and took turns reading from the Word of God.

When asked to read scriptures aloud, many children struggled.

After Nkrumah stumbled through his verses, Aunt Mary got frustrated. "Nkrumah! You don't know how to read that well!" He stared back at her. We all stared at her, wondering what would come next.

Finally she spoke again. "I had problems reading, too. Did y'all know that?" She looked around at us. About fifteen children gathered around the tables.

We shook our heads.

"Matter-of-fact, I still had problems reading even as an adult. When I moved out here to Alaska, I ended up going to the Fairbanks Literacy Council. Now I can read, and the Lord blessed me with a good job at the Borough. Can I get an amen?"

"Amen!" We all responded.

My aunt continued. "The Lord called me to work with children, and there are so many needs. And He gave me the idea to start a tutoring program to help children learn to read better. Clap for the Lord, children. Clap!"

We all applauded.

Then Aunt Mary turned back to Nkrumah. "I'm sorry, Nkrumah, did I embarrass you?"

He shook his head.

"I ain't mean it. I just know that the Lord is showing me. I got to do something. Something has to be done about helping you children read. Someone helped me. I know I gotta help you. Ain't nothing to be shamed for. The Lord is gonna bless you. You hear me? He gonna bless you." Then she walked over and gave him a hug.

Same Old, Same Old

August before 5th Grade, Age 10

The next week, we worked to clear the trash again. Afternoon sun beating down on us, made the work even harder. One layer of trash revealed new pockets of discarded items. Moving a few willow branches aside, I discovered a two-by-four with wood nails hammered into it. Were the last owners building something that they couldn't finish? I pushed that thought aside. We found more old toys, bits of plastic, and a blanket nearly baked into the earth.

I stuffed all of it into a bag and stepped forward. That's when my leg locked in pain. A nail stuck out of my shoe, straight through my foot and out of my once white canvas shoes. Immediately, I yanked my foot up. The nail coursed through it. Erect and unmoved, the board and its nail remained.

When pain found my brain, I remembered to scream. I limped forward a few steps.

Keenan clambered to my side. "What's wrong, Tawny?"

Tears rushed out of me as Brother kneeled down to inspect.

"My foot!" I whimpered.

"Let me see!"

At the bottom of the shoe, we viewed a single spot of red about the size of a penny and growing.

"I'm going to get Daddy!"

"No!" I screamed again with more tears. I couldn't be left here in this junkyard by myself, scared and bleeding. All the worst case scenarios came to mind. There could be another nail. I could fall on the same nail and stab my stomach. It could even go through my heart.

Keenan looked back at the shop and forward to the mobile home. I whimpered as he made his calculation. Since we could get to the mobile home sooner than the shop, Brother helped me limp home.

The Dogs

August before 5th Grade, Age 10

The next morning, the sun engaged in its ever present stare. I hop-walked into the dining room stretching my arms above my head. The doctor had told me not to put too much pressure on it for long periods of time. I sat in the cushioned rocking chair. Overlooking the landscape, I noticed the trash truck. The stray dogs had come. The black one with a mane of brown hair over his shoulders pulled down a bag. The golden dog grabbed the opposite side of the bag; together the two engaged in a tug-of-war. The blue bucket pieces dropped out and spilled back onto the ground among the high weeds and gravel. I watched, unable to move for several moments. A chunk of the pickle jar bounced against the ground and splattered against a boulder.

"No!" I yelled. I felt the power rush out of my mouth.

Sweat stung my underarms and my scalp. I hop-ran out the door and down to the last step. If I had not been injured, I would have run outside right to the dogs. Both dogs ceased sniffing and eating to raise their heads. They eyed me; I stopped and became aware of my large t-shirt and bare feet against the rough wood step. I held my breath. The front door closed and Keenan stepped onto the porch. He pulled on his last shoe as he came down the stairs.

The dogs resumed their pillaging, climbing on the bed of the truck. Grasping another bag in their teeth, they swung their heads until the goods were free and satisfied themselves with our left overs.

Keenan ran past me. "Get inside. You already got a messed up foot."

"I can't. They'll ruin everything."

"No. I'll take care of it."

Keenan grabbed a piece of old plywood laying on the ground. Swinging the wood, he rushed over to shoo them away. The dogs retreated and headed back down the dirt road towards the woods.

When the dogs left, I went inside. My brother walked down to the shop to tell Daddy.

Later that evening Daddy apologized. "From now on, I'm going to make sure I load the trash on a bigger truck so the dogs won't get to it."

From the window, I watched Daddy and Keenan picking up trash that we had already picked up. Once Daddy would get these rocks and gravel up, we would be able to plant some grass like we had planted the garden.

They threw the trash on the low truck again because Daddy would be going the next day to dump it.

Tutoring

August before 5th Grade, Age 10

Since I loved to read, my aunt asked for me to tutor the other kids at the church. Every Tuesday and Thursday night before Bible Study, we met with kids from the church and some from the neighborhood. On the first day, she paired me up with a boy named Harold.

As he began reading, the words came out haltingly as he stuttered. Every word challenged him, even simple words like if, and, on, and the. He couldn't read, and I almost cried.

Harold moved his eyes away from mine and shuffled uncomfortably. I placed my hand on his. "Don't be embarrassed. We're going to read together. You just haven't practiced enough."

"What grade are you in Harold?" I asked.

He had long and lanky limbs like he was older, but his goofiness always made him seem younger.

"I'm nine, but I'm in 2nd grade again." Harold's eyes seemed to plead with me, and I wanted so much to transfer my belief in his ability to him.

"You're going to learn to read Harold because I'm going to teach you," I told him.

Continuing to read, I encouraged him and guided him as he sounded out words. At the end of our session, I gave him a list of words to practice.

"You can read. You just have to practice at home, here, and at school. You'll get it."

If I didn't give him a lot of praise, I'd see his sad face. I couldn't deal with his sadness.

"You can do it," I kept telling him.

Harold came every Tuesday and Thursday. His reading improved.

By the end of the summer my outlook improved even though I didn't have Mama. Everywhere I went, I could make a difference—cleaning up our land, growing bountiful gardens, and helping to build stronger minds.

Ticasuk Brown

September of 5th Grade, Age 10

The rust colored, gold, and verdant leaves spread over the trees and sprinkled the school grounds. Barely 8:15 a.m. in early September, and the sun rose less than two hours earlier. The sign announcing Emily Ticasuk Brown Elementary gleamed in the bright morning.

Since many new families moved to the area, the borough opened another elementary, and my address determined for me to move to the new building. A fence of green mesh canvas surrounded the structure and blocked the view to the playground like wrapping paper hiding a present. The tan building, shaped like a capital E with a main building and three wings, had a similar design to my old school.

I got off the bus and filed down the stairs. As I moved along the sidewalk, the doors hissed open as we passed the row of yellow school buses parked in front of the school. Students in new baggy blue jeans and unscathed bright purple, orange, and pink backpacks spilled out of the bus doors. A chorus of tennis shoes scratching against the pavement moved around me as all the children approached the entrance.

This year, Keenan wasn't with me. He started North Pole Middle School as a sixth grader. I tugged my new evergreen backpack higher on my shoulder. Pushing out my chest, I strutted into the school entrance confidently.

For the occasion, Aunt Denise had cornrowed many braids into one ponytail.

I wore my favorite baby blue acid-washed jeans that tapered at the ankle with fuchsia and white ProWings purchased from Payless Shoes. My black zip-up sweater with shoulder pads (a hand-me-down from my cousins) made me appear more stylish.

Even though there was only a slight breeze, I shivered and realized goose bumps had formed on my arms.

A tiny girl's white frilly socks reminded me of my own first day of kindergarten when I had pushed Mama away. Back then, I had wanted to stride into the classroom by myself. But now that I was here alone, all I wanted was my mother to be here.

Inside, the school smelled of the cold and hollow newness of fresh paint. The floor still had the sharp surface of industrial carpeting, not yet worn down by heavy traffic. The rays spreading through the double-paned windows warmed the interior. Even the ceilings wore smooth white enamel. I wished the entrance would stay this way, clean and fragrant.

A picture of a bald and pale Principal Whaler hung near the trophy case. Beside his portrait, the school's mascot hung, a photograph of a ptarmigan in its fall colored feathers.

Dozens of students and parents spilled into the foyer. After hugging their mothers at the doorway, children ran to their classrooms. Others clutched their mothers' hands. Backpacks scraped against jackets. A frowning teary face blurred in front of me. Corduroy jeans shushed through the hall. Boots and new high-top sneakers clumped through the hallway.

I read the computer printouts hanging on the wall to find my teacher and room number. The suspended papers rose and fell as the front doors opened and closed. I would be in Mrs. Neil's fifth grade class, room 20.

I continued to my class, staring at the pristine walls. The rooms were numbered differently than at Badger Road. The bell rang, and the sweat began to collect along my hairline. Confused by the new numbering system, a headache began to throb at my temples. Instead of 13, 14, 15, the numbers skipped. I kept turning into the same wing and searching for the even numbers. There was no one to ask. No other students remained in the hallway. I decided to take a deep breath and start over. I retraced my steps and tucked into a different corner, I found myself staring at room 20. Underneath the room number on the door, bold black letters written in cursive read: Welcome to Mrs. Neil's Class.

Mrs. Neil's Class

September of 5th Grade, Age 10

In the warmth of the classroom, the rest of the students sat at their desks. Sunlight streamed through the windows, illuminating the neat rows of desks.

The thick nap of new carpet scraped into my tennis shoes, and I tripped a little bit forward as I stepped into the classroom. The door shut behind me.

Ms. Neil regarded me with a straight, stern face.

"Are you Tawny Hughes?"

I looked at the bulletin boards decorated in stark black backgrounds. I nodded my head.

"Come on in and sit right there next to Jennifer B. and Melissa," she told me.

Jennifer and Melissa were looking straight ahead with hands folded.

I looked around at all the faces in my classroom. I knew most of the kids from Badger Road Elementary. Like the previous year, there was one other black student in the class named Frank.

I hung my backpack on the seat, looking around at the other students. They all had papers and pencils out. I reached around to my backpack and took out my own paper and pencil. I had made sure that Daddy purchased a pack from Fred Meyer's. I didn't want to seem stupid on the first day of school. Jennifer's glittery Debbie Gibson backpack hung from the back of her chair. Melissa held a pencil with her name engraved in it.

"Go ahead and put your things away. We have a closet area behind this set of portable cupboards."

As I plodded to the closet, I spotted the kidney table positioned along the wall near the door. We would be separated into reading groups this year, too. Two Apple Macintosh computers faced me. The closet had hooks for the coats, hats, and gloves, as well as storage for inside and outside shoes.

Mrs. Neil continued speaking about her expectations, rules, and the academic requirements.

She pointed to the neat cursive letters with long, thick fingers, her shiny curls flopping as she moved. Mrs. Neil promised to work us hard. She emphasized the seriousness of school. Her voice did not curve up at the ends of sentences like all of the teachers before. She didn't smile when she spoke, her words came in short hard lines, using multi-syllabic words in her directions, which she promptly explained. Soon she would expect us to understand all of her words. "You're not in a primary grade any longer," she said, emphasizing the "p" sound in primary. Her tone made it clear that she would expect more from us than what we had given in the past.

I wanted a challenge. I wanted to be smart and craved more homework.

Our teacher even told us a little information about herself. She came from Illinois, which she pronounced without the s sound at the end.

After her introduction, we began taking turns reading to Mrs. Neil. She gave us a quiet assignment while she listened individually to each one of us. She handed out a packet of work consisting of three reading passages with questions, a map of the world to color and label, a set of science questions, a survey about our interests, four worksheets of simple math facts for addition, subtraction, multiplication, and division. As I got started, I watched Jennifer out of the side of my eye. The girl wrote so sloppy. On the other side, Melissa wrote very neatly. I tried to write even neater, so I wouldn't be bested.

One at a time, she called each of us alphabetically to read to her outside in the hallway. Each student came back inside with a different expression. Jimmy's face blushed crimson, and his once smoothed hair appeared ruffled. Carrie re-entered smiling and fluttered back in quickly. Sarah walked in with a smooth gait, like she usually walked.

When my turn came, Frank smiled at me. I glanced at him and went outside. My heart jumped a moment before Mrs. Neil put the passage in my hands.

My teacher sat on a nearby chair, holding a pencil and a clipboard. She set the stopwatch around her neck. "Begin reading," Mrs. Neil said. I read like I did every day at home and at church, smoothly, stopping at periods and taking a quick breath after commas. Reading was the most gratifying skill that I possessed. The passage was about George Washington and how he led the army during the American Revolution. Later he, of course, became the first president of the United States. I read a biography of George Washington last year.

When I was finished, Mrs. Neil smiled broadly, "Well, you are quite a reader aren't you?"

I giggled, "I love to read. I read all the time. George Washington had a very interesting life. Thank you, Mrs. Neil," I said and clasped my hands and twisted them in embarrassment.

"Please send Jennifer R. out next."

After everyone read, she explained that language arts—that's what she wanted us to call it—would be separated into reading groups. Although she had issued readers, we would be taught out of novels. I squirmed in my seat in excitement. Our reading groups would be determined by next week.

By the end of the day, Mrs. Neil had given an outline of every subject to be taught that year: math, United States history, health, and science. She also explained that we would deliver speeches and complete research projects. Despite it being the first day, she assigned us homework in two different subjects: a math assignment from our math textbook for review and a one page essay about the type of activities we participated in during the summer.

My head throbbed at the temples. I felt groggy from the long day, but excited about the prospects of learning more than I had ever learned before. It all fit with my plan to be a scientist. I needed difficult work and teachers who challenged me.

Not an Adult

October of 5th Grade, Age 10

A few Sundays later, I walked down to the basement after church. The overhead fixtures in the church basement cast a harsh glow across the folding tables and metal chairs. My Aunt Mary who sat at one of the tables, waved me over.

"Hey girl, how you?" she asked. I wondered how her twang persisted although she lived in Alaska for decades.

With my arms folded and my head towards the floor, I answered, "I'm alright."

"Come here, girl," she commanded, pulling my folded arms closer with her weighty arms.

I took a step closer. She insisted on pulling me even closer.

"Come here, girl. Let me tell you something."

I finally unfolded my arms and looked up into her eyes. She held me close so that I felt her warm breath on my ear.

"I want to tell you that I know that you are working hard, keeping the house clean and getting that yard cleaned up."

I just nodded.

"But Tawny, you are not an adult."

I dropped my head down again. Her long thick fingers caught my chin and tugged it upward.

"You hear me? You are not an adult."

Her stare made my eyes hot and a spray of moisture escaped her mouth as she spoke with a conviction and force that broke down my guard.

"You're really helping *yo'* daddy out. But you *cain't* worry about makin' everything alright again."

I shifted under this new proclamation.

"But we live in a junkyard," I said finally.

"Your Daddy's fixin' it up. It's gonna take some time though. You got to smile. You're too pretty for all this frowning."

Pretty—something about the word stung me. It didn't mean nothing.

She leaned down and cupped my chin in her hand. "So pretty. Smile. You're too pretty to be frowning."

I jerked away from her.

"What does pretty get me? Pretty, pretty? Or pretty for a black girl? Not pretty enough for my mother to stay around. Not pretty enough."

Aunt Mary looked as if she could see my destruction but couldn't do anything about it. Her mouth hung open. I really wanted the answers even though I knew she didn't have them. I was asking life, the universe, that great somebody that is nowhere but everywhere.

The hairs on her chin had grown back in two patches, either side of her chin. That new hair asserted itself like an unwelcome guest. And it didn't matter. It didn't make her any less of anything. I loved her the same, even more because those hairs hadn't stopped her from being herself. She didn't believe in her own beauty and didn't mourn it either. Her thick body was strong, and she was a force—much more than having fading beauty or weak womanhood or a victim of being black.

Outside, the darkness had won. We'd gone from fourteen hours of daytime in September to barely ten hours. The sun rose after 8 a.m. and set before 6 p.m. Every morning I woke in darkness, went to school in darkness, and came home to a darkening sky. The brief days felt like a cruel tease.

Helping Mrs. Neil

November of 5th Grade, Age 10

The weather didn't matter. In Alaska, we went out to recess for twenty minutes every day. By November, I couldn't endure the cold. So I tried to stay inside as much as possible by helping my teacher.

One afternoon, Mrs. Neil allowed Melissa and me to stay inside to help her cut out shapes for a new bulletin board display. After explaining the directions, I worked quietly and marveled at the scene outside of the classroom windows. A fresh layer of snow fell outside in the daylight.

Melissa broke the silence. "My dad takes care of us."

"Oh really, where is your mom?" Mrs. Neil asked.

"I don't have a mom. She died," said Melissa in a strange, but very comfortable way.

"Oh, I am sorry to hear that," said Mrs. Neil.

"It was a long time ago. Do you have a mom, Tawny?" Melissa said, quickly changing the focus from herself to me.

"What? Please," I said, laughing nervously and looking away.

When I looked back up, they both stared at me.

"Well, do you?" asked Mrs. Neil.

"Oh, yes I do, but she lives in California," I said, looking down.

"Wow, California," said Melissa in amazement.

She turned to Mrs. Neil, changing the subject again.

"I would love to go there. Why did you move here, Mrs. Neil?" Melissa probed.

Upset by Melissa's questions, I didn't follow the rest of the conversation. I stayed clear of Melissa after that—too nosy for me.

Water Still Freezes

November of 5th Grade, Age 10

Last year when the water froze, it flowed again after a few days. But this winter, two days turned into a week. We still didn't have water.

***

Before I left the house that morning, I asked, "Daddy, will the water be on when we get home from school?"

"Yes, it will be on."

At the end of the day, I ran off the school bus and into the shop.

"Daddy," I said exuberantly.

"Hey, girl, you haven't seen me all day. What do you say?"

"Good evening, Daddy."

"Alright."

"Did you get the water fixed?"

"No, tomorrow it'll be on."

He said it without a hint of doubt. I accepted his answer and ran on the trail through the abandoned vehicles. I made my way up the few stairs of our mobile home porch.

Every day I asked him: Is the water on?

After a few days of this, I stopped running off the bus. I passed the shop without stopping and continued walking home. Every day the walk to the mobile home got longer, and the sky darkened. Each day I came home, my steps slowed with another chip of hope gone, a pebble of respect for my father knocked away.

For dinner later that night, Daddy put the left over cornbread with mixed-in bell peppers into the oven to heat. I could barely stomach another evening with his bonehead cooking. Thank God for Kool-aid. Keenan knew how to make it just right, using more sugar than called for in the directions. I poured the remaining water from the blue jug into the large pot. "Daddy, we're out of water."

"That's alright. I got another jug in the back of the truck out there. We're fine." Daddy went outside to get the jug.

Since Daddy only reheated the food, I didn't bother taking the time to warm the dish water. As I scrubbed the hardened raisin bran flakes from the sides of bowls and wiped a glob of mayonnaise from a butter knife, I shivered.

The scent of the scorched chicken and sour cornbread reminded me that I hadn't eaten since school lunchtime. My stomach grumbled, and I sped up my dishwashing.

I finished washing the dishes in less than ten minutes. Inside the refrigerator, only a small amount of Kool-aid remained at the bottom of the pitcher. I dried off the table with a kitchen cloth. I set out an orange plastic cup, a shapely Coca-Cola glass, and one empty glass jar for the Kool-aid. We broke all the matching cups and glasses a long time ago.

Daddy, Keenan, and I all sat down to eat dinner in silence. I ate reluctantly, picking over the lukewarm cream corn. The dry chicken scratched at my throat when I tried to swallow it. Kool-aid helped to wash down the lumps of chicken.

Keenan ate like the food was about to run away, pushing chunk after chunk into his mouth.

Daddy, sitting at the head of the table, stuffed his mouth, too. His cheeks stuck out like a chipmunk preparing for winter. He chewed slowly until his cheeks were emptied before filling up again.

Learning More About Racism

December of 5th Grade, Age 10

Mrs. Neil pointed at the question written on the board. *In what ways was racism different during the Jim Crow Era than it is now?*

We were reading *Roll of Thunder, Hear My Cry*, a novel about a black family living in the segregated south.

I sat looking at her embarrassed, as if I should know. As if the question was for me individually.

"Everyone, turn to page 62, paragraph number 2," she said.

Leaves of the books rustled throughout the class; hard covers knocked against wooden table tops. Page edges scratched my thumb on the way to the correct place.

I read, but the answer wasn't there—at first. The passage discussed the white kids riding buses to school, and the black children walking to school. Then I realized that a lot of the racism in modern times comes from other kids calling each other names. The racism in this book includes adults. It includes the laws.

Mrs. Neil did this for me daily. She knew how to take an unfocused and unclear passage that I had read before and make it understandable.

I wanted to show Mrs. Neil that I could do it. She believed in our intelligence. I felt my mind changing as I became a better reader and a much better writer.

"Now on your paper explain the ways that racism is different during the Jim Crow Era than in modern day America." At my seat, I leaned in toward my desk, pressing the lead so hard into the page that I had to stop and shake out my hands.

"Look Jennifer, since we have to write so much, I have a hard skin on my middle finger," I said, rubbing the rough lump.

She cringed, "That looks so ugly."

"I know," Henry said, twisting around. "You must be a nerd." Inspecting his hands, he held them palms up and turned them backwards. "Look, I don't have any of those."

Melissa laughed. "Me either. You write so much that you have a callous on your finger. I got one of those on the bottom of my foot from ballet."

"I don't care," Shrugging, I went back to work. I delighted in learning and in hard work. I would continue to put in the work, no matter what anybody said.

Since Martin Luther King Day approached, Mrs. Neil told us a story about racism when she was a little girl. Any discussion about race caught my attention. I looked around to see the other children's faces, searching for a hint of laughter or indifference. I wanted to be ready to defend or offer my knowledge about black history.

"We used to go swimming after school," our teacher explained, "I had a good time swimming with everyone until one day, a little boy told the life guard about me."

We all stared at her expectantly.

"I couldn't go swimming after that," she stated as she walked to the front of the class, "It was an all white pool. Black people couldn't swim in that pool."

I stopped for a moment. Did she say she could not go to an all white pool? I looked at her for a moment. I guess those thick lips could belong to a black woman. Her shiny hair must've glowed from hair grease. And yes, the lilt in her tone when she got stern at times could be categorized as Black English. Although it had never occurred to me before this moment... My breathing stopped. A smile involuntarily ripped across my face.

"Oh! You're black?" I blurted out.

Frank, who rarely spoke in class, added, "I thought you were Chinese."

She stopped and looked at us with an expression between a frown and a smile. She placed a hand on her hip.

"Yes!" she answered matter-of-factly.

Promises, Promises

January of 5th Grade, Age 11

After school, the bus stopped in front of Midway Auto Body Shop at half past three. At 3:30, twilight settled in. The sky had that blue-gray quality of late afternoon in winter. A thick blanket of fresh powder fell as I got off the bus.

Two black birds balancing on the telephone wire fluttered off as the door hissed closed. The rumbling stall of the bus shifted to the revving of the engine, and the bus rolled away. A willow shrub, bare and shivering in the frost, grew in front of the shop. Ahead of me, the triangular roof painted the color of sour lemons interrupted the white, graying sky.

The deep brown wood room faced me, which looked tacked on to the front of the shop as an office. Through the foursquare windowpane, I could see my reflection in the glass. The interior lights made it possible to see myself against the gathering darkness. Mama told me I had a flat face and almond eyes; two traits I couldn't ever distinguish when I saw myself. I only recognized my red nose and weepy eyes that always rejected the cold. I needed some lip balm for my chapped peeling lips. I wished I wasn't so skinny; I craved the heat so. My fuzzy braids stuck out from underneath my beanie.

I heard Daddy working in the shop, painting or pulling a dent out of a wrecked car. He seemed to be always here. Just before I pulled the door open to find him, I paused.

I didn't feel like going into the shop, even though I had an inkling to use the restroom. It would have been easier in the shop because the water pipes of our mobile home were still frozen.

Every day Daddy told me the same thing: "The water will be on tomorrow." If Daddy broke his word one more time over the humming of the soldering gun, or yelled it over the drone of the drill, or muffled the words through a painter's mask, I wasn't sure what I'd do. I figured Daddy didn't make enough to pay anyone to fix the frozen pipes, and I don't know why he wouldn't just tell me that.

But each time he broke his promise, it took longer for me to get over it. I could no longer hide my disappointment while Daddy looked me in the face and lied.

"I can't do it," I said aloud to myself. "Not today."

By the time I turned toward the mobile home, the sky had darkened further. The office clock read three thirty, but it felt like evening. I turned and walked past the back of the garage toward home. Once I left the protection of the building, the wind became unhinged. I pulled my fur-trimmed hood further over my head and angled my face sideways so that it shielded me from the oncoming gale, hurling icy snow against my cheeks. I slowed down until I took one step every few seconds. The path to our mobile home stretched out before me. An intimate dusted white forest of baby birch, white spruce, and aspen limned out the right side of the path. On the opposite side, a row of seven abandoned cars, rusted and snow-topped, traced the path from the shop to our home about eight hundred yards away. As I walked, the tightly packed snow path sounded like crushing foam under my moon boots. The tips of my toes and fingertips began to tingle from the bitter cold.

Once inside, I set down my backpack and walked down the hall to the bathroom. When I opened the door, the rotten odor of the sewage pierced my nostrils. To contain the stench, we always kept the heater vents in the bathroom closed, so the heat couldn't reach it. The cool air inside turned my breath into clouds.

Soon, the bowl of the sky would trap us in darkness for another sixteen hours. Before I turned on the switch, I reached for the knobs on the sink and closed my eyes. "Jehovah God, in the name of Jesus, let this water flow." I turned the handle. Silence reverberated through the room. Nothing. No water. I was fooling myself; I had known all along there would be none.

A powder blue trash can sat in the middle of the bathroom—not too close to the toilet, not too close to the sink. I walked over to it. One foot first, then the next until I could just see over the rim—too full.

The toilet had long been filled with pee, toilet paper, and other waste. Then my father instructed us to relieve ourselves in the bathroom trashcan, which he now called the slop bucket. With Daddy, Keenan, and I using the trashcan, it also became too full.

Why hadn't Daddy emptied the slop bucket? I shifted my hips a little. Every day he dumped it out on an abandoned lot across from our place. No one knew about it since our nearest neighbors lived over a mile away.

I shuffled through the kitchen and into the dining room where I could look out the window to see if Daddy was coming. Soon it would be time for him to come home and fix dinner. I'd ask him to empty it then.

I took off my boots beside the front door and decided to wash the morning dishes. I began moving the plates, spoons, and bowls from the sink and placing them on the countertop. Lifting the partially filled red five-gallon jug, I poured water into a large speckled black pot we used to hold the dishwater. I squeezed my legs together and put the jug down. The trickling made the urge to pee worse.

Taking a few deliberate breaths and telling myself to calm down, I strode toward my room.

Having retrieved my comforter, I returned to the living room. As I crossed between the left side and the right half of the mobile home, the exposed seam holding the double-wide together felt as cold as an icicle. Daddy had promised to seal the split, but he hadn't gotten around to that either.

In the living room, I turned on the television. The VCR's digital clock read 3:45. *Duck Tales* was already halfway over; I turned the knob to watch the rest of the program.

I took out my math book, pencil, and paper out of my backpack and sat down on the couch. Covering myself with the blanket, I began my double-digit multiplication problems while laughing along with Donald Duck's family.

Minutes later, Keenan came home. The wind whipped through the opened door.

"Hey Keenan, what's going on?" I said smiling at my brother. His heart-shaped pecan face scowled back at me.

"I got a headache. I'm starved." He hugged his stomach. He must've forgotten to eat at school again.

"You stopped by the shop?"

"Yeah for a minute," Keenan said.

Daddy was probably mad at me for not coming to the garage after school.

"Did Daddy say anything?" I asked, looking at him carefully.

"No," Keenan said.

He pushed his high-top Converse shoes off his feet, but kept on his purple Lakers jacket. It had been a gift from Mama two Christmases ago. Like a security blanket, he almost never took it off.

As Keenan walked out of the living room, I thought of Mama. Her absence was as present as the coolness seeping in from the cracks. Even with every bulb on and the heater cranked as high as it could go, this double-wide would never be bright enough or warm enough without her here.

The bedroom door closed down the hall. I sat wrapped in my blanket as I continued laughing along with *Duck Tales*.

I looked at the time on the VCR: 3:51. Was Daddy ever climbing up those stairs? I had to use the bathroom badly. I thought about going back to the shop to use a real toilet, but I was unwilling to face the cold again. Wind caught in the pockets of our home muffled its howling outside. I held my breath as the mobile home swayed slightly. I prayed, Lord, please keep our home together.

Before I could decide one way or the other, Daddy stomped onto the porch and banged into the house. He wore a once-midnight colored jumpsuit faded to a pale, gray blue. "Hey, Tawny. I haven't seen you yet today. Why didn't you come by the shop and speak?" Daddy said, looking at me steadily.

Daddy held filthy work gloves in his hands. Raised keloid scars shimmered on the backs of his hands. I had to think of a good excuse.

"I'm sorry. Good evening, Daddy. I had a lot of homework I needed to get started on."

I crossed my legs and wiggled, "Daddy will you please empty the trashcan in the restroom?"

"Why?" His eyes darted around the room. "Keenan didn't put it out?"

"Keenan?" I asked.

"Yeah, I told *him* to do it." He rounded the corner into the kitchen toward the rooms. He knocked on the door. "Keenan!"

The VCR clock read 3:55. My bladder felt like it was about to bust. Why was he bugging Keenan about this?

I heard Brother's door open.

Daddy pointed toward the bathroom. "Go empty that slop bucket right now!"

I pulled the comforter over my head.

"What did you say?" Keenan's voice crackled with annoyance. "It is too full! Tawny let it get too full."

Daddy yelled. "Hush your mouth! We not talkin' bout Tawny. We talkin' bout you!"

Ordinarily I would have defended myself, but I was stunned to see this simple thing had gotten my brother in trouble again. This time he was innocent. My gut began aching from another worry.

I didn't want my brother to see me. If he saw me, the combination of his shame and mine would surface and both of us would burst into tears. But the job would still be there, tears or not.

"I told *you* to do it! Do what you're told!" Daddy yelled.

Maybe Daddy was tired and just did not want to do it himself. A twelve-year-old shouldn't have to dump out that bucket.

"What am I—How am I going to deal—?"

"I've got gloves. Use 'em!"

I could hear Keenan stumbling around in our room. I knew he was shedding his Lakers jacket—that was much too small—for something he could move in, for something he didn't care about getting dirty.

Before he came out, I ran to Daddy's room. I thought about those icy stairs.

I sat on my parent's bed, waiting out of Keenan's sight.

Finally he began to walk down the hallway, the floor creaking with each step. When I knew he couldn't see me, I peered around the doorframe and watched him. His whole body trembled as he staggered under the weight of the slop bucket. Even with his stick-thin frame, the hallway seemed too narrow, as if the walls had begun to close in.

In my guilt, I tried to follow far enough away so he didn't know I was there. Why hadn't I gone to the bathroom in the shop when I could have? Outside, the wind screamed now.

I raced to the window.

Darkness had already fallen. Full night pressed against the windows. I could see my brother managing the bucket with the help of the porchlight. Folding my hands, I prayed for him. *God, please let my brother get down those stairs without spilling it.* At the second step, Keenan slipped, but somehow managed to right himself as well as the bucket. He dragged it down, step by step until he reached the bottom. Gingerly, my brother crossed the snow packed road, taking one step and hefting up the bucket. He took another step and lifted it once more until he was finally across the road, completely out of sight.

I ground my teeth. I should have done more to save him from this humiliation. I should have spoken up for him.

Brother dropped to his knees at the edge of the path. I wanted to run to him, but I was still desperate, needing to pee.

Finally, Keenan brought the bucket back to the bathroom. I didn't dare move until I heard him closing the front door again.

Rushing to the bathroom, I used the empty slop bucket in shame.

Even in the storm, he crashed the soccer ball against the wall. With each explosive contact, my stomach dipped from a heavy pit of guilt. Keenan would've stood up for me.

I chose not to go outside to speak to Brother. I didn't know what to say. The barrage of the ball against our home also gave me evidence that he was all right—still kicking.

At last, the attack with the soccer ball ended. Keenan stomped the ice from his boots and sealed himself back inside his room.

My feelings shifted from guilt for my failure to defend him to a need to explain myself. I knocked on Keenan's door.

After letting me in, he stood in the far corner of the room. I entered his room and leaned against the door. A mess crowded the floor: a knocked over pile of cassette tapes, sheets and blankets on the floor stripped from his bed, and clothes pulled from dresser drawers that still hung open.

I shook my head and dropped my eyes, focusing on the legs of his baggy jeans. "I thought I could— I asked him to do it. He should have done it," I said.

"It's not your fault that we don't have water," he said, shrugging.

"Not yours either," I told him, looking into his eyes for reassurance.

"It's 'cause Mama ain't here."

"She left us," I reminded him with a bitter tone.

"I know. It's Mama. You wanna know what Mama told me?"

His voice fell, and I noticed a hardness had set into his jaws. The shine of a teardrop balanced on his bottom lash until it fell, traced his cheek, and curved under his chin.

He spoke with loose trembling lips, "She told me, 'We're going to find you a new daddy.' I remember it. I was only six, but I remember. She told me. She told me that would be the last time I would see Pete."

"What?"

Though Pete was our biological father, I didn't think of Damon as our stepdad. He was just Daddy, but Keenan made me remember. We weren't just living without Mama; we were like orphans with no parents at all. The hollow feeling inside of me widened, and goosebumps rose on my arms.

What if Daddy decided he didn't want to deal with us anymore, like Mama and Pete had? He was just a man. I remembered how they met. Damon first spoke to Mama in the stands at a baseball game. Despite her shyness, Mama ate from his bowl of sliced peaches and ice cream. We saw him again at KFC when he followed her out to the car and leaned into the window of our car. He had been just a man back then. Now he was our father, our sole provider.

In my silence, Keenan stared at me.

"She told me that. Do you believe me?"

I nodded. When we had left California, Mama was so thin like a teenager. She had been a teenager when we were born. Our existence required her to be more, much more. And she had been much more, but we became too much for her to handle, maybe too much for anybody to handle.

"Yeah, I believe you," I said, absorbing the rawness of his words.

"I know. She told me that shit," he said, pointing a finger at himself. I was frightened by his eyes, which had become hard and shiny as glass. I knew I couldn't hug him, because we would both shatter. I couldn't handle the tears building inside of me and the amount of emotion that he was trying to contain.

Keenan continued with a low rumbling whisper, "Then we moved away from California to this shit—away from our grandparents, away from most black people. And the next thing I knew, she had this motherfucker. We're calling *him* daddy. He's not my daddy! I know who my daddy is. You don't remember him, Tawny, but I do. I remember!"

Back in the kitchen, Daddy stood over the stove, reheating some burnt chicken from last night. The top of his head gleamed where his hair thinned. With his jumpsuit off, he looked calm wearing a dingy, stretched out tank top and palazzo pants. Even with Mama gone for five months, Daddy's meaty, muscular arms and stained hands still looked out of place handling the pots, pans, and mixing spoons.

I took the bag of sugar stored inside the refrigerator, chose two packets of cherry Kool-aid from the drawer, and took the measuring cup stored in the bottom cabinet. I set the ingredients on the kitchen table, hesitating.

"I guess I'll make the Kool-aid," I said purposely loud. I hoped Keenan would hear me. I walked slowly back to the refrigerator to take out the pitcher.

As I sauntered back to the refrigerator, Keenan came out of his room. He had stopped crying, but under the chandelier his moist eyelashes made his eyes sparkle. My brother kept his gaze focused on the Kool-aid. "I'll make it," he said.

I stepped out of his way. Keenan stood at the table, pouring the sugar directly from the bag into the pitcher. The measuring cup lay on the table, unused.

Daddy pulled a can of creamed corn out of the cupboard. After opening the can and putting the corn in a saucepan, he started preparing the plates. He took out a stack of four plates and began placing a wimpy slice of cornbread and dried out chicken on each plate. After a few minutes, the corn began popping and hissing on the stove. Then he spooned out a helping of mushy creamed corn on each plate. I hated creamed corn.

Keenan finished up the drink. With a damp rag, I wiped off the rectangular shaped wood table.

When we finished eating, we each carried our plate to the pot in the sink. Keenan washed the dishes this time. I swept the floor.

Daddy went back into the room to change back into his jumpsuit. He pounded down the stairs. He headed back to work at the shop like he did every night. His dark figure blended into the night.

In the slow climb back from December's darkest days, we had gained back forty minutes of day since winter solstice, but it didn't feel like much. We had months of darkness ahead before spring would return.

Brother cleaned the dishes then went back to his room. I finished my homework in the living room while watching *Little House on the Prairie*. The home we were used to had no Mama and no Daddy. Keenan and I dwelled in separate rooms, remnants of a splintered family.

The Testimony

January of 5th Grade, Age 11

In December, Daddy got saved and started attending church with us every Sunday. Church took up a larger portion of our lives. We learned how to follow God the right way—as taught in Church of God In Christ (COGIC) churches.

When we walked in, I read the plastic clock hanging on the wall of the old sanctuary. It was 10:15 a.m.—late again. Outside, the December darkness ruled. The sun wouldn't rise for another fifteen minutes, and even then it would barely clear the horizon. During December, we only got about four hours a day.

The church entrance opened right into the old sanctuary where the men's class met.

Sweat tingled under my arms, and my face began to heat up as a few of the men turned to gawk at us. The dull ceiling fixture made Elder White's forehead glow a faint aura as he led the men's Sunday school class.

Daddy walked up the aisle to join the other men, while Keenan and I continued through the old sanctuary, passing two columns of mismatched pews—some varnished a shiny dark brown, some with scratched paint worn bare over the years.

Reaching the door in the left front corner, I opened it and even more brightness pushed against my eyes. Aligned along the middle of the ceiling, round balls hung by a suspended cord. In this way, each section of the new sanctuary had a sun, a light of the world. The glowing gathering place reminded me of the hope that Jesus brought.

The women's class met in the far front area in the choir stand.

Keenan and I joined our junior class, for nine through twelve-year-olds, bunched together in the last few rows of pews in the back of the new sanctuary.

Mother Avery's shining face greeted me. My rushing blood and flushed face calmed. Our teacher Mother Emma Avery, co-founded the church with her sister. Even when Mother Avery scrunched her eyebrows together in a question, she was smiling. I agreed with Mother Avery's smile. Instead of at home—cold and without running water—we'd be here all day with four to five hours of flowing hot water and flushing toilets. I wished I lived here in this perfect place.

Our Sunday school teacher motioned a place for Keenan and me to sit on the pews beside her three grandsons—Masai, Olafintala, and Nkrumah. "Good morning. Come on in and have a seat."

I looked at the white Jesus with melancholy brown eyes and stringy brown hair hanging around his shoulders. I always wondered why artists painted Christ white when black people always quoted scriptures about his hair of lamb's wool.

Mother Avery leaned over the pew in front of us, so that she could face us.

"Tawny you don't mind reading, do you? You sound so good when you read," she told me.

I smiled and quickly flipped to the right page, "And having come in, the angel said to her, 'Rejoice highly favored one, the Lord is with you; blessed are you among women!'"

"Look at God," she said with a high squeaky voice and squinty eyes that shimmered.

Following Christmas tradition, our Bible lessons all led up to the birth of Jesus. This Sunday we learned about how Mary got pregnant as a virgin. Joseph still married her even with a baby by someone else. Well I am sure he didn't really believe the daddy was God, at least not at first. It made me think about how some people left and some people stayed.

Not one of us kids in the junior class had our real father caring for us. The three Avery boys didn't live with any parents; just their grandma and grandpa took care of them. The Rayburn girls, Eve and Mayleen, only had their grandmother. They sat side-by-side and shared their Sunday school lesson book. Day-ja didn't have her biological mother or father.

After an hour, all the classes left their individual meeting places and gathered in the old sanctuary. Each Sunday school class came up to report their learnings. Then Elder White preached about the Sunday school lesson, showing overhead slides and explaining Bible verses. He fascinated me with interesting details about geography, different translations of the Bible, and ancient customs. Still, I could only focus on Elder White's speech for about ten minutes before I started looking for something to pass the time.

Tucked into the back of the pews, I found a book that explained perseverance through the biography of Thomas Alva Edison. Edison focused on getting his education and reading a lot. He failed many times to perfect the electric bulb, but he kept working at it. I knew I could develop these qualities in myself. I wondered if my setbacks, trials, and tribulations (that the saints spoke of) were all a part of the journey to my inevitable greatness. I resolved to keep working and trying, never giving up.

When Elder White finished his talk, Mother Avery, who was also the Sunday School Superintendent, gave her report. "There were thirty-two people in attendance. Offering collected was $47.26. This is the report on December 4, 1988 at 308 Ladd Street, Fairbanks, Alaska 99701."

To finish up the Sunday School service Mother Avery would lead the singing of my favorite song in a high crowing voice:

"At the cross, at the cross, where I first saw the light, and the burdens of my

heart rolled away. It was there, by faith, I received my sight, and now I am happy all the days."

With the conclusion of the song, everyone moved from the old sanctuary to the new sanctuary for our afternoon service, which started at twelve and continued without a time limit. We've gone until four before and left as early as one thirty.

On the first Sunday of the month (according to the rules), we couldn't be downstairs in Children's Church. This Sunday we had to stay with the adults in the new sanctuary. Eve, Day-ja, Mayleen, and I sat together. Keenan usually sat in the front row near Deacon Wilson since he worked with him as a junior deacon.

Mother Nevins began the praise and worship service with a solemn dragging voice:

"I made a vow to the Lord," she sang.

"And I won't take it back," a few members of the congregation sang back to her and clapped to quicken the pace.

Brother Danny hit the piano keys a few times to warm up.

"I made a vow to the Lord," she called again, as slow and solemn as the first time.

"And I won't take it back," we responded with a slightly faster clap. Jenner hit the drums slowly, adding a little speed with each response.

Brother Danny caught on, and hit several piano keys all at once. Sister Jolene's voice reigned from the choir stand. Soon each note on the piano tickled my insides, reaching into a part of me that I couldn't define. Mother Nevins' voice, now overshadowed with Sister Jolene's buoyant energy, faded out. The notes twisted up and sashayed back down, tantalizing me with the rhythmic tune. I couldn't resist moving along with it. The church members lifted their voices together led by the younger sister's spirited voice. Tambourines shook in joyous hands, and the drums massaged the worldly ills from my memories. The music roused me in such a way that I couldn't worry about who was watching me. I had to clap, had to wave my hands and smile when people shouted. I felt so good that I couldn't deny myself the pleasure of joining in the Praise and Worship portion of service. Everyone sang along with the soloists and the harmonies that the saints offered to the Lord.

Next, saints took turns standing up and testifying. The head mother of the church, Mother Wright stood up to testify first.

Her backside stuck out because she couldn't stand up straight any longer. "Holiness," she said, her mound of stomach punching out with the force of her voice, "Holiness is right." She squeezed her gray eyes and shook her head, on which the last few strands of her once silky hair survived.

Sister Dakota delivered a muffled testimony about how she witnessed to a co-worker about God's Word. Brother Matt spoke about how he was pushing his way to get to church every Sunday. I saw a few of the teenagers' eyes roll when Matt spoke. Matt only came to church between Thanksgiving and Easter every year ‑ a holiday Christian. He even skipped Sunday school, just arriving at twelve to attend the afternoon service. Whenever Matt came, there was always the threat of being at the church an extra hour while he worked it out on the altar. Keenan didn't see why he couldn't come to Sunday School and get an extra two hours in the morning.

Other people's testimonies felt normal, but not Daddy's. He had a testimony nearly every Sunday. I didn't want everyone to know that we didn't have running water and heat in the house. But he did what the Christians described as 'laying it at the foot of the cross, giving it all to Jesus'. He didn't even know how to testify right. Everybody else stood up, stayed in one place, and said a short little speech about how God helped him or her "get over" and sat down. But not my dad. He started by looking all around and speaking really loudly.

"I am asking you all to pray for me and my family."

"Amen!" One sister called out.

"Hallelujah!" Exclaimed one brother.

Give me a break, I thought. Hopefully he wouldn't go too deep into the reasons why.

"I'm praying that my wife will come back!" Daddy confessed looking around.

"That's right!" The agreements rang out over the congregation.

Mayleen and Day-ja stared at me. The more he spoke, the more I cowered into the cushiony red pews. I thought about how stupid we would look if she never came back. Eve sniggered. Day-ja cut her eyes at Eve. Then she scooted over to me and squeezed my hand. We sat there together for the rest of service, her hand in mine.

"We're having a real tough time right now!" He hollered louder with each sentence.

He stepped out into the center aisle.

"That's all right!" yelled a man in the front row.

Daddy took another step forward and threw his hands up, jerking suddenly as if something had shocked him.

"That's alright!" Another woman called out to him.

"I know I'm waiting in line for my blessing." He yelled now.

Again he threw up his hands as if electrified, and let out a roar.

Aunt Mary, seated just two rows back, let out a, "Haa-ay!" her head jerked and her left hand shot up. She shifted her body as she stood to her feet.

"Keep me in your prayers, saints! Keep me in your prayers! I feel it working!"

I tightened up my free fist and drew my lips together. I held on to the sadness and anger inside without crying. I wouldn't let myself be set up for disappointment. It was fun to play the tambourine and sing and clap, but when you laid it all out for Jesus (someone we couldn't even see) we ran the risk of losing everything. Nothing worked right in my life. The water pipes remained frozen. Mama removed herself from our lives. Everything was falling apart.

Daddy finally finished his speech and walked back to his seat, but the energy boiled over before he sat down. Aunt Mary began to shake her hands as if on fire. She let out another "Hay-ay!"

I sat up to look, immediately forgetting my shame. I heard her heels striking the carpet with a steady beat. Brother Danny, on the organ, struck up the Holy Ghost music: dun, dun, dun, dun, dun, dun, dun, dun, dun. Jenner got on the drums. Mayleen grabbed the tambourine and began to pound and shake in a rhythm that created a trifecta of spiritual enrapture. Brother Danny sped up to match Aunt Mary's trotting: dun ta dun dun, dun ta dun dun. The drums quickened and the tambourines popped faster. The people sharing my aunt's pew filed out into the aisles. Now Aunt Mary was in the center aisle. She ran away from the pulpit and back up again near the altar, the floor rumbling under her weight. "Hay-ay! One shinta la shunta la! Hallelujah! One shinta la shunta la! Thank you Jesus!" Her voice rang like a bell over the congregation and alerted others to action.

Now because of Daddy taking over the testimony time, we were going to stay at church longer and stay hungry longer.

Mother Nevins rose out of her seat, dropped back her head, and waved her hands. In the choir, Sister Jolene beat her heels into the Jesus Blood Red carpeting. A long brown tear streaked her foundation flawless face. It took at least twenty minutes for everyone to settle down.

Next, Deacon Wilson got up to take the offering. He started with his customary low, calm voice. All of a sudden he jumped up and stomped on the floor, shouting, "Woo!"

A couple of the other kids jumped in surprise and giggled. The choir sang "The Lord is Blessing Me" as the offering was being collected. Deacon Wilson counted the small stack of dollars and lingered.

"Saints, I know someone out there is waiting for a blessing!" His eyes searched the congregation.

"That's right," he continued. "You have to give to receive! We have all these beautiful lights. It ain't free to burn them. We have electricity bills to pay. It costs $300 a month. We have a beautiful new sanctuary, saints. But it takes money to run. If we can have five saints with twenty dollars that will help us out."

Deacon Wilson held out his arms and searched the faces of the mothers, brothers, sisters, and visitors seated in the pews. His eyes widened, magnified by his glasses. No one moved. He took a kerchief from his pocket and wiped the sweat from his face. Pastor got up and dangled a twenty-dollar bill from the podium.

Brother Wilson looked around and smiled. "Well praise God. Pastor, going to get his blessing!"

Pastor nodded his head in exaggerated fashion, "That's right. I'm not going to miss my blessing!"

Daddy got up to give more money, and so did three other brothers. We barely had money for food, but get Deacon Wilson up there screaming, and he's giving away money. That's exactly why we were having hard times. He had a hard time saying no to stuff. I had heard Mama tell him that before. Deacon Wilson gave another jump, stomp, and holler. "Thank ya! Thank ya, Lord!" He shouted as he exited the sanctuary to count the cash.

Pastor began his soft-spoken sermon. Instead of straining myself to hear, I just resigned myself to whispering quietly with my friends to pass the time. He repeated his favorite verse loudly: 'For God so loved the world that he gave his Son that *who-so-never* believe in him should not perish but have everlasting life.'

By now I knew that our pastor had been mispronouncing the *'whosoever'* all this time. No one ever corrected him.

I wished we had Children's Church every Sunday. In December darkness, spending time with other children gave me a boost. We'd eat breakfast with interior lamps, wait for the school bus in the dark, and come home at nightfall. The only daylight we saw came through classroom windows and the brief playtime at recess.

Trying to Be Normal

January of 5th Grade, Age 11

By January, I mastered the recipe for baking cornbread muffins from scratch: Albers cornmeal, baking powder, granulated sugar, butter, vegetable oil, milk, and a couple of eggs.

I thought of the Huxtable family staircase that the children trotted down to reach the living room. When I couldn't watch TV, I'd bury myself in books such as *Phillip Hall Likes Me, I Reckon Maybe* and *The Lion, the Witch, and the Wardrobe*. But if I wasn't watching television or reading a book, I was trying to get closer to the ideal family by cleaning up the house and learning how to cook.

Outside, the black night persisted.

"Ooh isn't my cornbread good you guys?" I wanted them to talk, and I wanted their compliments.

To cut the silence Daddy said, "It is really good, Tawny. You are really good at baking."

"Well thank you. I also cleaned the bathroom. Did you see it, Daddy?" I asked eagerly.

"Yes, I did. Excellent job," He spoke with stuffed chipmunk cheeks.

Keenan nodded as he scarfed down his food. He didn't really give praise even when I prompted him. His empty plate showed me his appreciation.

Boiling Mad

January of 5th Grade, Age 11

Every morning without water became more difficult. Monday mornings felt impossible. Peeking my foot out of the warmth of my covers, I quickly retreated. My nose, left bare all night, felt red and numb.

I heard the floor creaking outside the door. My dad must have been up. Soon his form blocked the doorway, silhouetted against the lit hallway.

"Come on! Get up."

"It's too cold," I complained.

"I know. The heat is out," Daddy answered with a heavy whisper that matched the dark morning.

"Okay, Daddy," my head dropped. I pushed myself out of the bed to get ready for school and endure the frozen air.

"I'm sorry; I'll have to get up earlier to turn on the oven."

"When will it be back on?"

"Today, when you get home from school," he uttered the repeated promise.

I rushed to the kitchen to boil water. I wanted to wash up every morning. I wanted to smell good. At first, my dad would warm up the water every day and carry it through the long hallway. I had recently begun doing it alone.

I half ran and slid through the kitchen. After waiting fifteen minutes, the big pot of water boiled. I stood on the chair to get to the pot. It took a second to steady the chair legs from wobbling on the uneven and ripped linoleum. Letting the steam hit my nostrils, I carefully poured part of the hot water into a plastic basin. I got off my chair and slowly picked it up.

I made my way through the hallway, carrying the water steadily. Halfway there, I could imagine the warm towel on my face, neck, and the back of my legs.

The basin of water strained my grip. I tottered just a moment, and the water tilted and spilled all over the carpet and drenched my left foot. My sock held in the heat. I fell to the floor screaming. Yanking off my sock, I saw a bubbled blister on my foot. My brother appeared as I screamed in agony.

"We need to take her to the hospital," Keenan yelled to Daddy.

"Just calm down. She is alright," Daddy said in an unconvincing voice.

"She is hurt!" Brother insisted.

"Aw, it's not that bad. She's strong." Daddy said.

"Please let me see the doctor," I cried.

"Let me take a look," he said.

He looked at it carefully.

"Oh, it isn't that bad," he said softly.

I looked at Daddy, eyes fixed on him while trying to process this latest move. *Should I trust him?*

"Let's get some cool water," Daddy told Keenan. Brother ran to get it.

"Can you make it back into your room?" Daddy asked me.

He helped me up. I held up the foot, and limped forward one step. I nodded.

As I hobbled away, he called after me. "You know, doctors can't do much, except tell you what you already know. Then they'll charge you for it," He said.

I remembered the doctor's office after the rusty nail. The nurse cleaned and bandaged my foot. At the front counter, Daddy couldn't believe the high cost of the bill. He didn't reveal the amount, but it stressed out my father.

Half an hour later, I got fully dressed alone. I covered up the burned foot with a thick sock and a snow boot. Daddy had already gone to work at the shop. I made my way down the stairs and shuffled the length of the trail to the bus stop. As the bus pulled up, I hid the pain and walked erect on the bus. Would Daddy get in trouble if someone found out? Everyone would know that we didn't have running water.

I sucked in the air through my teeth when the burn ached. Filling my lungs and letting out the air slowly, I tried to ease the pain without drawing attention. Once off the bus, I hobbled to the bathroom. I took off the sock, and looked at my foot. I noticed the bubble had plumped with liquid as I pressed tenderly into it.

The Bills

January of 5th Grade, Age 11

That Sunday, Daddy watched television while I busied myself with cleaning the kitchen. My foot felt a little sore, but the bubbled burn on my foot burst and released the fluids. I cleaned it daily and changed the bandage. I didn't even hurt that bad.

From the kitchen entrance, I could see my father sitting in the living room on the sectional. Evening sun filtered weakly through the windows at 4 p.m., but it already slid toward the horizon. We had less than six hours of daylight.

As I cleared the kitchen table, I removed plates, cups, and picked up a pile of opened mail from the large oval table.

I looked over at Daddy again.

"What should I do with these papers?" I asked him.

"Uh, I don't know. Take a look at them."

I read the first letter from his bank.

I read aloud, "Dear Mr. Damon Hughes, your check for $8.33 has been denied for insufficient funds," I paused, "Daddy, what does this letter mean?"

"What letter?"

"This one from the bank says insufficient funds. What's that?"

"That means there is not enough money in the bank to cover the check."

I raised my eyebrows, "Not enough money for eight dollars? That small amount?"

"That's right," He answered, never looking up at me.

The Heater

February of 5th Grade, Age 11

By February, we could actually see the sunrise before school and watch the sunset after we got home. The endless darkness dissipated, though winter's cold showed no signs of loosening its grip.

Daddy walked into our mobile home fully suited with his ski mask hat folded above his eyebrows. Bunny boots chained his feet. He wore a faded, splotched jumpsuit when he worked in his auto body shop. His shop wore him now as much as he wore his work gear. I read it on his hands and smelled it in his sweat: car grease and fuel, paint splatters, and exhaust. He began working when we boarded the school bus around 7 a.m. He'd still be toiling when we got home.

"Hey Daddy!" I greeted him.

"Hello, how's it going?" he replied, looking around at Keenan sitting in front of the television.

"Alright," I answered.

"Keenan, y'all watching T.V.? Is your homework finished?"

"Yeah," Keenan answered.

Daddy turned left into the kitchen and walked into the hallway, he stopped in front of the wall heater and popped open its door. Keenan and I gathered around. Kneeling down in front of it, he pulled an empty vegetable can from the corner and turned a small knob. Daddy's palms wore a permanent tint to them.

Darkened lines hardened the natural creases on his hands. Deep cuts blackened by oil fringed his fingers.

Golden liquid poured out of a spigot at the base of the wall heater. It flowed out, filling the container. He reached for another can, filling it halfway until it sputtered out.

We hadn't seen liquid pour out of the heater like this before, and Daddy always tinkered with the heater in our mobile home.

"What is that?" Keenan asked.

"Diesel," he answered, looking at the heater and shaking his head in apparent frustration.

"Wow, it *stinks*," I squeaked and waved my hands in front of my face.

"*You* stink," Keenan said and pushed me playfully.

"Whatever," I said, pushing him back harder.

I turned and ran away, but Keenan grabbed my arm and twisted it. I yelled for him to stop.

"Hey, y'all quiet down," Daddy told us.

"That's Tawny," Keenan answered.

My brother let go of my arm. I stuck my tongue out at him. Keenan stomped his foot as if he were going to go after me. I screamed and ran into the living room.

"I said be quiet!" Daddy roared, "Now I'm going to get some ass!"

I gasped. Keenan stood frozen. I walked back into the den where I could look at Daddy through the kitchen into the hallway.

"That's a bad word," I informed him.

"No, it's not. It's in the Bible," he answered with his eyes fixed on the heater.

He'd never cursed at us before. The Bible used to be the reason he didn't use that word. If Daddy was cursing now, maybe he was getting frustrated with us like Mama had. We might end up without any parents. I looked at Keenan. Judging by the fear in his eyes, we were thinking the same thing.

Daddy continued to catch the leaking diesel from the heater. The scent saturated the air inside our home.

For the rest of the week, the furnace malfunctioned. Keenan and I slept in the kitchen with the stove on all night. We huddled together to stay warm. Throughout the evening, we sat around the stove. Its door hung wide open. We got as close as possible, trying to compromise comfort out of wooden kitchen chairs and blankets. Our covers kept us warm because Mama had quilted squares from old fabric, infusing her love and extra layers onto my old Cabbage Patch Kids comforter and Keenan's old He-Man comforter. Throughout the evening, we scooted forwards and backwards to navigate the worn places in the linoleum and balance being close enough to stay warm and far enough not to get burned.

Personal Hygiene

February of 5th Grade, Age 11

A few days later, I tried to involve myself in more school activities to develop my mind.

"Who would like to be in the geography bee?" I waved my hand wildly. Mrs. Neil obviously overlooked my hand.

"I will, I will." I called out.

"Tawny, you are not allowed to yell out without being called upon."

I put my hand down. Mrs. Neil kept looking around the room. She nodded her head at two other students instead of me.

"All right John and Morgan, you can start practicing during recess tomorrow," said Mrs. Neil.

As everyone filed out for recess, Mrs. Neil pulled me to the side. When all the students had cleared out of the room, she spoke.

"I didn't call on you because you already were in the spelling bee, oratorical contest, band, and Battle of the Books."

"Okay, but——," I started to defend myself.

Mrs. Neil interrupted me. "Other students need a chance to be a star and shine like you already do so brightly."

I smiled at this metaphor and Mrs. Neil gave me a tight hug.

"I would also like to talk to you about something else."

She went to her desk and pulled open a drawer. She returned to my side with a plastic bag.

"Thank you, Mrs. Neil," I let out an excited giggle as I looked into the bag.

The smile melted into a frown as I realized the contents: a white box of Dove soap, a bottle of coconut scented lotion, a face towel, and a blue container of Secret deodorant.

Mrs. Neil spoke to me about hygiene. She explained I needed to check if the pocket edges of my jeans were dirty before wearing them again. My teacher also told me to keep the deodorant in my backpack just in case I forgot to put it on in the morning. I could not explain to her that I was only able to take a real shower about once a week. According to Daddy, the water would be on when I got home from school that day.

I didn't know I smelled. What did my friends think? Should I talk to them about it? I couldn't stomach the idea of them thinking I was funky.

When I returned to class after recess, my head remained sunk on the desk and hidden by my arms. My eyes blistered from the pain of holding back tears.

Holy Water

February of 5th Grade, Age 11

That weekend, we came into Sunday School class late. This time when we sat by the Avery brothers, Nkrumah whispered, "Y'all smell like diesel."

I felt my eyes getting glossy as my neck stiffened. We had tried to get rid of the diesel smell. Until this moment, we had thought we had. The leak of diesel fuel out of the water heater stank up everything in the house. At Denise's, we had cleaned our clothes with Tide. Every day, we cleaned our bodies as best as we could without a shower.

"I know. It's our heater. It isn't working," I answered.

"Thanks for letting us know, man," Brother whispered back to him.

My brother and I looked at each other and shook our heads.

I asked to be excused to the restroom.

The church bathroom still smelled of paint and had a new coat of baby green. Workers installed a new pair of sinks and a mirror. The lounge area included a new couch of plaid, tan and brown. It reminded me of grandma's furniture in California.

The whole church was being renovated, which is the fancy word they used for moving things around, rebuilding, and adding on new parts. I took off my shoes and felt the comfy, warmth of the amber plush carpeting even through my thick ribbed tights.

My life was going through a type of renovation, but I didn't know why. I could see why the church needed to be fixed up a bit; the mismatched pews had grooves where rumps had rubbed the varnish raw.

When Mama lived with us, my life didn't need anything. I had a mama and a daddy who adopted me like I was his own. Now Mama was gone, and I had a lopsided life again.

I did not want to go back to Sunday School—too much embarrassment that I couldn't even change. In this bathroom I had water, plentiful water.

I walked over to the sink, beige colored with streaks of bronze mixed into the countertop. What if the pipes froze in the church? I bet they'd collect an offering and get the water flowing again right away.

Water had always been a big deal: to wash or not to wash. When Mama was still here, it felt alright to be dirty. A bath seemed to be too much, too hard to manage when it was time to go to bed or wake up in the morning. Mama had *forced* me to take baths. Now I wanted to be clean, especially after Mrs. Neil's "gift".

All these thoughts splashed around my head as I let the water run over my hands, cool at first then drifts of warmth covering my hands. My hands were always cold with fingertips in mid-thaw, but there was never enough time to get fully defrosted and warm.

The cool water heated up until it steamed and at once the water was too hot. I quickly removed my hands from the scald and turned the knob off. Touching the silver faucet, my fingertips felt the heat of the feverish water that it had carried. In the mirror, strings of water slid down my forearms, revealing streaks of dirt, dark brown. Just how dirty was I? More water, I thought. I turned it on again. More. I closed my eyes and thought about the gift pouring through my hands.

Above the bathroom sinks a mirror hung, stretching nearly the width of the counter. So I stared at myself and wondered if I looked poor. Did I look like I was about to fade away, like my family was disintegrating? My week-old braids looked fuzzy. That's why Mama used to rebraid my hair every Sunday. I raised my wet hands from the streaming faucet and smoothed down the fuzzies. A stream of water trickled down my wrists and crawled along my arm until I wiped it away. Turning my head to look closely at the braids, I discovered a bunch of white flakes dotting the roots of my hair. I started to pick out a couple. Then added a little water. No help, just wet hair. A few drops started to roll down my cheek where sideburns grew on men.

We could live here. No one used the church most of the time. Besides church all day Sunday, there was Tuesday night, Thursday night, Friday night, and choir rehearsal on Saturday. Most of the week no one used the church. The church stayed warm at night. It could work even if we had to sleep on a pew or on the floor.

In the mornings, we could take a wash up in the sink or maybe bathe in the baptismal pool. I brought my lips together and felt a smile tuck into the corners of my mouth.

I could wash up right at that moment. Too bad I didn't have a washrag and guaranteed privacy. Anyone could walk in at any moment.

The vanity fixture lit up the mirror just right, and I could see bright, round dots inside my black irises. I would look a lot better if my hair could get rebraided. I was a mess.

I wondered how long I had been here. I dried my hands on a paper towel and left the restroom.

Those shiny eyes in that mirror belonged to me. I even looked better at church. Jesus would take care of me.

Moose Sighting

February of 5th Grade, Age 11

The next day, I set out toward the bus stop in the pre-dawn darkness around 7 a.m. In mid-winter, the sun wouldn't rise for another three hours. The Big Dipper and Orion's Belt sparkled overhead in the black sky. The shop's floodlights created pools of harsh yellow along the path, outlining the packed snow and casting long shadows into the surrounding darkness.

My boot crushed against the hard-packed snow at a rhythmic pace, lulling me into mesmerizing thoughts.

Mama may never come back. I'd literally have to be on my own with Keenan. Daddy was here, but he wasn't really. The shop took up most of his time—it always had.

Maybe Mama's existence without us was less angry, less upset. We irritated her so much, perhaps she enjoyed a happier and a calmer life. I remembered how her refreshed appearance numbed me when we had visited her at The Regency. But maybe I was just being selfish. Mama needed a break. After her break, she'd be back. She'd feel happy to be our mother once more.

Something moved in my peripheral vision. I stopped walking and began searching the bare trunks in the forest and the smooth blankets of snow covering the trash and cars and gravel. I had made it to the middle of the path from our home to the bus stop. There, caught in the glow, a moose calf nibbled a willow bush, revealing a row of ivory teeth. Its coat shined reddish-brown against the snow. Its fragile shadow stretched long across the snowbank. It stepped away, one limb at a time, but faltered on the outer shell of hard snow as its hoof sank a few inches. With twig-legs, it walked lamely along the backside of the shop.

Behind me a branch snapped, and I swung my head to the opposite side of the path. There a moose cow stood erect, head held high. She watched at a distance, just outside of the forest, where my garden had grown in summer. Each moose stood on either side of me: the mother on my left and its calf on my right. Usually without thinking, I would have let my fear take over, let fear control my voice and send it toward the sky. Something held me back. Mr. Beu reminded us to never get between a mother animal and her offspring. Already halfway to the bus stop, I was too far away from the mobile home to run back to safety. Whispering to myself, "*Get to the bus stop, Get to the bus stop*" cleared my mind of fear.

Mother moose moaned a low baritone call to her baby. My only thoughts were the bus and school. If I ran, the mother would suspect me of trying to harm her offspring. She'd interpret my panic as guilt, and it could get me killed.

Be normal, act normal. I took one step, put the other foot forward, and took another step. One more step ahead and another until I was walking, not looking back, just walking and forcing myself to breathe evenly.

The Camper

February of 5th Grade, Age 11

When I got home from school that day, I trudged the path to our mobile home. At 4:30 p.m. dusk began, casting everything in gray shadow. In early February, we only got about eight hours of daylight. As I opened the door, the familiar chill of the house greeted me—even colder than outside. I flipped on the switch. Nothing. This time no digital clock lit on the VCR. The stove wouldn't come on to heat the house. No electricity in the whole house.

I gathered up my backpack, and I stomped down the stairs.

When I got into the shop, I nearly burst when I saw Daddy bent over a car, working the engine under an open hood.

"Daddy, the house is too cold and the lights won't come on!" I shrieked as I entered the shop garage.

I stood in the garage doorway bundled up with gloves and a hat, expecting answers.

"I know. I thought you would stop by here first," Daddy spoke, but he didn't turn around to look at me.

I shifted my weight onto my right foot and put my hands on my hips waiting for him to continue.

"We're going to stay here now," Daddy motioned towards the space in the front corner of the shop.

How would we live here? I couldn't believe that things had gotten this bad. Like an idiot, I thought the water might be on today. Instead more things had been taken away. First no water, then no heat, and now we didn't have electricity.

Daddy didn't have to tell me. I already knew that all of these problems came because the bank had insufficient funds - not enough money to get the pipes fixed, not enough to pay for the heater to be repaired, not enough for more fuel to heat our home, and not enough to pay for the electricity bill. Too many things had gone wrong for us to continue to live in the mobile home.

Now we had to share our home with cars while they were getting repaired. My dad rebuilt engines here. He gave cars a fresh coat of paint and knocked dents out of fenders. My eyes widened as my book bag slid down to the concrete.

Daddy kept his voice as cheerful as possible. "You and Keenan are gonna sleep in the pull along camper. It's the one we took on the river a couple summers ago."

I didn't say anything as I walked toward the familiar pull-along trailer resting on bricks.

I turned the latch and as I opened it, the fresh air on the Tanana River banks replaced the scent of car exhaust. I knew the smell of Mama's cooking again. Its aroma floated and twisted in the air as I was transported back in time. The miniature gas stove and the cozy bed offered comfort on a family fishing trip. Outside the dull trailer windows I recalled the Tanana River strolling by the sandy beach, instead of tools and contraptions against the shop wall. The wind mildly stroked the trees on the opposite shore. My mind returned to the time when my skin roasted under the sun's gaze. I wore a halter-top and home-sewn print shorts.

With the sight of Mama, my lips joyfully curled open to reveal my large protruding front teeth. She returned a matching gap-toothed grin. Outside, I could hear Keenan popping the ball off his legs and arms. Daddy and Uncle Jessie walked the edge of the river laying out the nets, hoping to catch our portion of the rushing salmon.

"Keep going. Go inside!" Daddy nudged me from behind as the memory dissolved.

With Mama, the pull-along camper meant luxury. We had used it to laze on the banks of the Tanana River and watch the silt cloud the river bottom. The trailer had represented plenty of time and space. But now it became another source of shame.

Returning from my trance, my eyes searched our newest temporary home. The small sink's metallic glow stared up at me. A tiny closet emitted a moldy odor when I unsealed the door. A tiny bed occupied the back third of the camper. Two adjacent mats worked as mattresses laid over a wooden platform.

That night and many nights afterward, I slept beside Keenan.

The next morning, I looked in the clouded mirror above the bathroom sink. Daddy told us to wash up in the shop bathroom. My eyes weakened, and my nose shone pink from the freezing temperature. We last visited Aunt Denise more than two weeks ago. Newly growing hair filled in the once perfect separations between my braids. I needed to take down these braids and scrub my scalp with sudsy shampoo—all of the loving tasks Mama used to perform.

Writing About It

February of 5th Grade, Age 11

At school, my fifth grade class followed a predictable pattern. Mrs. Neil taught us how to take stories and break them down. Using those stories as models, she instructed us on how to write from inspiration. She told us about how she started with ideas and captured them whenever or wherever she might be, scribbling them on scratch paper in a car, composing in a corner of an old newspaper at a restaurant, or scrawling on paper bags during a meal. Later those ideas formed into sentences; sentences gathered into paragraphs; paragraphs expanded into reports and short stories. Published authors, she explained, turned reports and short stories into books.

Mrs. Neil taught me that anyone could be a writer. All I had to do was hone my ability to revise and edit. One of my compositions prompted us to write about a difficult time in our life. I felt comfortable writing about my current life, entitling it "Gypsy Days."

I did not include all the details about how we had to wash up in the restroom of the shop or needing to bathe at Aunt Mary's, Aunt Denise's, or at whoever's home we visited. I called this period 'gypsy time' because we didn't live in a permanent home or a mother.

Well—we had a mother, but she was… Should I call what she was doing vacationing? I don't know what she was doing or why. Daddy called it being "separated". My mother always took things to the extreme. Who else had a mother relocate so far away?

Proud of my work, I read my composition to Daddy.

"Oh girl, you don't know anything about gypsies," He said when I finished.

I smiled sheepishly.

"What do you mean?" I asked.

"Do you know what a gypsy is?" He asked.

I didn't answer.

"Huh?" He pressed.

"Yeah… It means that you have to move around a lot. You don't have a set place to live. I think," I said, with my certainty lessening.

He took a moment to clear his throat.

"Well, I don't know about that, but you should look that up and tell me what you find," He said, walking away shaking his head.

Somehow, I lost that paper after I showed it to my dad.

Weekend at Aunt Denise's

February of 5th Grade, Age 11

Thankfully, Daddy brought us to Denise's house with bags of clothes for washing and dropped us off in town for the weekend. Brother and I could relax in a normal home with Denise's kids. My aunt braided my hair and treated us with the same mixture of burden and love, just like Mama had.

Denise's apartment stayed neat. Angel would use her broad shoulders to skillfully sweep the carpets until it looked as if the house had been vacuumed. Her long and lanky body was always stooped over while dusting or picking up out-of-place items around the house.

My aunt's apartment seemed to be the center of the neighborhood with visitors ranging from old women, to young men, young women, and old men. She would take them into her room or make us go to one of my cousin's rooms so that she and her company could puff on a joint and talk about grown-up matters.

On Sunday night, with freshly braided hair, the three of us returned home in the oily shop filled with exhaust. My sorrow burrowed itself into my psyche. Contrasting Denise's house with our own existence, highlighted the dire situation in which we lived. Keenan and I needed to weigh the severity of my father's folly. I needed life to make sense. We had been hiding the lack of running water and the burn on my foot. But now that we lived in the shop, I began to wonder if we had concealed too much.

The Short Bus

March of 5th Grade, Age 11

By early March, the days were noticeably longer. We gained nearly ninety minutes of daytime since December. The sun now rose around 8:30 a.m. and set after 6 p.m.

Three of us remained on the bus. The unsecured windows rattled over the gravel road. As my dad's shop came into view, I pulled on my hat, readying myself for the winter outside. Jason and Bobby sat in the back of the bus across the aisle from me. Bobby stood up and looked out the window, and smiled with his buck teeth stained with white circles. When Bobby nudged, Jason rose to sit on a folded leg and craned his thick neck to get a better view. Nodding, Bobby tossed his head to move away his limp blonde hair.

"Whose bus is that?" Jason said. He brushed a tuft of dark hair from his eyes and turned to me.

Pushing myself to the window, I saw that a short yellow bus had turned into the shop parking lot, and was in the process of backing out. Our bus driver stopped down the road from my stop, allowing the other bus to maneuver itself. I hadn't ever seen another bus on this road. It must've been Keenan's new school bus.

"Yeah, whose bus is that?" Bobby said, looking at me.

They watched me. Jason and Bobby flashed yellow teeth at one another laughing, instant allies.

No shame, I pushed out my chin. "I guess it's Keenan's bus. He got kicked out of North Pole Middle School for attacking an eighth grader with a volleyball pole. So they made him go to a new school."

Jason cackled, a high-pitched laugh only reserved for teasing. Our bus groaned forward.

Bobby stood up, excited, "Your brother? Whoa, I knew he was crazy. That's why they put him in a retard school and—"

Cutting off the taunters' words, I stepped towards him, and only stopped when I stepped on his boots. Bobby took a step back. "Hey!"

I steadied myself by holding on to the seat-backs as the bus lurched to a stop. Time for me to get off, but I knew he wouldn't have said that if Keenan were here. I cinched my eyes at Jason, and he silenced himself. A thing rose inside of me, electricity in my fingers, stiffening lips, solidifying my abdomen. Anger became my super power. Pointing at Bobby, I drew the rest of my fingers into a fist. "You sorry bitch ass. You talking about *my* brother?"

Rage flowed out of my heart.

"He's just at that school for a little while, until he gets his anger together. You're so dumb, no use trying to give you a chance. Everybody know you almost out of elementary and can't read." I hadn't really noticed before how scrawny Bobby was. His eyes glowed like hungry African children on television.

"Whoa, you got burned," Jason said, hopping around acting goofy.

Bobby waved me off and let out a nervous laugh. Eye-level with his chest, I held my arm up in an upward angle. My braids shook around my shoulders as I spoke. "If you say shit else 'bout him, I'm going to whup-your-ass." I delivered the threat like three punches hard and fast, as I had seen Mama do. I didn't care that Bobby was bigger than me or a boy. I would win any way that I could—be it a volleyball pole or a two-inch thick hardcover book inside my backpack. My breaths were loud. I kept my pointing-fist in his face and waited for his next words or actions, whatever came.

Bobby looked down sheepish and shrugged, "Damn, it was just a joke. Keenan's cool. Relax."

"Hey, Tawny. Time to go," my bus driver called from the front.

"That's what I thought, punk."

I grabbed my backpack and strode off the bus like a new girl, no more sweetness. For the first time I hadn't soaked up the criticism. I wouldn't be ashamed of my brother; there was no one who I wanted to be more like.

The Monstrosity

April of 5th Grade, Age 11

Outside, the sun felt stronger than it had all winter. In early April, we basked in up to fifteen hours of daylight, gaining nearly six minutes every day. On the ride home, we enjoyed that sharp quality of spring, bright but not yet warm.

Back at home, I felt stunned that Daddy had resumed construction. There used to be a foundation with walls behind our mobile home, waiting to be finished. The mobile home changed. Now the structure fused altogether: the foundation at the bottom, the walls in the middle, and the mobile home on top of it all. I wanted to be excited that Daddy moved forward, but it just looked crazy.

All my fantasies—*Little House on the Prairie* and the study and canopy bed and the green grass for soccer—disappeared. I had been fooling myself if I thought that my Daddy would be able to give me any of that. All those thoughts were for little kids. My imaginary home had been like believing in Santa Claus and the Easter Bunny. Kids like me didn't have any reason to believe that I would be living like people on TV shows. Yes, the Cosbys might have been black, but they were a type of television fiction that just worked to fight against all the stereotypes of slavery, black criminals, and angry black women. In reality, I was lucky to have a Daddy even if he wasn't my real one. So what the hell was I feeling sorry about?

Mama would be back when this place was together. Any real woman would.

Return to Civilization?

April of 5th Grade, Age 11

I forced myself to visit the mobile home to get a few items. Once it had been lifted in the air, Daddy nailed a set of stairs to the side of the building so that we could get inside. Where the stairs and the plywood met, I could already see large nails pulling away from the siding.

Even while stepping lightly, I slipped on the loose board of one step and nearly fell. I managed to grab hold of the railing, but I scraped a hole in the left knee of my jeans. I gritted my teeth and heat prickled along my scalp in a wave of rage. I only had three pairs of jeans, and this was my favorite. Luckily, I had on thermal underwear, or I would have skinned my knee as well.

Later that evening, the singular ceiling fixture in the shop office buzzed faintly as I talked to Keenan about the state of our family.

"What do you think we should do?" I asked Keenan, reading his brown eyes. He dropped his head, shrugging.

"I don't know, Tawny," He said and moved his arms around aimlessly.

"We can do something," I urged.

He looked up again, eyes steady.

"Like what?" He asked.

I moved closer to him and dropped my voice.

"Call Child Protective Services."

"What do you mean?" Keenan asked, looking at me frowning.

"I mean we don't have to live like this."

He remained silent, scrunching his eyebrows into his eyelids. I continued.

"If someone came here and saw how we live—"

"You know that's what Aunt Mary does," Keenan said.

"I thought she worked for the state."

"Yeah, as a social worker. She goes around and checks on people and their kids."

"She wouldn't let them take us... probably."

Keenan asked, "Would they take us to Mama in California?"

I stopped to think about this. I hadn't thought that far.

"Probably not. She's not here. California is too far away."

"Where would we go?"

"I don't know. Probably in a home with some people."

His head began to shake left and right.

"No, they'll separate us," he said.

"We'll tell them to keep us together."

He shook his head.

"It's not that easy, Tawny."

"We'll be split up."

"No, we won't!" I declared planting my hands on my hips.

"Tawny, there won't be anything you can do about it." His chin up, eyes pushing into mine. The pointedness of his gaze made me surrender. I dropped my arms to my sides. He continued.

"Look, Tawny, there is nothing you can do to stop these people when they get involved. I'm stuck at stupid Pearl Creek Elementary in a class with a bunch of retards. I know I don't belong there, but I'm stuck there anyways. Trust me, you don't want to get these people involved. We really won't have any control."

I took a deep breath.

"I guess you're right."

"I am. Trust me."

I wanted to, but Brother operated differently—meaner and suspicious of everyone.

When the phone rang, I reacted too slowly. Placed high on the cobwebbed wall, a bell echoed the ringing through the garage and the office area.

Daddy picked up before I could. He answered with his characteristic throat clearing followed by his booming tenor. "Hello, Midway Auto!" The hello caught his upper register, hanging on for a moment longer than the rest of his words.

My mind remained stuck on my brother's insistence that calling for help would cause more trouble, trouble that would surely lead to regret.

Parent Conference with Daddy

April of 5th Grade, Age 11

Walking through the school with Daddy made my emotions jumble. Since parent conferences interrupted his work day, he attended the meeting wearing his faded and stained Carhartt coverall. His bunny boots thudded on the industrial carpeting. A thin layer of sweat developed on my scalp from the embarrassment as we walked through the hallway.

At 2 p.m., the sun blazed at an angle we hadn't seen since September. The long days made everything feel possible again.

I felt protected with Daddy walking beside me despite the shame of his work gear. A few kids and their parents walked by. Daddy greeted them with, "Good afternoon!" as he had taught me.

When we entered the classroom, Mrs. Neil stood up and shook his hand.

"Hello, Mr. Hughes. I am Mrs. Neil. I would like to tell you that Tawny is a very nice young lady. She is a joy to have in class and is very motivated to do well in school. She has excellent grades and is on the path to being a very successful young woman."

I smiled proudly.

"Alright that's good to hear," Daddy said looking at me, patting me on the back.

"What do you want to do when you grow up, Tawny?" she asked.

"I want to be a scientist—a chemist."

"Oh alright, well you need to make sure you take lots of advanced math classes in middle school and high school. You should be able to get an academic scholarship to college."

"What's that?" I asked.

"Well a scholarship is money that colleges and different organizations give to pay for tuition."

"But that is for people who play sports, right?"

Mrs. Neil smiled.

"Yes, scholarships can be for athletes, but they can also be for people who earn excellent grades in school."

My eyes widened.

"Really? I can go to college for free just by getting good grades?"

Mrs. Neil chuckled.

"Yes."

I never knew that. I could go to college for free.

Mrs. Neil revealed a clear path to reach my goals.

Daddy delivered a slap to my back. I jumped with the force of it. "All you have to do is keep on keepin' on."

With the sting of his enthusiasm reverberating through my back, I marveled at the possibility of attending college for free.

Asking Aunt Denise

April of 5th Grade, Age 11

A week later, we visited Denise's house again to spend the weekend and get my hair done. The stove light beamed down on my aunt as she cooked dinner. Outside, the snow banks began to recede as the temperature no longer dipped below zero. The cool steady breeze of forty degrees slowly melted the snow.

As she cooked, I spoke to her about us not having water and no heat. That's it. I couldn't tell her that we also lived in the shop.

"Denise, can we stay with you?" I asked her as she fried chicken on the stove. She gripped the handle of the skillet and used a carving fork to turn over the drumsticks.

Auntie put one hand on her waist and leaned back. Instead of really listening, she just used humor to smooth over the situation. "Oooh Lord!" She said letting out a cry as she reached out for an invisible savior—someone she couldn't see, touch, or believe in. "I'm taking me and my *four* kids to the welfare office and get some help!"

She didn't understand how we lived. Maybe she thought I was being dramatic. I looked to my brother for back up. Keenan's shame quieted me; his lips closed tightly like a drawstring. He wouldn't look up, just stood there scuffing the tip of one of his sneakers into the floor over and over.

Later that evening, I showered at my aunt's. The hot water heated the bathroom. I unclothed myself and stepped into the tub. Stretching my neck, I dropped my chin toward my chest, allowing the water to drum on my nape to the crown of my scalp. Down my back, the water streamed, steam rising around me. I tried to relax, but my aunt's megaphone voice echoed inside of me. I thought of trying to explain it to her again, laying out all of the details. She needed to know that we lived in the shop, too. Someone should know, but something wouldn't let me. It was too scary to think what might happen if we told her or anyone.

Crisis Call

April of 5th Grade, Age 11

In the shop office, I sat on the fake leather couch that had cracked, revealing the inner browned foam lining. The stench of dust and stale air made me feel hopeless. Outside, the darkness felt isolating. At 7 p.m., the sun had set an hour ago. The one functioning light in the office hung above the desk, throwing weak yellow shadows across the cluttered space. The hum of the furnace switching on filled the silence.

Keenan had come home grumpy and had fallen asleep in the camper early in the evening. I don't know how he continued sleeping with Daddy working in the shop. Periodically metal clinked against metal. Tools clanged against the concrete of the garage floor.

We still tried to adjust to living in the shop. I used to brush my teeth and wash my face before bed every night before sleeping. Now I avoided the filth of the shop restroom. I did not know how to clear that level of dirt: oil splatter, dried paint clumps, and permanent grime on the cruel concrete floor. Washing up in the restroom also proved challenging without a counter, hooks, a cabinet, or shelving to lay toothbrushes, toothpaste, a brush, wet towels, dry towels, and clean clothes.

The phone rang, and this time I picked it up right away. On the other end, I heard Mama's voice, soft and familiar. She had not called us, had not written any letters or sent any packages for two months.

If she never called, it would be better than for her to call sometimes. We didn't have her number —just had to wait for her call. I needed to hear her voice.

I had gotten a B on a test, and lost the Spelling Bee. It felt like everything was unraveling. Mama put it in perspective.

"Girl that Spelling Bee don't mean nothing, and that is just one test. You're the smartest kid I know. Don't let one test or contest make you feel like a failure."

I sobbed for a few minutes into the phone. I cried until the receiver was slick and my nose was runny. It felt spooky to be talking to Mama on the phone in such a dark room, with only that one weak bulb and the vast darkness of the shop surrounding me.

"Ain't nobody perfect. So everybody can do better."

"Okay, Mama."

"It'll be alright, girl. You'll do better next time. Learn from your mistakes. Okay?"

"Mama, I love you. I want you to come home. I miss you."

Another stream of tears dripped out of me. When I was able to take a deep breath, the air rippled through my body.

Mama continued the silence. I thought maybe something was wrong with the phone. "Mama?"

"Yes, I'm here."

"Mama, we need you." I couldn't hold anything back any longer. Daddy was trying his best, but his best couldn't pay for electricity, keep the water running, and fix the heater in the house. One of our teachers might find out and call someone to investigate. We kept it quiet for ourselves—not for him. But this was Mama, and she ought to know. She should know what life was like without her. I didn't know anyone else who could take this burden. I gave it to her, hoping that she would end my hopeless suffering.

"Your Daddy is taking care of you now. You can come visit in the summer."

"We live in the shop, Mama. He don't know how to take care of us."

"The shop? What do you mean?"

I felt the words sting my tongue, and I gained energy, an anger that I hadn't felt toward Mama before. "We live in the shop. That pull-along trailer that we took to the Tanana River is our new home inside of the shop."

"Wait, how did that happen?"

"You haven't called. We don't know how to reach you. We couldn't tell you that the water had been off for months, that the heater broke, then when the electricity was shut-off we couldn't stay in the mobile home."

"I didn't know. How long have you been living there?"

I couldn't say everything, couldn't tell her that Keenan and I worried that no one would want us. The only person who was here wasn't even really related. Daddy was falling apart; our home was falling apart. There was no way that my brother and I could risk being split apart.

"Why Mama? Why didn't you know? Why aren't you here?" I couldn't keep the whine out of my voice. Tears slid down the back of my throat. I choked them back and shivered.

"Tawny, let me talk to your father," Mama said, low and raspy.

Daddy and Mama stayed on the phone for a few hours that night. I could hear Daddy, but I didn't understand what he was saying. At first he spoke in husky whispers, quick and rushed words. Then the conversation changed. Daddy's responses softened. There were longer silences between when he spoke and when he listened.

Every night for two weeks, they spoke to each other. I still couldn't hear most of what he said, but periodically I heard Daddy say in a tender voice. "Damita…"

The Return

May of 5th Grade, Age 11

A month later Mama, Daddy, Keenan, and I entered the church holding hands.

The morning sun lit the old sanctuary windows. This day would stretch sixteen hours. We arrived early that Sunday around 9:30 AM. Only about ten people had arrived, praying with knees on the floor and elbows on the benches. Half of the bulbs stayed dark, providing the praying folks with a tranquil atmosphere. Mother Nevins moaned a melancholy prayer. Mother Avery mumbled a lamentation unto the Lord.

Near the entrance, I heard, "Jesus, Jesus, Jesus," Aunt Mary prayed in a fierce whisper.

Daddy stood over her and tapped her shoulder. When she saw us, she rose up and began stomping, stomping, and screaming.

"Hallelujah," she sang out, shaking her hands as if they were too hot for her to keep still. Her thick feet drummed against the floor as she began her Holy Ghost dance.

Daddy laughed from deep in his chest. "Well praise God."

After a few moments, she stopped her shouting dance and hugged Mama. My mother and aunt held onto one another for a long moment. Mama closed her eyes and kept still. Aunt Mary patted her on the back.

Keenan ducked out of the sanctuary.

"I'm going to the bathroom," he said.

While he relished being part of the excitement at school, Keenan didn't like the spotlight at church. I felt open, like I could cry at any moment. Mama had returned happier. She didn't even drink or smoke anymore.

A few minutes later, Keenan was back from the restroom. All four of us lined up on a pew and knelt together. Mama, Daddy, Keenan, and me on our knees in the new sanctuary of the church. I didn't close my eyes, though. I watched Mama closely. The skin around her eyes moistened. Then the tears dropped from Mama's cheeks and soaked into the cushioned pews. I wondered if Mama would get saved, too.

Good Again

May of 5th Grade, Age 11

Mama, Keenan, and I stayed with Aunt Denise while Daddy worked to restore the electricity and repair the heater. Now that the season changed, the April weather thawed the pipes. I can't explain how it all happened, but I think some people from the church helped. During the last week in April, all four of us moved back into the monstrosity: mobile home on top, incomplete foundation at the bottom.

The late afternoon sun shone through the dining room into the kitchen, producing rays filled with dancing lint. I sat at the kitchen table with my science worksheet and math workbook stacked beside me. While reading *To Kill a Mockingbird* for homework, I had a full view of Mama gutting king salmon at the sink. Daddy had worked with Uncle Jeff, helping him set out a fishing net on the Tanana River. He brought home dozens of the state fish, which were abundant during the annual spring Chinook run. Mama's wide shoulders and muscular arms moved fluidly. She sliced into each fish's belly and cut smoothly under the head down to the tail. With one more incision, she cut the head off. Water gurgled as the organs slid out into a colander.

Daddy walked up behind Mama and clasped the counter on either side of her. As my mother rinsed off her hands, the two of them stood apart with the light between them. She turned and united with my father, extinguishing the sun. After months away, Mama had returned more in love with Daddy than ever. I watched them kiss for a moment. Daddy closed his eyes and Mama allowed her eyes to droop seductively.

In mock disgust, I wrinkled my face and interrupted them. "Excuse me, I'm trying to do homework. That's despicable."

Mama said playfully, "Well don't worry what we're doin' over here. Mind your business."

With Daddy's huge arms around her, I felt certain that everything would work out. Puckering her flat wide lips, Daddy kissed her once more before letting go so that she could return to the fish.

Daddy smiled at me and pointed at my schoolwork. "That's right. Focus on your studies." I smiled back at him and continued reading.

From the living room, we heard Keenan dribbling into the house. Brother let the door slam behind him as the soccer ball scratched against the floor.

"Hey Keenan," Daddy said. He appeared at the threshold between the living room and the kitchen holding his soccer ball under his arm. Daddy beckoned him closer. "Don't slam that door."

"Sorry, Daddy."

Our father nodded.

"By the way, you finished your homework?"

He told Daddy the same answer every night. "I don't have any homework."

I never believed him; I didn't know why my parents acted like they did. They just left him alone unless they got phone calls from school or when progress reports showed up in the mail peppered with D's and F's.

"OK," Daddy said. Keenan bounced to the room, hugging his ball.

"Baby, I need some lemon to season the fish and some avocado for the salad," Mama said with a sweet voice. She had never called him that before.

"Right away, dear," He gave her a peck on the lips, grabbed his keys, and left for the store.

Dear? I am not sure why they were talking to one another so strangely.

Mama remained at the sink singing "Ribbon in the Sky" in a scratchy falsetto. Leaving my book on the table, I walked over to her.

"Wow, you're almost finished," I said. On the counter, lay a pile of cleaned fish.

She nodded.

"Mama," I said, waiting for her to look at me.

When she finally did, I reached out to her. She pushed me away. The pang of rejection returned.

"Mama, I need hugs and kisses. You hug and kiss Daddy all the time."

Instead of looking up, she slid a clean salmon on top of the pile.

"Oh be quiet," she said.

It didn't make any sense. I wanted to know her reasons. Mama concentrated on the fish as if the shushing water would quiet me. But I stood there.

"Why Mama?" My back curved inward. It didn't matter what she said, no excuse would make me feel better. Mama wouldn't turn her head again.

"You better go sit down somewhere," Judging by the threat in her tone, I did just that.

To complete dinner, Mama sliced cucumbers, chopped beefsteak tomatoes, and boiled eggs for the salad. The salmon was rolled in cornmeal and fried in a bubbling skillet of Crisco. To set the table, I laid a fork, spoon, and a butter knife on top of four folded napkins. Then I placed four plates so that each of us would have a place to eat.

Lying in my bed that night, the spring's first mosquito buzzed in my ear. Outside my window, the sky still glowed pale blue. In early May, the sun barely set, and true darkness would never really come. The sky would go from blue to purple to that strange twilight that passed for night before lightening again by 4 a.m.

I couldn't stop concentrating on the image of Mama and Daddy kissing, the sun shining around them. What made her return? Why had she gone away? They hugged and kissed like Mama had never left. But she had. Maybe I shouldn't have questioned her this afternoon. Maybe I was the reason she left in the first place. I did need a lot of attention; I couldn't help that I wanted a lot of hugs. But everything should be good again. Since she got back, there was no scent of weed and no alcohol. At least she stayed out of the bedroom. Instead, she busied herself with cooking and cleaning around the house. Should I trust her?

PART III: TEENS

High School Life

September of 11th Grade, Age 16

Five years had passed since Mama returned. By sixteen, I had grown a little taller, and Mama became a holy woman. But the pipes still froze, the trash continued to pile up, and the mobile home remained perched on its incomplete foundation. Some things stayed the same too: Keenan played soccer, and I made honor roll.

Through the hallways of North Pole High School, my best friend, Day-ja, and I walked side by side. We laughed about an episode of *Martin*.

I felt a sting from a smack on my ass. I stopped and jerked my head around. Harold stood along the blue lockers, looking up at the ceiling and sucking on his bottom lip. "Harold! Stop it!" I yelled, and I kept my mouth tight to make sure I didn't smile.

He looked around as if in a search to find the guilty person, then grinned. Harold had grown from a goofy kid into a tall, muscular teenager. Something about his form, his presence made it hard for me to be serious with him.

At this age, people often told me I looked like a twelve-year-old. I barely had titties, and didn't have much height on me at five-feet.

"Leave her alone!" Day-ja said, mean-mugging him and stepping toward him with the boldness afforded by her 5 '7 height. "Don't play like that! That's not cool!" Both of them were very protective —maybe because they towered over me.

Everyone else grew much taller, but I grew like a snail. I still wore clothes out instead of growing out of them.

"Wait a minute. Tawny, Tawny," he said looking at me. Harold came closer and bent down from his six foot tall perch to lower his hands around my waist.

He hugged me as he explained, "I was just playing with you. You know that right?"

Warmth spread inside my chest and belly. I had never been so close to him. Avoiding his eyes, I focused on the deep brown of his arms and his pectorals carving out shapes through his tank-top. Smelling the bubble gum on his breath, I noticed his soft lips. Trying my best to glare at him, I nodded.

Day-ja walked behind him and pushed him in the back of the head. He released me and stomped at Day-ja, feigning to go after her. My friend flinched. Harold waved her off.

We locked arms and walked away laughing. We turned down the next hallway.

"Day-ja," someone called. One of our classmates used the kind of voice that resonated on radio waves, that fake voice that teen boys make for a girl they want to impress. Turning around, we saw Kevin wearing a green Celtics hat with the bill to the side. He lifted up his chin and smiled at her with open arms.

"Hey, man!" Day-ja said, smiling wide to match that arm span, wrapping arms and emotion around him. I stood watching. Day-ja had this way about her—made everyone feel close to her. We both met him last year when we had the same P.E. class.

"Hey Kev," I said. Neither of us had seen him since last year, but I couldn't show him that type of affection—no matter how long it had been.

Boys loved Day-ja. They always asked her out or gave her extra attention even if they were too scared to admit their interest.

Day-ja's physique had transformed from a pre-pubescent girl to a young woman. One day she was skinny like me, just a few inches taller. Then last summer, she grew four inches and developed curvy hips, cleavage, and a big booty.

She wore skin-tight jeans, acid washed with a zipper at each ankle. The way she strutted beside me made things worse.

I wore a jean skirt, one with pleated ruffles that hung to the ankles. For my hair, Aunt Denise had fashioned me a basket-weave bang with blond braided hair intertwined with my natural dark strands. The girls always complimented my hair, but that didn't matter. I knew that no matter how modern the hairstyle, something about my ankle skirts made the boys stay away. Besides Harold, no boys paid attention to me.

Day-ja and I parted ways. She had to get to her class on the third floor. "Catch you at lunch!"

Further down the hallway, Keenan closed his locker. Now as a senior, he stood a few inches taller than me at 5'3. This caused him more agony the older he became. As a teenage boy, he had outgrown the cuteness of being tiny.

A dark-haired white boy shouldered Keenan as he walked past. My brother turned around immediately, slid his foot between his and the boy's, and tripped him. Dark-hair was about to get up with gusto, but Keenan gave him this look. He got the message that he'd be in for a fight. So, Dark-hair exhaled, letting go of the energy. Keenan smirked at him and held out his hand to help him stand.

My brother was used to this. Other guys always tried to punk smaller ones as a way of proving themselves. Keenan knew how to defend himself, gaining strength all the time. He learned to strengthen his body with exercise.

Moving alone through the hallways, I walked as slowly as I could without distracting others. If I moved too fast, my skirt would twirl and twist. Fear of getting caught in someone's path slowed me; that skirt could do damage in a crowded high school corridor. The derision I'd face would be unbearable. Most of the time no one dared tease me because every once in a while, I'd go off on people. No one had seen that side of me since sixth grade.

Now that Mama got saved, our family lived as full-time holy rollers. We attended church too much: Tuesday, Thursday, Friday, Saturday, and all day Sunday. I no longer had church clothes and school clothes. All my clothes served as church clothes—suitable for the Lord.

Just in time, I side-stepped FaKeem. He and his pregnant girlfriend had stopped, suddenly engaging in a lip-lock in the middle of the hallway. What would've happened if I ran into them?

FaKeem had been known for being loud and clowning girls. He got real disrespectful with Sierra last week, calling her a bitch and a hoe. A few of his friends were around laughing at her, backing up his ignorance. I could deal with one taunting idiot, but not a group of them.

Steady walking would take me from class to class unnoticed. I learned to ignore the runners that whipped into my skirt, and the swinging arms that swatted it inadvertently. High school still had awkward kids—unaware of their bodies. I just breathed deeply and floated away. That's how I imagined I looked in this floor length pleated jean skirt.

Church Teachings

September of 11th Grade, Age 16

"That's my wife right there. We've been together for over fifty years," Pastor said pointing at Mother Margaret. Light filtered through the sanctuary windows, soaking into her vacant eyes. The first lady of the church sat on the front pew, staring at the back wall behind the pulpit in a daze from Alzheimer's.

"Amen," Mother Wright said.

"Hallelujah," said Elder White.

Pastor paused to look at everyone, starting on the far left where Mother Avery and Mother Wright sat. He slowly expanded his gaze to span the congregation.

"Yep. That's a long time. Over the years I've learned something about husbands and wives. Amen. That's right! 'For God so loved the world that he gave his only begotten Son that *who-so-never* believeth in him should not perish but have eternal life!'" As usual, Pastor yelled out his favorite verse at random times, reciting it incorrectly.

"Well..." Brother Montgomery said, sounding a note deep as a bullfrog.

"The Bible says not to let the sun go down on your wrath. It says 'Do not go to bed angry with your wife.'"

"My, my, my," Mother Avery said, shaking her head.

"I said don't let the sun go down when you're angry."

"That's right," a group responded from the pews.

"So in over 50 years of marriage we haven't once raised our voices to one another."

"Praise Him!" the church-goers answered again.

This wedding tale sounded like foolishness. It had been a hard life for many of the sisters sitting in this sanctuary.

Mama and Daddy sat together on the third row pew. Both of them nodded their heads. Day-ja and I sat on the back pews. She looked at me and cut her eyes, and I almost started laughing. Trying to contain the laughter, I closed my eyes and rolled my lips inward. Neither one of us wanted to say it. Day-ja and I had back-slidden. We didn't feel the same way about religion and God as we once had.

I used to think that God's love could sustain me. My breasts had grown from non-existent to A-cups, and I felt tinglings and other preoccupations much stronger than God's love.

Mama dedicated our whole lives to holiness. She reminded us daily that holiness started inside, in the soul, and manifested itself outwardly. So according to the scriptures, holiness affected the way we walked, the way we talked, and the way we dressed.

Holiness especially affected the way that women dressed. In a holiness church, you just couldn't walk in with any type of clothes. You had to wear dresses and skirts below your knees and pantyhose for women. Little girls had to wear tights or their parents would be judged for not caring for them properly. At one time, all of the COGIC ladies wore dresses at church and everywhere else. No pants. Now only certain folks believed in following the no pants rule. Back in the day, some believed it to be a sin to straighten your hair, but that didn't last.

"Blessings!" said Mother Wright in a scratchy voice. She waved her hand, holding a used tissue. Three times wed, and she had outlived every one of her husbands.

"The Lord says when you find a wife, you find a good thing."

"Well,'" Brother Howell said, looking around nodding.

"Thank you, Jesus," Sister Dakota said and clapped her hands.

"When you find a wife, you find a good thing," Pastor said again, slower this time emphasizing each word.

"Hallelujah!" Aunt Mary's voice rang out as she clapped.

"The Lord told me the first time I saw her. My jaw hit the ground when I saw her. She had those pretty brown legs. The voice was loud as my own. It told me. That's going to be your wife. I just walked right up to her and said. I'm going to marry you."

"Ha. Ha!" Deacon Wilson stood up nodding and clapping.

I wondered if Deacon Wilson had found Sister Wilson the same way. Had the Lord shouted in his ear and pointed out his destiny? I looked around the sanctuary. The saints never let on that they didn't believe in his narrative, just amen-ed and applauded as if their real lives didn't play out the exact opposite. All these single mothers raising these children alone had been in church for years, lonely and overworked.

"Praise him."

"Thank you, Jesus."

Pastor kept spinning his tale. "Her eyes bucked out, she just looked at me, and said 'he hasn't told me anything yet.'"

The saints looked at one another laughing.

"Look at her. My sweetheart is so beautiful, still beautiful and just as sweet. See, she come 'round eventually. At some point the Lord told her the same. We were in agreement, and we lived happily ever after."

"Amen."

"All right now."

Clapping. More hallelujahs and more pretending. Some of these mamas who existed without a father and child support just clasped their hands in embarrassment.

"I know some of you women want to find a husband. You been waiting on the Lord. Some of you are getting impatient. But the Lord has sent word. You not 'posed to be looking. The Word say 'He who finds a wife, finds a good thing.'"

Silence. Pastor threw up his hands and turned as if to walk away.

"See. Y'all don't want me to preach!"

"Praise him anyhow."

"Amen."

He kept on going. "You got to get your relationship with God in order first. He will bring the man to you."

Pastor moved his arm pointedly from left to right.

"You need to get *right* with God. He'll send you a man when you least expect it. But it ain't going to happen by *you looking*. Ya'll need to stop *looking* at the conferences and the revivals and the…"

He stopped and turned around, walking a few steps away from the podium.

"Preach!" The congregation pushed him to continue. "Preach!"

"Some of y'all coming to church with dresses and shoes and hats you can't afford. *Looking!*"

"*Looking!*" Deacon Wilson and Brother Montgomery repeated.

The organ sounded an echoing ripple.

"Tell it," a married sister shouted from her seat.

"Some of y'all can't pay your tithes and offerings because your hat broke the bank."

The organ played.

"Well!" Brother Montgomery sang it out now.

"My, my, my," Mother Avery said.

"Too busy *looking! Looking!*" He made exaggerated blinks at the church members.

"*Looking!*" the people repeated.

The organ mimicked his tone.

"I want everyone to say '*looking*'!"

"*Looking!*" the congregation echoed.

"Instead of *looking*, you need to be spending your time praying. You ought to be on your knees asking God to send you a husband. You ought to be investing in the future of the church with your tithes and offerings. Give and it shall be given unto you."

"Yes, Lawd!"

"Hallelujah!"

"Stop *looking* around and get your eyes in the Word of God."

I couldn't help but think that a "right-now man" or "right-now father" would be a lot better than a fairytale husband.

"Listen to the words of the Lord God. He said he will supply all your needs according to the riches in heaven. If you find your own husband, you'll be disappointed. But if you *wait* on the Lord…"

Some of these women had grown children already. What was there left to wait for?

Pastor stopped and turned again, hanging his head. He rarely preached like this.

"Ya'll don't want me to tell it."

"Tell it!" A few sisters called out.

"Yes, Lawd!" Someone hollered.

"If you let Jesus find your mate, he will give you a husband that will last forever. That no man can tear asunder. He will give you the desires of your heart if you just wait on him!"

"Wait on Him!" Brother Montgomery repeated in his sing-song way.

"Yes, Lawd!"

Aunt Mary stood up and shook her hands as if a crab had caught hold of her fingers, turning and shaking in a circle. Pushing herself into the aisle, she ran back and forth, moving her heels faster than the drummer. Jenner beat the drums, steadily growing speed. The preaching time had ended; shouting time had begun.

Near Grown

October of 11th Grade, Age 16

Mama stood near a sink full of dishes as afternoon light streamed through the window. Her eyes flashed with irritation.

"Is it your turn to wash the dishes?" she said, looking at me.

I cut my eyes at her. At mid-day on a Saturday, I had already seen the sink's worth of dishes, the caked up oatmeal, hardened grits, and egg scrapes.

I held up a strong hand to quell the current of anger traveling through my spine.

"You know if it were my turn, the dishes would've already been washed." I took liberties when I said it too—with a hands-on-hips stance that threatened to say more.

I never mentioned my earned independence when she lived thousands of miles away in California. So why would she think I needed her to tell me what to do now?

I reminded her again and over that I washed and cleaned without being told or reminded. The whole year when she had abandoned us, I made it a habit. Nothing changed in the five years since she returned. Before Mama had left, I would never posture to her this way. Now, her edge had dulled where mine had sharpened.

She nodded. "Whatever. Well, where's your brother at?"

So annoying. Keenan let her tell him what to do and accepted her back with full privileges of a real mother. But she had quit for a while. Who else got a mama who quits for a while and comes back?

I turned and walked over to Keenan's door. I tried to open it, but the knob didn't move. I banged twice to identify myself. Upon opening it, he gave me an up-nod.

"Dishes."

Keenan's headphones fit askew on his head so that one ear could hear. With jacket on, shoes on, I could tell he had been balled up at the foot of his bed. He only locked the door when dressing or listening to non-sanctioned music. Behind him, his black toy chest lid lay open, revealing a dozen or so tapes. His Wrestle Mania ring lay sideways. He hid the secret, secular music cassettes under the toy wrestling ring. He dropped his head for a beat. Then he returned his Walkman and tapes to the chest. Shifting around the contents, he put his Wrestle Mania ring on top of his "worldly" music tapes.

I shook my head and closed the door before walking through the kitchen to the dining room window.

Mama sat at the kitchen table now shifting through some bills. From the calls we received on a daily basis, I knew she needed to decide which ones to pay, which ones could wait.

When I grew up, I would be prepared to pay bills on-time. One day I'd be able to proudly invite people into my home where the water always flowed. Sometimes I thought about my friends with absent parents. Maybe we would be better off if she had gone and stayed away. For all I knew, she could leave again. Giving all my power back and allowing her to be my regular mother again... Too risky. I didn't have to accept her back unconditionally, and I hadn't. I loved her now with a long-armed type of love. I no longer sought a hug or kiss in earnest, only in jest to get on her nerves.

I had read too much, seen too much. Looking out that dining room window felt like a bully thumping me on the head. The dogs had repeatedly ripped up trash bags. Debris had long blended into the rocky bed of earth that lay before me. My parents would do nothing about it, but I was still going to say something. I wouldn't let them feel comfortable in this mess. Keeping it all in wasn't going to work for me. It just didn't make any sense.

"Why didn't He dump that trash before the dogs got to it?" This is what I called the man I used to call Daddy now—just He.

"You got to ask yo' daddy that question."

Keenan came out of the room and started running the dishwater. From the window, Mama sat at the dining table along the far wall. Keenan stood between us at the sink.

"But why don't we get some landscaping, get some grass?" I turned from the window and looked at Mama. I wanted real answers, some type of solution to be thought of or attempted.

Keenan was washing dishes as quickly as he could.

Mama turned to me and put her hands on her hips. "You got some landscaping money?"

My brother looked up from the dishes to me, holding my gaze for a moment before getting back to the dishes.

"No, but I am a kid. I am not supposed to pay for it!" I cocked my head to the side.

Mama crossed her arms, put her head down, and let her eyes drill into me with a condescending slant.

"Well until *you* paying bills, *you* need to concentrate on school. Children should be seen not heard - like I care what you think."

"Amen!" Keenan laughed at that old saying and faked a church voice.

I waved him off. Someone at church had said they read it in the scriptures, that God supported adults not caring what kids thought. But I countered with another verse. "The scripture also said, 'A little child shall lead them.' I have ideas that could work, and if you listened —"

"We'll see how *you* do when you grow up." She cut me off and threw up her hands.

That same warning: one day I'd understand how hard it is, how impossible it will be for me. Such a comment could not go unanswered, especially when uttered with such certainty and pity.

Keenan shrugged his shoulders at me. He, too, had heard it before. My brother had told me that he did not see a reason to ignite these conflicts with our parents.

"What is *that* supposed to mean?" I pressed.

She only rolled her eyes.

"With all the people in the world who have nice houses and can pay bills, why do you think *I* won't be able to pay *my* bills? Most parents want better for their children."

She finally repeated, "We'll see how good *you* do when you grow up."

I scoffed, "We sure will. We will see." I spoke deliberately strong. I stomped to my room and slammed the door.

My mind raced. Mama wouldn't let me go anywhere, wouldn't let me talk to friends on the phone longer than five minutes. How could I be free when I was locked up? I read Maya Angelou's *I Know Why the Caged Bird Sings* because I felt bound and restricted. I angrily snatched my clothes off. Under my long skirt, I wore tights. Over the tights, I wore socks. Over the socks, I wore tennis shoes. I didn't have any clue where that scripture came from—the scripture demanding we wear extra long skirts. I got down to just an undershirt and panties. Then I punched at the air.

No matter what she predicted, I could see my future clearly: a carpeted green lawn, repairmen hired to fix all problems, money to pay the handymen promptly. My children would not have to repeatedly answer bill collection calls. Her pathetic warning only made me plan more carefully, study harder. I would not be some United Negro College Fund commercial waiting to happen. I had worked so long on this damn junkyard we lived on—many tries and many failures.

She didn't believe in me, and I decided right then that I was giving up on my parents and the idea that they would provide for me - emotionally or otherwise. From that point on, I rejected their rule over me. If they didn't care what I thought, if they didn't believe in me, I would no longer believe in them.

They couldn't tell me what to do anymore. I had lost all respect for both of them. I wouldn't take it - not one more punishment, not one more whipping. If they tried, I would be moving out that day.

Snow and Soccer

November of 11th Grade, Age 16

By the time we reached our stop at ten minutes after four, the November sun had already surrendered to darkness. Fall in Fairbanks meant losing day hours fast, hemorrhaging six minutes daily. We had less than seven hours between sunrise and sunset. On the hour-and-a-half bus ride from North Pole High School, I watched what little daylight we had drained away into dusk.

Reluctantly, I zipped up my goose down coat and pulled on my insulated gloves. I wished we were the last kids to get off the bus and no one could see that we lived here. I followed Keenan's short, emaciated frame off the bus.

As the door hissed closed, the rumbling stall of the bus shifted to the revving drone of the engine as it rolled away. When we stood together, I felt bolstered.

The snow fell in heavy flakes, covering the ground in clumps. Dropping steadily, I could tell that this time the snow would stick—the first permanent snowfall of the winter.

Luckily, we didn't see Daddy working outside the shop. So we passed the front office and trudged up the path to the rear of the garage towards our home. Mounds of snow began to cover the bags of newspaper, oil bottles, broken pieces of plywood, and TV dinner boxes that we picked up last summer. As usual, our father had told me he would remove the trash a few days after we had collected it back in June.

With eyes burning like cinders, Keenan dragged his feet on the dirt and snow covered path. I pressed my lips together, knowing that he wanted to talk about the national soccer tournament he missed last summer—again.

Without neighboring houses or businesses to tame the wind, I felt attacked whenever I went outside. I just wanted him to hurry home so I could get out of the elements.

When we made it to the side of the shop, Keenan's backpack slid from his shoulders. He stopped and sat down, letting the snow build up on the sleeves of his Lakers jacket. The snow and dirt clung to his pants as he settled himself. Keenan pulled his elbows over his knees and rounded his back into a slump, dropping his head.

The shop's security lights made the falling snow look like static on a TV screen.

The wind siphoned away the heat from my nose. I inhaled deeply and put my hands on my hips. Clouds of air escaped our mouths as we breathed. We were only a few hundred yards away from home.

"You should be happy to be in your senior year. I have to survive this place another year after this one." With hands planted on my hips, padded by gloves, hat, and down coat, I felt like a bossy woman emphasizing the roundness of my shape. The winter air nipped at my wrists, finding the tiny crack between my gloves and coat.

"Trevor and Fred have been talking to a soccer scout from Arizona State University." Keenan's words came out in a staccato through gritted teeth.

His teammates often irked him because they liked to show-off. This new information pushed my brother further into depression. From the pulse of his jaws beneath his skin, I knew to wait for him to continue. I scanned the woods to see if any moose lurked. I hoped that Daddy wouldn't come around the building and want to talk.

"Have you ever paid attention to how stupid Trevor and Fred look when they play? They're sorry players. But they got to go to the National Youth Soccer Tournament."

Keenan dominated on the Arctic Knights. Our parents thought that if they didn't show interest in his playing, Keenan would stop wanting to play. They didn't want to drive the nine miles into Fairbanks for practices. They hadn't come to any of his games since he was ten-years-old. Not even the weather could keep him away from soccer. He kicked the ball off the wall of the shop during the winter, splashed the soccer ball through the mud during the spring break-up, competed in tournaments all night in the midnight summer sun, and scattered multi-colored leaves while shooting the ball during autumn.

As I stared at my brother who already entered his senior year, I shook my head. My heart dipped with the sight of his sunken appearance. Sitting in the snow, I could see him conceding to failure—letting the cold soak into him. I felt the icy wind against the slit between my neck and clavicle.

"It's not fair to you that Mama and Daddy didn't have the money," I said.

His gloved fist rammed into an exposed patch of dirt. "It's not the money. The team fundraised all year—car washes, bake sales, skating parties."

"Why didn't you—"

"Every time Mama wouldn't let me go. They wanted me to work at the shop."

I flexed my arms into a boxing stance. "I would have told them—," I wasn't sure what I would have told them, because it didn't happen to me. My arms dropped limply. "I don't know." I decided then and there that it wouldn't happen to me. As heat prickled along my scalp, a bit of the cold subsided.

"Daddy told me he would have the money for the trip."

"He told you he would have the money?" I couldn't close my mouth. And since I didn't want to push him over the edge I didn't say what I was thinking. *You believed that?*

My chest began to rise and fall more quickly. A warm, moist layer of perspiration condensed along my hairline as I glared at the shameful landscape. Three months later, trash bags still sat beside the broken down cars. According to our dad, each useless car was like money in the bank. When we first moved here, he had assured us that the two cars wouldn't be here long. Instead, he had allowed more cars to be dumped on our land. The powder blue 1962 Ford was now rusted along with the blue and gold Alaska license plates that he had been certain tourists were sure to buy as a souvenir. The faded brown 1982 Volkswagen Beetle with its money-making engine had been here for five years. Although the 1980 red Camaro was totaled, Daddy had been confident the unscathed right door would pay off in the near future. Even though he didn't like people to call our home a junkyard, nine cars had been littering our land over four years.

My brother's eyes focused on the freezing ground, at the mixture of dirt and ice underneath his feet. The snow dissolved into his thin black and white Converse and seeped into his shoes.

Finally I spoke quietly. "They couldn't buy us groceries. We were getting barely edible donations from The Food Bank."

I couldn't understand what my parents wanted for us. What did they want from us? How could my brother be successful if he didn't even get the chance to pursue his goals? If we weren't able to challenge ourselves to go to the next level, we would never get there. Success, I knew, was not Midway Industrial Park, not working for a business that barely had customers. It didn't make sense to pick up bottles, cans, empty bottles of anti-freeze, and flattened paper KFC buckets every summer so that the trash could be thrown right back onto the face of the earth.

We should be clearing the land so that I could plant larger gardens. I knew how to grow tomatoes sweeter than cherries and nurture bunches of carrots that could make anyone's eyes shine. I could do better than the heaps of mildewed corncobs and expired chicken noodle soup from The Food Bank.

"Let's get out of the cold." I rubbed my nose and wiggled my numb toes inside my boots.

Keenan stretched out a bent leg and stiffened. My brother could not become the man he needed to be if he stayed here. And he could do better, but I was no longer sure that he still believed that.

Why couldn't they see? Why couldn't Mama understand that a successful life was not living in squalor and on diesel fumes, or collecting feces in a trash can, not being told that we didn't have enough when they didn't even try to have enough?

From the shop's garage, the loud clank of metal pounding metal rang through the air, the familiar sounds of our father working outside. The gnawing cold had already found my fingertips and toes. I wished Keenan would hurry up, so we could get home before he could see us.

"Tawny! Keenan! Come here for a minute," Daddy's voice roared.

Too late. I stopped, breathed in slowly with my eyes closed for a few seconds before facing him. Behind us, our dad stood next to the shop, a couple hundred feet away with one arm stretched, beckoning us.

We stumbled back up the path as my stomach sank like the snow falling around me. Keenan's footsteps crunched behind me. When I got a few feet away from Daddy, I stopped and adjusted my backpack. Keenan caught up to me. Even though I was seventeen-years-old, I felt like a little girl standing in front of his 6-foot-tall bulky frame.

Our father smiled with glittering eyes, which moved from Keenan to me. Dressed in a midnight colored jumpsuit and ski hat, he smelled of the strong nauseating aroma of car exhaust fumes. His bunny boots blended into the forming snow heaps.

"Well hello and good evening." Daddy's voice sounded crisp and melodic.

"Good evening." I spoke in a monotone. *What's so damn good about this evening? It's freezing and now that you've seen me, I have to be out in the cold longer.*

Brother kicked the edge of his shoe into the ground.

He took a step forward and repeated louder with emphasized enunciation. "Good evening, Keenan."

Keenan kicked a loose rock and mumbled good evening below his breath.

"What's wrong with you, Keenan?"

Before answering, Brother looked away and followed the soft wave of the few cars driving down Richardson Highway in back of him. "I'm alright."

He's not alright. He's hurt. If he looked into my brother's eyes, he'd see water that wasn't going to freeze—even in this weather.

"Well you look like you need to get some rest." *He needed someone to help him raise money for the damn soccer tournament you promised you'd pay for when you couldn't even pay for groceries.*

Keenan mumbled something I couldn't understand.

"I can hardly hear you. What's going on with you, Keenan?" He said.

"Have a lot of homework."

The winter air had already permeated my moon boots, and my feet felt like ice.

"Tell me how's school," He said, turning to me.

"School's fine—always is." I pursed my lips together and raised my eyebrows.

He turned his head toward Keenan and waited for his reply.

Keenan finally said, "Alright."

"Well, I got to get back to work."

"Yeah, I have a lot of homework, too," I said.

Keenan and I turned and continued home. Like mid-winter snow, he didn't realize Brother's hardening. Last summer the determination in his eyes had turned to anger. He no longer desired to prove himself, just wanted to defend himself. Keenan stopped again and kicked a mound of snow beside the path.

"Apply to colleges and try to see if you can get into a soccer program that way."

"It doesn't work like that. My grades are shit," he told me through gritted teeth.

Soon the moon and the Big Dipper would submit to the penetrating darkness of seventeen hours of night. Around us, the snow continued to collect, hiding the trash and camouflaging the abandoned vehicles. We would be in a frozen prison of ice and snow until April.

Every summer I had brought a new energy for gardening, for making it a home where I wasn't embarrassed to live. But looking around this dump, just thinking of the recurring cycle of trash collecting—the chain of broken promises—I knew I had already spent my last summer trying to make this place better, trying to grow food in a place where the weeds ruled. I didn't know how it would happen, but I was already gone.

Honors Classes

November of 11th Grade, Age 16

In my first period honors English class, I was the only black student.

Through the classroom windows, I could see the parking lot lampposts against the November darkness. First period started at 8:30 a.m., but the sun wouldn't rise for another hour. The hills beyond were barely visible in the pre-dawn twilight. The overhead fluorescents would stay on all day.

My black friends all enrolled in regular classes. Harold still needed me to proofread his essays for English. Day-ja also needed a lot of support with Algebra. I liked helping, but the low level of the work in those classes surprised me. The difficulty my friends had completing the work concerned me more.

Our parents didn't care about school either—not really. They would get upset about Keenan's low grades, but they never helped him improve. They never even checked if we had finished our homework.

I understood that they didn't know how to help us, just like my grandparents hadn't known how to help them. Both of Mama's parents dropped out of high school. My grandparents met in night school.

I often thought about the conversation that Grandma had with Mama before we moved to Alaska. She talked about all of these problems being a part of a cycle. For generations, the women in our family had become mothers without being prepared. The results were disastrous: violent deaths, prison, and another generation of teenage mothers. More teenage girls gave birth to babies and more teenage boys acted out the frustration and anger inherited from their impatient, frustrated mothers.

No threat of it happening to me. Even as a by-stander of teen love, I felt the danger. I never understood until I became a teenager how the flesh could be weak. Sometimes when one of my classmates walked by with streaked mascara and red-teary eyes, I felt safe in my long sleeved sweater and ankle skirts.

Other times, I felt that I was locked out of the feelings, good and bad, of being a real teenager. I missed out on the thrill for being too holy. My clothes kept me from being an all the way friend and out of reach of becoming a boy's girlfriend.

I used to think that anyone could make it: go to college, get a good job, improve their situation. I had thought that all anyone had to do was complete their homework and pay attention in class. After helping Keenan, Day-ja, and Harold, I knew better. They didn't know how to do the work, and—most of the time—there was nobody to help them.

My parents didn't even value my achievement in school. Although there were times I felt discouraged, I knew that education was the only way to get away from my parents, to prove to them that I could do better than they expected. I wasn't going to fulfill those statistics I read about black kids. I was going to be more.

Midway Man

November of 11th Grade, Age 16

"I'm so tired of this shit, Tawny. I don't know what to do. He act like this shit is going somewhere, like he going to do something. He ain't ever gone get this shit together."

Keenan was walking around his room speaking in a roaring whisper. Late evening darkness permeated his bedroom window.

We didn't want anyone to hear. Mama and Daddy slept in the next room. Around eight, Daddy had come home and went directly to bed. Now at nearly midnight, neither of us could sleep.

"You remember those damn blueprints?" I asked.

"Yeah, they still in the corner of the kitchen!" Keenan said with a dry laugh.

"That shit was make-believe!"

My brother dropped his head and let his shoulders rock. He bent over, laughing so hard.

"What's so funny. You laughing out the blue like you crazy!" I said cracking up, too.

"Wait, listen. I'm Daddy."

Keenan put his hand up, stretched his pinky down by his lips and his thumb by his ears as if it were a phone receiver. "Ring, ring." He said in a high pitch. Then he changed his tone to a low baritone. "Hello, this is Midway Auto."

He sounded just like Daddy; I laughed. We did this sometimes—acted out our lives as if it were some play in an alternative universe.

This time his voice changed into an old white country man's, "Uh, yeah. I have been searching various junkyards."

I spoke up now in my best Daddy voice, "Hold on, now. This is Midway Auto, not a junkyard. This is Midway Industrial Park. We have high quality junk cars and souvenir license plates…"

Keenan cut me off, still imitating the old country guy, "Well anyway I was looking for a—"

In turn, I cut him off in Daddy's voice. "No hold on there. I said this isn't a junkyard. Before we move forward, can I get an apology?"

"Listen Midway Man all I—"

I whooped and did a little dance as I felt my bladder about to burst. "Midway Man? Oh my goodness, that is so funny. That is him: Midway Man!" I yelled inside of my whisper.

I couldn't bring myself to call him Daddy anymore. With that skit, we renamed him. I named him after Midway Industrial Park, our sprawling property inhabited by abandoned vehicles, layers of trash, and a failing auto body business.

As I had grown older, his reins had tightened until both of our supplies of patience had worn past thin into livid. I prided myself on unbroken promises, straight A's, and taking responsibility. These qualities conflicted with his broken chain of promises.

Boys Are Bad

November of 11th Grade, Age 16

By November, Harold had become a constant object in my stream of thought.

As I looked down at my hands cracked from the whip of the dry spring air, I thought of Harold seeing them. He may not want to hold my dry hands. I should keep them moisturized because of the need, but lately every thought led to Harold.

In early October, I'd spend hours daydreaming about him when the light streamed through my bedroom window in the evenings. By November, when darkness fell by the time I returned from school, those thoughts had intensified into dreams that woke me up sweating.

Last night, I dreamed of us kissing. The make-out session had changed from shy ten second pecks to minutes, to explorations. I bit his lip after tracing the edge of his lips with my tongue. He sucked my neck. I bit his shoulder. In the dip between the clavicle and mound of shoulder, I feigned a pool from which I lapped water from stone smooth skin. So weird and so right, our strange brand of love. He nudged my arm up to find the dark meat under my arms, burned by razor cuts and irritated by deodorant. He sucked the shame out of it like a thirsty baby. Thrusting my tongue into his mouth, he sucked more. I woke up sweaty.

I needed to talk to somebody about how those eyes of settled brown devoured me. If I could just go on a date with him... If we could just hang out sometimes, maybe I could get him off my mind. Day-ja thought Harold was gross. She didn't even want me to talk about him because she could only view him as the goofy boy from our church. Maybe my parents would let me go on one date.

When I came home, Mama sat at the machine sewing patches on some old thrift store jeans. She cut the seams out of the pants in the process of converting it into a skirt, an old fashioned 70's style.

She wore her hair blow-dried and rolled up in a bun. She wore an ankle-length black skirt and a blue turtleneck—caught in a time warp. One calloused foot pushed the pedals. Her hips rounded out the sides of the chair. That once skinny figure had long been lost in the comfort of hallelujah and praising Jesus. Almost all the church ladies were big. Maybe it was a sign of their blessings.

I stood beside her while she finished a seam, waiting for the machine to stop droning.

By 3:30 p.m., the chandelier's muted light didn't quite reach the far wall. The sewing machine's weak bulb guided her as the rest of the room grayed and darkened by the minute.

"Mama, I need to talk to you about something."

"Humph! Like what?" she said, already giving a defensive tone without knowing what I wanted.

"You know, about dating and having a boyfriend," I said.

Mama grabbed the scissors and cut the thread from the old jeans. Then she turned to me. Her nostrils flared.

"All you need to know about boys is this: they are bad. You don't need no boyfriend. Get your education first."

That was so dumb. She acted like she had never been my age before. Shit! She got pregnant (twice) as a teenager, but she wanted me to pretend that boys didn't affect me.

"I know, but can I just go out on a date?"

"A date? With who? You ain't got no boyfriend. You're not allowed to date."

Why not? I wanted to scream.

"You know what Pastor said. Teenagers shouldn't be dating. You just probably feeling hot because you're going on your period in a few days."

"How do you know? That's so intrusive."

She even monitored my bodily functions. What the hell could I do without her knowing?

"We're synchronized. So I know when you're going on yours."

"I have 4.0 G.P.A. I don't get in trouble at school."

"Better not be," she said, taking her foot off the pedal and looking me in the eye. She narrowed her eyes trying to read me. Mama wanted to see if I was threatening to drop the "good girl routine" if she didn't allow me this. She didn't understand: I wasn't going to change that. School was my only way to get away, to one day take control of my own life. I reluctantly took another step forward.

"So one date?"

"Get away from me," she said, turning back to the pants-skirt.

"Mama, I am not trying to bug you. I just need to discuss some things with you."

She stopped the machine. But instead of giving me any more attention or time, she bent down, bit a piece of thread, repositioned the jeans, and kept sewing.

"Mama," I said, trying to talk over the whirring.

She kept on sewing like she didn't hear me.

"Mama," I said louder.

"Girl, don't make me hurt you."

I got the same familiar pang every time I needed something real, something above the basic fruit or vegetable or greased up scalp. I just wanted to be able to come to her about something real. But the scar tissue allowed me to keep going, not fatally wounded just eternally scarred.

I needed more than a Bible verse and more than Jesus' invisible love. I wanted—needed some right here next to me love. I needed to be able to feel it tightening around my waist or holding my hand. She could pretend that boys weren't real, but I knew they were. It didn't matter how silly she thought it sounded. A good man, or a teenage boy, could make a girl feel better, could make *me* feel good.

Before I let the hurt sink in, I walked out the kitchen and into my room.

Another Perspective

November of 11th Grade, Age 16

Day-ja and I had to work on a chemistry project after school. Her mother picked us up on her way from work. We went straight to her room to get started.

The smell of chicken a half hour later lured us into the kitchen. Sister Barner worked over the stove. At 6 p.m., darkness soaked the scenery outside. Inside, the warmth from the chandelier relaxed me. Sister Barner had changed from her work clothes, now wearing a tank-top and a pair of tight jeans.

"I didn't know you wore pants," I told her.

The grease crackled and a layer of smoke spread throughout the house.

"I sure do. I know what they say at First Church, but these aren't men clothes. Do I look like a man with these pants on?"

She leaned out one leg and jutted out a hip. I tilted my head. Though I didn't say anything aloud, I answered in my head. No, she didn't. She looked pretty and comfortable with a fist on one hip and her hair slicked up into a puff of curls.

"If a man put these pants on, he'd look like a transvestite. Pants don't change who I am inside. I love the Lord no matter what I am wearing."

Day-ja and her mother slapped hands.

"That's right, Ma. They ain't gonna have me all stuck in the Medieval Times. Ain't nothing wrong with a little fashion."

"I never thought of it that way. That makes sense because in ancient times the Roman men wore togas, not pants."

"Exactly," Day-ja said.

"Shoot, it would be so cool if I could wear some jeans—I'd be warmer."

Sister Barner nodded her head and hummed in agreement as she forked the chicken, turning it over one drumstick at a time.

"Tawny, you ain't ever cared before. You trying to impress somebody?" Sister Barner asked.

I stared real hard at Day-ja, warning her not to say another word. She waved me off.

"Ma, you know goofy Harold?"

Day-ja's mom turned from the stove so she could look at me sideways. "Don't tell me…"

"Um, no… Uh… Day-ja is just… He is…"

Her mother held up a hand. "Nuff said."

She and Day-ja met eyes and got to laughing a chorus of guffaws and chuck-chuck's in an easy melody that let me know that this was the way with them. Sister Barner put down the fork and bent over, too tickled to stand straight.

I felt my underarms sting. I hid my face under my hands. Warm hands pulled on my wrists. Day-ja's mom stared at me and opened my arms as she enveloped me in her bosom, rocking me and rubbing my back. Her shirt smelled of grease, Lawry's seasoned salt, and scented talcum. She led me to sit down on one of the chairs. She sat down across the table from me.

Sister Barner looked me directly in the eyes. "Girl you don't have to be ashamed about liking that goofy boy." She smiled wide and winked at me. Then she turned to her daughter. "You know Day-ja likes some funny looking boys, too."

"Mom," she said with a sudden straight face. "No, I don't. Mark is cute."

"So *you* say," her mom said, wrinkling up her lips and scrunching her eyes.

The situation flipped. Day-ja's mother and I laughed together while Day-ja rolled her eyes at us.

"Day-ja, you know we just messing with you. Go see about that chicken. I don't want it to burn."

At the stove, Day-ja picked up the fork and turned a couple of legs.

"But, I do agree with Sister Barner. Yo' boy funny-lookin'."

Her mother stuck her tongue out at Day-ja.

"Whatever. Mom, show me how to know if it is done or not." While she got up to go to the stove, I panicked. She might tell somebody and that somebody might tell someone else. What if Harold found out?

"Harold's not my boyfriend. I just think he's…"

Sister Barner shook her head at me. "Well none of that matters—how he looks or anything. What matters is that he cares about you, that he treats you right, and respects you. Child, you don't want no girlfriend who have the same taste in men no how. That is a good recipe for a bad mix up."

I nodded. Just the way she put things together, the way she scooped out advice and served it like a good meal, made me wish Mama could be like Sister Barner.

"I thought you were going to act like being attracted to a boy was a crime, too."

Sister Barner's eyes went soft when she looked at me. "You are absolutely right about you and pants. You're so beautiful, girl. Your parents might be scared of boys getting out of control. If you had some jeans, you couldn't beat 'em off with a stick."

I shook my head.

Day-ja said, "I know that's right. I got a few outfits I'm going to give you that I can't fit anymore. You might wear a pair of pants to school. The boys already be bothering you with those Little House on the Prairie skirts on."

"Shush, Day-ja," Sister Barner said.

"I'm just saying…"

Sister Barner pulled me into another hug. Up close, I could see a dozen strands of shiny gray hairs mingled in her poofy hair. Sister Barner had already raised four adult boys who lived wonderful lives in the lower forty-eight. I remembered what the Bible said about gray hair and wisdom.

Letting me go, she looked at me. "If you ever need to talk, you just let me know. You got our number. Call me."

"Ok."

"I want you and Day-ja both married off someday. The only way that happens is if you learn how to deal with boys—the right boys."

Pants

November of 11th Grade, Age 16

A few days later, Mama sat on the couch when I came home at a quarter past four in the midst of twilight. As soon as she saw me, she jumped off the couch. "Let me see your backpack."

I froze. Cinching her eyes, she held out her hand. "Let me see," she spoke through gritted teeth.

"Oh okay. I just have some pants in there because Day-ja told me she wanted to give me some old clothes..."

While I spoke, she kept moving and unzipped it so fast. Before I could finish my excuse, the pants were out in her hands. With flared nostrils, her eyes moved from me to the jeans.

"You didn't wear these?"

I shook my head. She nodded, held the middle so that the legs fell. Then she crumpled them up again and brought them to her nose. She inhaled deeply.

"You're a liar. You stink, and your funk is in the crotch of these jeans."

"I just—"

She held up her hands, "Stop. I don't want you to say anything else. You lied enough for one day."

I crossed my arms and dropped my head.

"So you're wearing pants now, huh?" she smiled and leaned against the doorframe. I fluttered my eyes in surprise. So maybe it didn't really matter to her.

"Yeah, I guess so," I said shrugging.

Mama changed her face into a grimace.

"So you think you're grown? Can do whatever the hell you want to do?"

"No I just—"

"Shut up," she said, "Stay right there."

She walked away swinging the pants. When she returned, she held her sewing scissors. I wanted to snatch the pants out of her hands, but I just watched as she cut each leg down the seam.

Mama threw the pants at me. "Now let's see you wear those again."

I closely inspected the jeans; maybe I'd sew them back together. She was already halfway down the hall.

"Mama, just listen for a minute. I read about it. You know when I did that report on the Romans?"

"You mean the one I typed for you?"

"In ancient times people didn't even wear pants. And those pants were made for women. If a man wore those pants, he'd look like a transvestite."

"The scriptures say that a woman shouldn't dress like a man. I'm standing on God's word."

She stomped to her room and slammed the door.

Late Night Talks

December of 11th Grade, Age 16

To clear my head, I would speak to my brother about all of the issues that plagued me. I always had trouble sleeping. He often had the same problem. So when I knocked on his door at 12:30 a.m., I knew he'd be up. I knew what to listen for: the faint sound of music. I could see the light from under his door.

"Come in," He said. I entered ready to clown.

Feigning a deep voice. "Hey, what is that you're listening to? That better not be no worldly music," I spoke authoritatively.

"Whatever, Midway Man," Keenan said.

I attempted to prolong the scene by trying out another character.

"Boy, you should be in the world, not of it, Keen-nern," I spoke, using Aunt Mary's voice.

My laughter subsided and the reality sobered us.

"Man, I am so tired of this. We can't even listen to Mary J. Blige. What is wrong with Mary J.?" He said.

"I don't know," I said, shaking my head.

"It makes me sick. Nobody says nothing about those white people singing country music for gospel. But when we try to modernize the 'chuch' music, it is the devil music," Keenan continued.

"We can't do anything." I added. "We can't like the opposite sex. We can't go to the movies. We can't wear make-up, or listen to worldly music."

We looked at one another and shook our heads.

A Date?

December of 11th Grade, Age 16

On the way to Spanish class, I passed by Harold. He clutched my hand and held on. I kept walking, but slower as I said, "I don't want to be late."

At 2 p.m., the hallway windows already showed that gray quality of fading winter light. In December, we only had about four hour days with the sun rising after 10 a.m.and setting around 3 p.m. The interior lights made everyone look washed out.

"Stop for a second."

"What do you want, Harold?" I said, trying to look stern for a moment. The way he stood with his chest caved in and dull eyes confirmed that he really liked me. I remembered him as the little boy with pleading eyes I had met years ago. I couldn't help but smile at him and took a couple more slow, short steps.

He made a hoarse sound in his throat and wet his lips. I could see he desired me, and I wanted that. "Just a second. I want to talk to you."

I stopped walking. Still holding my hand, he led me a few steps around the corner just off the main hallway beside an emergency exit. Taking the books out of my hand, he set them on the floor.

His deep brown skin and soft licking lips, I mean soft looking lips made me avoid his eyes as warmth spread over my chest and into my belly. Harold's torso stopped right at my face—well-defined pectorals, biceps, and a six-pack. I forced my head and eyes upward, opening them wide and slowly lowering them.

"Do you think we can go to a movie sometime? Hang out?" He asked in a pleading voice.

"Yes."

He put his arm around my shoulder and brought me closer to him. Hunching down to my eye level.

"What's up, Tawny?"

"I don't know."

"What's wrong? I really like you. You're..." he shook his head.

My whole face began to heat up, and I felt my nipples prickle into goosebumps.

"I can't get over how pretty you are."

"Thank you," I blushed.

Not brave enough to compliment him, I touched the tips of his eyelashes. As soon as I did it, I knew it had done too much. It would have been better to tell him how handsome he was or about the curves in his muscles. He closed his eyes and loosened his grip. We laughed.

"Will you kiss me?"

I stiffened. Not a kiss. He wasn't even my boyfriend. What kind of girl did he think I was? Looking around the hallway, I noticed that most of the kids had entered their classrooms. It felt late, like the bell would ring any moment. I scooped up my books.

"The bell is about to ring!" I shouted over my shoulder as I ran to class.

Rushing through the hallway, I kept thinking about Harold. He loved me. I loved him. We loved each other.

From all the romance novels I had read, I knew my feelings were overblown in my mind. But just having him that close to me... A hundred compliments from one hundred different adults couldn't compare to his one sweet sentence about my looks.

Making it just in time to Spanish class, I slid into my seat as the bell rang.

Breaking Point

December of 11th Grade, Age 16

"Get up!" Mama yelled from her room and beat on the wall. I tried to rouse myself in my bed in the adjacent room. Last night, like most Saturday nights, I stayed up until two o'clock in the morning to watch <u>Soul Train</u> and <u>Amateur Night at the Apollo</u>.

While my parents wouldn't tell me when to go to sleep, they'd definitely tell me when to wake up. This morning I didn't want to get up, and I couldn't shake the drowsiness. I even felt more exhausted when I thought about the frozen water pipes, about lugging water, waiting for it to boil. The morning tasks were too much to ask when the plumbing didn't flow, when I had to coordinate hygiene with a five-gallon jug of water and three other people.

I had fallen back to sleep when Midway Man banged on the door.

"Come out and boil some water so you can wash up!" he directed.

It took me a moment to prop myself up, before I opened the dresser drawer and looked for a satisfactory blouse and a skirt. My eyes wouldn't open long enough to pick out a Sunday outfit. Minutes later when he opened the door, I had my head buried in a drawer with my eyes pasted shut.

"I told you to get up and start heating up that water!" he said.

"I just need a few more minutes of rest," I mumbled.

I heard Keenan coming out of the bathroom. Why didn't I go to sleep at the same time as Brother last night?

He ignored my request and stomped down the hallway. The door remained open as he moved back to the kitchen to continue cooking breakfast.

Pulling myself up and off my knees, I stood up to close the door. Midway Man worked over the stove where the stove light glowered on top of his bald head.

I picked a sweater from the drawer, stretched out on the bed, and fell asleep holding it.

He pounded and opened the door simultaneously.

"Girl, what did I tell you?" he slit his eyes at me as he pointed, and again he walked away.

I pushed myself off the bed, took a few steps to the door, and closed it again.

Minutes later, he pushed the door open, holding a belt. He was about to whip me. I promised myself the next time they whipped me, I'd leave.

We stared at one another. I did not whimper. I wanted to communicate my fearlessness. My thighs tightened and butt stiffened. He swung the long brown strap. I took the hit on my thigh. I felt the sting, and I fell on the bed. Remaining calm, I took each swat with soundless, balled up lips. I kept angry eyes steady on him. He changed directions and whipped it again as I rolled to my other side. The belt collided into the other thigh. I stood up slowly and got swiped on the buttocks. Midway Man hit me one last time. He breathed heavily as his energy dropped with the belt. Pushing myself out of the bedroom door, I made two more steps into the bathroom. Once inside, my angry reflection confronted me in the mirror.

Getting Out

December of 11th Grade, Age 16

I looked outside my bedroom window at the black of the evening. At 5 p.m., darkness had claimed the day hours ago. Although the snowdrifts already stacked up ten feet around the mobile home, the real chill began this month. In December, the winter moves from a bitter twenty degrees below zero to a hypothermic freeze of forty below and lower. I pressed my eyelids closed and let the stale, cool air inside my room filter into my lungs.

I had to find a new place. I rejected my parents' unreasonable rules and their hollow authority. I could see my reflection in the window glass, ghost-like against the black.

In my isolation, my things had become my only comfort: my bookshelf and my drawers of folded clothing, the lamp near my bedside stand where I read into the early hours of the morning, and the abandoned box of toys. The Cabbage Patch comforter that Mama remade into a quilt faded into the twin bed. Two straw hats and old trophies lined the top shelf of the closet. My immaculately neat room made me hesitant to leave.

Midway Man whipped me. The belt had not left any marks, and I had resisted crying. None of that mattered. I would not accept any of their attempts to rule over me. His whippings were just a manifestation of his inability to communicate, his unwillingness to listen, and his refusal to treat me like a soon-to-be adult.

I told myself, promised myself, that I would not let them discipline me ever again. I would no longer live without the flow of water or without the flushing of toilets. I found it intolerable to have the scent of diesel fuel ground into my clothing, my nostrils, so deeply that I could not detect the fumes until I was at church or at school, and someone pointed it out.

At church that day, my anger gained intensity. The whole day, I kept quiet while I formulated a plan. No one needed to know. Keenan would talk me out of it. Day-ja wouldn't take me seriously. If I talked about it, I feared breaking my promise to myself.

I considered various options: staying with Aunt Denise in town, living with another church family, or going to a foster home. How I would make it on my own or make it to school—I did not know, but I would.

I grabbed some white drawstring trash bags out of the kitchen cabinet and banged it shut. My parents watched television in the living room. The TV's blue flickered across their faces. Mama's flat, wide lips hung open gently. Her eyes, colored by the screen, stared straight ahead and the skin of her inverted triangular face rested calmly. Mama leaned into Midway Man's chest with his arms spread out over the back of the midnight sectional. He wore a white v-neck undershirt and palazzo pajama pants. As he focused on the television, his legs lay listlessly against the recliner and Mama spread her legs over the couch cushions.

Obviously, Midway Man had forgotten about the whipping he had given me this morning. They didn't know about the promise I made to myself. I kept my promises to myself even when I didn't tell anyone about them.

Increasing my switch-walk down the long dark hallway, I re-entered my room.

I started at the wide chest of drawers where I kept old jeans I used to wear neatly folded in the middle drawer. I quickly dropped the jeans into my white trash bag. As I pushed the pants down to the bottom of the bag, a whiff of the wood's dry odor rose from the cloth. I opened the next drawer below the emptied one; then quickly closed it. I wasn't sure if I wanted to take the old sweaters in that drawer or not, but I knew I would freeze if I did not dress in layers.

Then I went to the top drawer. I grabbed the first place medal from the North Star Borough District Speech Contest, a blue ribbon won for the short story I entered into the Tanana Valley Fair a couple of summers ago, and a savings bond I won from the District Spelling Bee Competition when I was twelve. I tucked all of these things into my plastic bag between the sweaters and the jeans so that they wouldn't get chipped or tear up the bag.

In my closet, I pushed back the clothing on hangers and began to pull each piece towards me for inspection. I stared at the blue satin Christmas dress that fit me like a parachute and decided not to take it. The long jean skirts, I would keep. Where would I end up? I realized I probably should take all of the clothes—just in case. I pulled every piece from the hangers and rolled them into a tight neat bundle to make room for everything.

I picked up my purse from my bed before heading to the bathroom. I held my breath long enough to grab the Noxzema and rolled my toothbrush into some toilet tissue before tucking it into my purse.

I looked at my box of toys in the corner of my room. Of course I'd leave those. I threw my second pair of moon boots into the third plastic bag along with the rain boots, and black patent leather church shoes, a couple of belts, two hand-me-down purses, two jump ropes, an honor roll plaque, an African mask won from a black history speech exhibition, and a science fair grand prize ribbon. I looked at my Bible on top of the chest of drawers for a moment. I picked it up and pushed it into my purse. I turned to take a moment to look around my room. Taking another deep breath, I blinked away the mist rising in my eyes and sniffed the moist saltiness forming in my nose. Done.

I grabbed one stuffed, white plastic bag and dragged it. The heaviness, the friction caused a hole near the drawstring closure. Stopping, I picked it up, carried it down the hallway to the kitchen and dropped it. Immediately, I turned to get another bag. First dragging it until a hole formed in it, then carrying it into the kitchen. I carefully placed this one on the floor because I didn't want to draw too much attention. Then, I retrieved the last bag.

When I finished, I walked into the living room and intentionally blocked the television. My eyes focused on the tops of my parents' heads, a technique I learned in preparation for speech contests so as not to make direct eye contact. "I'm moving out."

At first, they acted like they didn't hear me. Then Mama spoke, "Stop playing and move out of the way, Tawny."

Clearing his throat, my dad said. "Where are you going to go?"

My mom interrupted then, "You going to live on the streets? It is twenty below zero outside," she said. She pressed her lips together and pushed them into exaggerated smirk.

"I don't know," I said, pushing my chest forward. "I just want to go to the church."

Midway Man put his arms down to his side and straightened up on the couch. "Do you want a ride?" A smile crept from the corners of his eyes.

"Yes, thank you." This time I allowed our eyes to meet, to hold the moment accountable.

I was glad that he had offered. I really didn't want to ask them for anything. But we lived at least a mile away from the nearest neighbor and nearly seven miles away from the church in Fairbanks.

The crinkles in his eyes disappeared as he cleared his throat.

"Well, Tawny. I need to talk to you first."

"Alright," I said with a shrug. He really thought his lecture was going to change my mind.

"Well I'll be in your room in a few minutes."

I figured, in that moment, he had forgotten who I was. I had a will that would move mountains. Shit, I was the one who willed him into my life. So certainly I was leaving. I was far too proud for running away. I was fed up. I was moving away, because I wouldn't run away from anybody.

As I walked back to my room to wait, Mama's heavy steps followed behind me. She wanted to talk now, I guessed. But as I reached my room, I heard the grind of her heel turn. Her bedroom door clapped shut behind her.

I sat on my bed and stared into the memories of my life. I swallowed a gulp of air as the rhythm of my flowing blood quickened. That was Mama. She caused me to grow up mad—no peace, no happiness my whole life. When the situation got too hard, she escaped. Other times, she used to tell me to get out of her sight. The seal of her door made me certain that I had to care for myself.

Midway Man came to the threshold and looked inside my room. I got up, straightening my back.

"Can I talk to you for a minute?" Midway Man said to me as I was grabbing my favorite books, *Where the Red Fern Grows* and *The Color Purple*.

"Yes, when I finish packing." I said, stuffing a black church shawl into my backpack. He waited, silent for once, as I stuffed and closed my last bag.

"You done? We may as well come into the living room."

Once I sat on the couch, he began a lecture that I refused to take in fully. It concerned something about how he had always loved me; I should know that; I did not have to leave. I just stared ahead at the television where I feigned interest in the PBS special playing. I knew I would remember it even though I did not listen. He had told me the same things over and over.

"I've never done nothing wrong to you—I've always loved you."

That's what he said, but he actually never listened to me. They both said they didn't care what I wanted or what I thought.

He continued speaking, "This is not because of me. Your mother did not show you that she loved you. I have always loved you. I have always shown you that. I am going to pray for you."

I wanted choices. I had to care when I earned 4.0 or student of the month. I won third place in the district Spelling Bee and won the District Speech Contest. Did anyone come to see me—support me? No. Did anyone help me? No. But I knew that if I stood out through my academics and extracurricular activities, I knew I could escape poverty and the substandard living conditions that plagued my childhood.

Midway Man's tone changed to a short clip. "Oh, you're too bull-headed to listen? Yeah, all right. We'll see how you do."

With my chin to my chest and my head cocked sideways I stared at him so that he would know that I saw through him. The television screen flashed in his eyes. I couldn't even take pleasure in the jump of his cheek, his signature glitch whenever he got mad. We both stood up from the couch, and I strutted to get my bags, carrying all three this time for emphasis. I carried them a few steps to the walkway of the front door.

Yes, he had loved me. Yes, he had been the only one sometimes when he didn't have to be. It wasn't enough—not when we didn't have enough food, not when I couldn't urinate in a toilet that worked.

New Beginnings

December of 11th Grade, Age 16

On Sunday nights, First Church always had Young People's Willing Workers (YPWW) at 6:30 and Evening Service at 8:00 p.m. Soon the church folks started arriving.

Outside the church windows, only darkness pressed against the glass. The sun had set over three hours ago, leaving that long Arctic night that wouldn't lift until late morning.

Day-ja found me nestled on the bathroom sofa, bags at my feet. Her widened eyes took in the bags, took in my hardened expression.

"Hello, Tawny."

"Hi, Day-ja."

"What is all of this stuff, girl?" Her North Carolina accent stuck out of her words with squeaks.

"I moved out."

I shrugged my shoulders, locked on her eyes and waited for more questions.

"Are you serious?"

"Yeah, I packed up and told them to drop me off."

"Where are you going to stay, Tawny?"

I shrugged my shoulders again. I didn't want to broadcast that I planned to stay at the church.

She touched my arm and moved in closely.

"You're staying with us."

Outside, the temperature had dropped to thirty below. The church's warm interior served as a beacon against the endless black night.

A Real Home

December of 11th Grade, Age 16

When I entered the Barner house, they gave me my own room. Their home had two floors full of modern furniture and appliances. The Barners' house felt warm and bright, a refuge from the cold dark winter.

Day-ja led me upstairs. My friend insisted that I take her room. She would take the guest bedroom in their finished basement. Sister Barner's room was across the hallway from my new room. I breathed in heavily and let it out slowly and calmly. This is how real families should live. Instead of a mobile home sitting atop of an incomplete foundation, I deserved to live in a home with a complete foundation, and a functioning plumbing and heating system.

On the first Friday night I spent with the family, Sister Barner called us into the living room. Day-ja came and sat on the overstuffed loveseat, totally relaxed. Her long legs stretched over the couch.

"So what do you all want to do this weekend?" Sister Barner asked.

"The movies," I heard Day-ja say. She got to choose an activity every weekend.

I would not ask to go somewhere different than Day-ja. I didn't want to be told no. While worrying over what I should say, I hadn't noticed Sister Barner talking to me.

"Tawny, Tawny," Sister Barner repeated.

"Yes?" I asked.

"Do you want to go to the movies with Day-ja?"

"Yes, can I go?"

"Yeah, that is why I asked you," she smiled.

"All right. You guys tell me what you have to do tomorrow."

Day-ja said, "We have choir rehearsal."

Day-ja spoke for both of us. I felt grateful because I didn't want to cause any inconvenience.

Watch Night Service

December of 11th Grade, Age 17

On December 31, 1993, I attended First Church of God in Christ's annual New Year's Eve Watch Service. In the sanctuary, the lights hung from the ceiling as if round crystal balls, bright and optimistic. Although everything appeared the same, everything had changed. Instead of sitting with my parents this year, I sat near the front of the church beside Sister Barner and Day-ja. When we entered, Mama and Sister Barner nodded at each other.

As the church members entered the sanctuary, I reflected on my own life. Having already claimed freedom from my parent's home a few weeks prior, I felt like celebrating. Annually, we gathered to celebrate the New Year. None of the other church members shared the roots of this tradition, which I had learned the previous week. In Advanced Placement United States History, our textbook explained that in December 1862, at an important turn in the Civil War, word spread among slaves about a life-changing announcement coming from the President. The few privileged slave messengers whispered the news to the house Negroes, the house Negroes whispered it to the stable bucks, and the stable bucks spread the word throughout the plantations. Anticipating the great announcement, our African ancestors gathered in the church shacks and along the waterways where they met to praise the Lord. They waited for the messengers to send word that the Emancipation Proclamation, granting their freedom, had been delivered by Abraham Lincoln. Since then, black churches all over the

United States held New Year's Eve Watch Night Services to commemorate our freedom from slavery.

This history about my people fascinated me, but the church folk didn't want to hear anything from me. I figured I was the reason that Sister Barner wasn't the M.C. for the evening. Aunt Mary led the service. My aunt gave me a hard look. I lifted my eyebrows and blinked at her a few times.

After my aunt delivered the opening prayer, Midway Man entered dressed in a white button-down shirt and a plain navy blue tie. Neck fat spilled over the top of his collar and the cuffs could no longer cover the protruding bones of his wrists. He had gained weight and appeared tired. Finding a seat in the opposite column of pews, he turned toward me to make eye contact; I glared at him. When I saw my brother, I felt his pain and hopelessness. The new year should represent hope for betterment and progress. I should pray for Keenan, but my faith had withered. Had God willed my life to be so agonizing?

During the praise portion of the service, we all joined in to sing Christmas songs for the last time in the season. Aunt Mary started us off with the upbeat "Go Tell it On the Mountain." Then we sang the slow, contemplative lullaby "Silent Night." Then Aunt Mary started singing the traditional "I Don't Know What You Come to Do." Shaking a tambourine and singing along, I felt good again.

Sister Jolene got up to testify.

"I just want to thank God for my children being safe and in their sound mind. These disobedient children think that they can just do what they want to do, but the Lord said turn from your wicked ways," she said, wagging a finger in the air. "I just want to thank Him," she said and sat down. She hugged eleven-year-old Rufus and ten-year-old Tracy sitting on either side of her.

It didn't take an honor student to figure out she was talking about me. From the response from the congregation, they agreed with her.

"Amen," said Aunt Mary.

"Tell it," exclaimed Mother Nevins.

"That's right," hollered Deacon Wilson.

Just in case another accuser rose to testify against me, I got up to visit the restroom. Too angry to look into their sanctimonious faces, I stared at myself in the bathroom mirror. The overhead lights revealed shadows under my eyes. I appeared to be the same short girl with the slicked back ponytail. But I wasn't the same agreeable girl that just accepted substandard living conditions and excuses with a smile and a prayer. I didn't care if anyone understood or not. I had done everything I could to do right: excelled in school, helped at home, and even tutored other children. I wanted to be successful when I grew up. It would be foolish of me to sit back and allow people to suck the possibilities out of me like they had done to Keenan—even if they were my parents.

I couldn't articulate these words to anyone. Everything inside of me had told me to leave, and I didn't regret it. I deserved more. Everybody in the church deserved more in their lives than poverty, than broken homes, than ignorance generation after generation. Was I the only person willing to try? I wiped my face with a cool, damp paper towel and went back to the sanctuary.

By the time I had returned, Sister Charles was shouting, speaking in tongues loudly. "Ameekla oshakleeda."

Flinging her long hair backwards then forward in an arc, she ran around the perimeter of the church. I had never seen anyone raptured in the spirit like this before. She made her way to the center aisle. Her tongue talking turned into English words, "Thus saith the Lord." Her words came crisp and deep throated, unlike her soft regular voice.

"She's about to prophesy," Sister Barner whispered as if dazed. Goosebumps rose all over my body. Brother Danny stopped playing the organ, and Jenner set down the drumsticks. The whole church stared in rapt attention. Everyone in the church fixated on Sister Charles. Gazing at the ceiling, she stood with her arms folded behind her. One arm shot up with a pointed finger. Her head jerked. "I am displeased with the youth. Honor thy father and thy mother so that your days would be lengthened." Deep and raspy, like the Holy Ghost itself spoke through her.

"Yokley-a-shock-lada," she said.

Even though I didn't know if the words meant anything at all, I felt spellbound, waiting for the next words.

"These are the end days. The days of youth burning against the authority of their mother and father," she stumbled backward, her eyes squeezed closed.

"Amen, Hallelujah," Aunt Mary yelled. With all the shouting, the air had grown moist. Sweat thickened under my arms.

Deacon Wilson shouted, "Hallelujah!"

Mother Avery chimed in with her honey voice, "My, my, my."

"Prophesy," said Sister Jolene, a thin stream of a tear mixed with her foundation and ran down her cheek. She wiped it away with a wad of tissue.

My legs shook, and I bit at a hangnail. The goosebumps persisted. I tried to steady myself by clutching the edge of the pew.

The voice soaked into the congregation. "There are consequences for disobedience. You will see my face. You will know that I am real when you are called home in my presence. Death will come for those who fear not the Lord's word. I see a body, I see another body. I see dark clouds gathering and a streak of lightning. I see love slipping out the window."

Whose life? Mayleen, Eve, and Day-ja met eyes with me. I couldn't believe that death would claim unfinished lives in a world of endless possibilities.

"Two cold, youthful bodies will await burial."

Sister Charles's neck jerked back, and she opened her eyes. She stumbled back to her seat.

The pastor stood at the podium with buckshot eyes. He wiped his eyes with a handkerchief. "The Lord's presence is in this place!" he said, holding both of his arms out to the side. "Praise him!"

A moment later Sister Charles got back up, marching around the sanctuary, speaking in tongues, running up and down the center of the church.

Aunt Mary stood up, shook out her hands as if scalded with hot water and screamed. Her thick legs created a rumbling on the floor. With hands and legs vibrating, she made her way out to the center aisle and twirled her flowing blue dress. Sister Charles was on her second lap around the sanctuary. Sister Barner grabbed a shawl off the pew and walked near her. Holding up her hands and shaking her head, she said, "Praise Jesus!"

Sister Charles put both of her hands on Sister Barner's shoulders. A moment later Sister Barner caught the Spirit and whipped her hair and jogged her legs vigorously, as if following the beat of an invisible African drum. Midway Man waved his arms. Brother Wilson waved one hand and clutched the back of the pew in front of him. Before long he screamed from the depth of his lungs. "Thank you."

All the jumping and running, produced thunder and their screams electrified the place. In the presence of a ferocious God who would kill children, I couldn't help thinking that they were celebrating on top of the future graves of the youth. My stomach flipped and turned as I watched them, unable to move.

For over an hour, the adults took turns igniting each other with the Holy Ghost. Long after midnight, the Watch Service finally calmed. With everyone seated, they prayed quietly or moaned melodies to the Lord. Aunt Mary dismissed everyone with a brief closing prayer.

As usual, we all moved into the basement to eat the food that everyone brought. I descended the stairs bewildered and frightened. Mayleen and Day-ja were already in the basement whispering to each other. They turned to face me as I approached. Searching both of their eyes—from Mayleen's wide flung flecks of coal to Day-ja's round pair—I measured their expressions. I desperately wanted someone else to start the conversation. Who did they think would die? Before this, I hadn't considered that any of us would ever die. Now this unimaginable prophecy proclaimed that there would be two dead young people before the end of the year. Had Sister Charles seen faces that she recognized? Mayleen started talking first, "Ha Tawny, Sister Charles prophesied about you! You're going to die if you don't go back home."

"You don't listen to your father and mother!" Mayleen said.

"So you think it's me, too?" I asked, hanging my head.

"Pretty much!" Day-ja said. "You moved out. I won't even talk about how you cursed out your dad last week."

I made a list of all the things I'd done: moving out, cursing out my father, talking back, and not having faith that Mama would return when she left.

No one talks about that anymore. Mama left first. I left because all I ever wanted was to be loved, to be treated fairly, and to be normal. I was willing to die trying to get these things. I had suffered my whole life. So I might as well live freely and be unconcerned about damnation.

"It's not too late. Go back home, Tawny," Day-ja said.

What would I look like going back home? I wasn't some stupid schoolgirl who threw a fit and later realized her error. They were wrong. I was going to prove that to them when I got my college education and a great job and a big wonderful house.

"No."

Instead of Dating

January of 11th Grade, Age 17

For two weeks after the Watch Night prophecy, I couldn't shake the feeling that I was going to die. Every time someone looked at me from the church, I saw judgment in their eyes. They wanted me to be one of the 'cold, youthful bodies' Sister Charles had envisioned. But fear would no longer control me. If I was going to die anyway, I might as well live the way I wanted.

I decided to hang out with Harold. I didn't care anymore what my parents said. I didn't care what the church said, either. The only answer they ever gave was no. No's and more no's without explanation, without reason. That's why I didn't trust my parents or the church. Some of those no's didn't make sense. Sometimes they said no because they just wanted to be mean. Even though I earned straight A's, they didn't trust me. So I decided to do what I wanted to do.

I wanted to have sex. They're probably forbidding sexual experiences because of the pleasure. Not because of the problems, but because of the good things. They wanted to keep the good things for themselves. They told me and showed me repeatedly that they didn't even want better for me.

Outside his apartment, Harold jiggled the key in the lock. Holding the door open, my boyfriend followed me into the dark living room. As I stepped inside, he touched my waist with a shaky hand. He mumbled something about not expecting me to come. His parents wouldn't be home until after eight. When he turned on the switch, I stared at the old, soiled furniture.

His parents had married young and lived in a two-bedroom apartment on the southside of Fairbanks for the past seventeen years. Their furniture consisted of a thrift store couch and a lean-to television stand. His father sold odds and ends to the church-goers and worked various retail jobs. His mother was a mainstay at McDonald's, always smiling, always a friendly face. The scent of day old fried chicken hung thick in the air.

Could he make me touch love, feel love that I had craved for so long? There was something so sweet and trembly about him. I didn't worry about it turning into a negative situation later. He'd be grateful, and I'd be safe from his criticism. Because he loved me. I could tell it by the way he spoke to me, the way I felt when he looked at me. Mainly, I needed to see if sex would feel like love. It could be exactly what I needed. Harold could be exactly what I needed.

Inside the bedroom, Harold's daybed presented the opportunity. Sitting beside him on the bed, I leaned in for a kiss. I sucked one of his thick lips that had a trace of watermelon Jolly Ranchers and inhaled his Irish Spring scent. When he put his hand up my shirt and kissed my breasts, I tingled.

Harold pulled off his shirt, his pants slid down, and he kicked his jeans to the corner of the room. His muscular body shamed me until he pulled up my skirt. As he poked his fingers between my legs, he kissed my lips. I could only think about the want I had for him. He pushed up my legs. His penis stung inside of me, and I tightened my thighs.

He held on to my shoulders for a couple seconds. Then, his eyes exploded. "Oops!"

"What?" I yelled, "What happened?" I scrambled to right myself, searching for my clothes.

"Uh, I don't know."

His voice sounded like it had when I first met him. I remembered that he wasn't very smart. Had I really been this dumb?

"What do you mean?" I aggressively interrogated him.

"Nothing," he said, trying to be calm.

My eyes remained on him, studying him.

"Did you come?" I asked.

"No," he said.

He didn't look cute anymore. Harold shrank back to the same goofy boy again with a crooked smile.

"I thought I had, but I didn't."

A horn honked outside, and I jumped.

"Are you sure?"

"Yeah," he said in a high pitch.

I knew him long enough to know when he was lying. I put on my clothes and walked out the bedroom as he shuffled toward the bathroom. I caught a cab back to the movie theater with the money I had been given for a movie ticket.

On my way back, the experience worked its way through me. I dwelled in the vision of his bare chest facing me, feeling me, a part of me. I needed more of his attention on me. Remembering how our lips met and his breath quickened because of me, how it feels to matter when we're together. He whimpered and sweated because of me. He chose me. Nothing—no one could come between that moment - not guilt, not God.

And I wanted it again and again.

Between January and May, winter slowly released its grip on Fairbanks. By March, we got up to twelve hours of daylight. By April, we had fifteen hours. Longer days returned in a rush, six minutes per day, like the world awakened from hibernation. As the snow melted and the sun stayed longer, I focused on my grades, spending time with Harold, and tried to forget the Watch Night prophecy.

Keenan's Graduation

May of 11th Grade, Age 17

The graduation ceremony started at 2 p.m., and the late May sun created spotlights of the gymnasium's high windows. With the approaching summer solstice, we had up to nineteen hours of daylight. The overflow made everyone squint. The blue and red graduation gowns glimmered as the North Pole High School class of 1994 lined up outside of the gym like neatly wrapped gifts. When the class entered, their rows of chairs formed two rectangles, one a glossy blue and another block of fiery red gowns. The ceremony dragged on: scholarship announcements, university acceptances, special awards, the salutatorian's speech, the valedictorian's speech, the principal's speech, and a guest speaker. I barely paid attention to any of it.

Keenan graduated as a top soccer player, a state champion, and the hardest working athlete at the school. No one recognized him for it.

I sat in the bleachers excited and nervous for my brother. Mama kept exhaling loud breaths as if settling into relief and exhaustion after running a long race.

As Principal McKenzie handed Keenan his diploma, he took it in his hands and strode on the stage – wide steps and swinging arms. I screamed Keenan's name like a lot of other people – always the popular kid. Mama raised her arms and Midway Man clapped.

As "End of the Road" played, the new grown ups in red and blue gowns broke formation.

We snapped pictures of Keenan with his friends and the four other black kids in his class.

I couldn't believe Keenan's day had come. Nobody cared, not the school or my parents. Graduation symbolized readiness for the world yet nothing had been prepared for him to make it in the next stage of his life.

A joyful dinner at Royal Fork disguised the sadness of the event. Through the restaurant windows, the evening sun persisted.

At the end of dinner, our parents allowed Brother to go out with friends who picked him up from the restaurant. Sunset wouldn't come until 11 p.m. The endless light made everything feel suspended, like time had stopped.

The Job

June before 12th Grade, Age 17

A week after graduation, Midway Man gave Keenan a raggedy car that he had fixed up. He drove over to the Barners house to show me his weird looking yellow car like the one in *Wayne's World*. My brother's 1976 AMC Pacer appeared dusty with pale yellow paint that had long ago lost its sheen. This simple machine with its rear windows reminiscent of a bubble ushered in a new era for my brother. With graduation, he earned his freedom.

"I already got a job, Tawny!"

"Where?"

"Jeffrey's." The sun shone on him brightly. With his hands swinging, I knew he felt happy.

"Jeffrey's? What kind of job?" I asked him. I already felt let down, but his level of confidence made me pause.

"I'm a dishwasher over there. It only took me one day to get a job."

"What if you keep looking and ˗"

Keenan threw up his hand, cutting me off. "Naw, I'm good. Mama and Midway Man aren't tripping, either."

"Well alright," I said nodding. *A high school dropout could wash dishes. You could at least have applied for a job that required reading skills.* That's what I really wanted to tell him.

"Look, I just swung by real quick. I'm on my way to work."

While the rest of his soccer friends went off to college to make the transition from teen to adult in the lower forty-eight states, Brother stayed to live a teenage life at home with our parents working a part-time job. He just didn't have to go to school anymore. No one made him, either. He could go wherever he wanted, whenever he wanted.

Keenan grabbed something from the back seat. Pulling it over his head, he cracked a smile at me. In his work uniform — a white button-up smock — he looked like a ghost. He didn't even seem angry anymore that he hadn't been scouted to play soccer.

On his key ring, he kept a car key and a house key with a soccer ball trinket. The sport had become just an ornament of his past.

We all noticed this new Keenan. Aunt Denise talked about it. But Mama and Midway Man's attitude toward the situation confirmed my decision had been the right one. How could they be satisfied that a star soccer player settled for washing dishes instead of playing soccer at a university somewhere? They gave up on him, and I hated them for their complacency. My brother could do so much more, but this was what they wanted. This proved they had won the argument. Keenan wasn't doing better than them.

The words from our repeated argument rattled inside of me. *Let's see how good you do*, they had told us - warning us that life would be much harder than we thought.

On his time off, Keenan started hanging out with this military guy named Gant. They met over Denise's house. Gant was Angel's boyfriend. One day Keenan rode with Gant to the store to go pick up some ribs and hog maws for Denise. They dropped off the meat and went to smoke weed together - a new habit nobody could tell grown up Keenan not to do.

Teenage Realities

June before 12th Grade, Age 17

Walking down the street at nearly 9 p.m., the four of us spanned the road. The warm air felt like midday though the streets had emptied of passing cars. Coming from the convenience store, we took our time getting back. In early June, we almost enjoyed twenty-four hours of daylight with the sun dipping low around eleven, skimming the horizon before rising strong again. Now that Mama wrapped herself in the church, I got invited to the church girl gatherings.

Suddenly, I felt a whack on my head. I spun around to see Eve's back running away from me. I chased her down and slapped her with an intensity that turned my palm bright pink. She yelled and stopped running mid-stride to cover her face. I rolled my eyes and kept walking. May nudged her and said, "What? You gonna cry?" She shook her head and pushed her sister.

"Shut. Up!" she said laughing. Eve turned from sad to happy in two seconds. When she removed her hand, I saw my palm and fingers imprinted on her cheek, stretching all the way to her temple.

Such a silly girl. How could anyone take her seriously?

At four months along, Eve's bump just started to show. I couldn't see her as anyone's mother. But here she was sixteen and pregnant, and—at the same time—still an annoying girl.

For science class, I had read about the teenage brain. "Teen-age hood" is a type of pregnancy, a metamorphosis happening inside of the body. The reasons why we loved or hated certain things or people didn't quite make sense.

At sixteen, Eve would be seventeen by the time she gave birth, the same age as Mama when she birthed Keenan. Mama had two kids a year apart. She did good for a while, but when we actually became children, things started to fall apart.

As Eve formed physically and emotionally, how could she be having a baby when she—when we all—were in the infancy of adulthood? We were trying to learn how to possess ourselves—but to add a baby to it…

Mama hated me and Keenan. She didn't have the same patience for us older kids and teens as she did for us as babies. She didn't quite know what a teen needed, probably because she didn't know what she needed.

Eve's pregnancy surprised me because I didn't know she was that kind of girl. She didn't even have a boyfriend. I didn't ask questions about who and when. If she didn't trust me to tell about her escapades, I worried that she would view my questions as an intrusion. Would she be like Mama, or like her mother? Or would she be a whole new brand of a parent?

With Mama, we didn't go hungry. She wouldn't allow us around wayward folk and made sure we stayed clean. But she lacked the understanding and patience that a mother of a mature age should have. As a result, the love-hate persisted between the two of us.

The Gun

June before 12th Grade, Age 17

At the end of the week, Keenan wanted to show me something after work. He drove up to Sister Barner's house at nearly 8 p.m. when the sunrays felt like noon. I came outside, and he lifted his shirt to reveal something in his waistband: a gun.

The scrape against his waistband and the way he held it, tanked my stomach.

"It's a .357 Magnum Revolver," Keenan said. He threw his chin in the air, now dressed in confidence.

"Put that thing away!" I whisper-roared at him. Brother had to know he was doing too much!

With his first dishwashing paycheck, he bought the gun. He said he had to protect himself and me if anything happened.

"Why would you need protection?" I asked him.

"Let me tell you something, Tawny," Keenan said with a rigid finger. "I gave this one guy, Angelo, $40 so that he could buy us some weed one night. I didn't see the guy or the weed for two weeks. When I finally saw him near a liquor store, I got in his face. I said: 'Give me everything in your pocket, and I won't knock you out.'

My brother recalled the encounter with wild, unfocused eyes. That dude just smiled at me and lifted up his sweatshirt. He had a gun there stuck inside his pants. I took one step back, hit myself on the chest, and was like, 'If you gonna show a gun, you better use it.'"

I didn't know what to think. "Why would you tell that to somebody with a gun?" I asked, stunned by his hubris.

Keenan waved me off, "Please! Angelo is this white boy with a curly red afro and freckles, looks like Ronald McDonald. I couldn't really be scared of him."

I felt too afraid to ask what came next, yet Keenan stood before me as strong as ever.

"So what did he do?"

Keenan started laughing. "We were right outside of a liquor store, right. When he went inside the store, I walked in after him, grabbed him from the back. I swung on him in the middle of the store. You not going to believe it, but I K.O.'d him. It was crazy. I dropped that dude in one punch. He was out. I left before the police came."

Brother acted it out, the movements, the dialogue. I felt like I had been an invisible witness.

Every time Keenan talked like this, I didn't know what to say. I knew Brother well enough not to argue with him when he got like this. His unpredictable behavior caused a cramp in my stomach, worry that made it hard to swallow.

When he left, my stomach discomfort lingered. I couldn't sleep for the rest of the night.

Dinner after the Movies

June before 12th Grade, Age 17

The next week, Mayleen, Eve, Day-ja, and I went to the movies together. Afterwards, Sister Barner let us go to Jeffrey's around ten o'clock. Even this late, the manager kept the curtains partially closed or the glare would be unbearable from twenty-two hours of day. Even the brief night never got dark, only a prolonged sunset that stretched a couple of hours.

A host seated us at a booth. Since I knew Keenan's work schedule, I wanted to go see him in the back. I told them about his dishwashing job. The church girls' surprised expressions said it all. Day-ja didn't say anything, just sipped on her soda. Eve nodded her head in surprise. "So Keenan works in the back?" Then she whispered, "He washes the dishes?"

I nodded, "Yes, he does." I looked each of them in the eye.

May had her own issues. Rubbing her belly, she let out a few chuckles. "Well alright!"

I shrugged. They did not expect Keenan to have such lowly employment, but they were too polite to say more. Maybe they knew that I would go off on anyone who talked negatively about Brother.

I left them with their shocked expressions to talk to him.

When I found Keenan, he complained about the manager at Denny's not caring about his need to rest, to have a real life. Since the restaurant opened twenty-four hours, he scheduled him to work through the upcoming Summer Solstice and through the weekends. On this Saturday night, he worked until eleven o'clock. The next day, he started work at seven o'clock in the morning. All this for $4.25 an hour.

Preparation

August Before 12th Grade, Age 17

Keenan finally had a Friday off from working at Jeffrey's. Brother and I hadn't hung out since I had moved into the Barner's house over eight months ago.

Sister Barner got off from work later than she expected. When Day-ja's mom dropped me off at Aunt Denise's house after 6:30, I arrived over an hour after our 5:30 meeting time even though the sun remained positioned high in the sky.

In Denise's apartment, my aunt and her boyfriend Ben laid on the couch watching a horror film and eating cranberry sauce to create an extra bloody effect.

I looked around for Brother.

"Girl, Keenan left. A couple of his friends came over—that tall black one and that chubby guy. He waited for a little while, but Keenan said he had to go."

"Really?" I stamped my foot in frustration. "Man, I thought he'd wait."

"Girl, please. Where were you anyway?"

I rubbed my stomach to ease its sudden throb.

"What's wrong with your stomach?"

"Nothing, I think I might have eaten the wrong thing."

"Do you know where they went?" I asked, thinking that I could walk or get Ben to drop me off.

"I think they were talking about going to smoke at his friend's on 28th."

I rolled my eyes. I wasn't going to walk eight blocks so I could watch them smoke. I sat on the love seat next to the couch and watched *Freddy's Dead* with them while I let my stomach settle.

Around 7:30, Ben and Denise decided to head out for dessert at Jeffrey's—the only all-night diner in town. I told them I'd stay, that I'd call Harold to come keep me company. I wasn't in the mood for crowds.

Harold wasn't sure if he could come. So I watched Yo! MTV Raps and ended up falling asleep.

Elimination

August Before 12th Grade, Age 17

A knock on Denise's door had awakened me. When I opened it, Gant handed me a ring of keys with a tiny soccer ball attached. At the sight of him, I let the keys jangle to the floor. Red and wet, Gant's empty hands trembled. His unfocused eyes unloaded too much meaning. Gamaliel stood behind him, keeping his gaze toward the carpet. Both of them shook like they had just come out of the cold. I finally faced the ache, the pang in my belly; I ran and screamed.

At some point I realized Harold held me as Gant recounted the details without crying, without breathing.

I writhed away from Harold and went to my aunt's room. Grabbing the blanket from her bed, I pushed on my white round-toe flats and left.

Even though I hadn't been there, I could envision my brother and Redhead acting out their fates like characters on the silver screen. The last time Redhead pulled out his gun, Keenan knocked the boy out in the liquor store. Brother told him at their last confrontation: "If you show a gun, be prepared to use it."

When Redhead took out his gun this time, it had to be different. Redhead had something to prove. Keenan pulled out his own gun this time. Gant told me that they both pointed their guns at one another. Both aimed to prove their manhood. Keenan's friends watched. Redhead's friends watched. Both dedicated themselves to this performance. Each fired a shot. Each hit his target.

As sirens raged down the street, I walked steadily. Streetlights flickered on one by one along my path.

At 9:01 p.m., evening began fading to darkness. The sun had finally dipped below the horizon, leaving a long Arctic twilight. When the sky transitioned from gold to rose to purple. We lost nearly six minutes of daylight each day, summer dying as quickly as it had exploded into life.

The wind blew in between my braids and played with the hem of my shirt. My shadow followed me along the sidewalk. Just walking, until the distance disappeared, and I rounded the corner onto 28th.

Sirens flashed as I walked. A crowd had gathered into a tight fist of onlookers. People filled the street and the sidewalks. I reached the crowd. Using my arm and side body to cut through the gathering, I pushed past a man wearing pajama bottoms and a wife beater. Then I bumped into a woman in a plush baby green robe. Finally I saw police officers who tried to talk to me, attempting to stop me from getting to Keenan. I didn't slow down to hear their words. I heard someone yell out to them.

"She's his sister."

The blue-gray twilight made everything feel suspended between worlds.

Keenan's body and Redhead's body still lay on the pavement. One officer grabbed my arm. I started to jerk away before I looked at him. I recognized Tim, Keenan's elementary friend. I threatened him with my pointed finger. He nodded and stepped back as I bent down to Brother. Placing the blanket on the street beside me, I scooped my hands underneath his lifeless arms. I hugged him because I couldn't remember the last time that I had hugged Keenan. Since I was eleven years old, I had known he'd break. He carried that bucket of shit down the stairs because I hadn't stood up for him that day. I let him bear that load, and I didn't say anything.

I witnessed my brother slain on the concrete. He had thrown his life away. I loved him enough to give my own life for him. But he didn't think I cared—that no one cared if he lived or died. I never told him I loved him. Mama didn't hug him, and I didn't hug him. The only human contact he had was when he played soccer or fought. He couldn't rid himself of the need to prove his worth. The plague of anger and abandonment caused his demise. He had shown me how much he loved me so many times, but why the fuck couldn't I reciprocate? So many ideas focused clearly in my mind at that moment. Funny that I didn't know any of this the day before when I had my brother, when he still had his life.

My hands scraped the asphalt as I cradled my brother's back and the curve of his ribs. His blood slipped against my cheek. Rocking him in my arms for a few minutes as I felt the warmth leave his body. Finally, I had to let go of him slowly, gently. I spread the blanket over his body.

The Blame

August Before 12th Grade, Age 17

In the coroner's office, we sat waiting for something. I sat across the room from my parents, three rows of chairs. Aunt Denise sat next to Mama and Midway Man. My cousins Angel and Lamar sat on either side of me. Angel held my hand. Lamar crossed his arms with eyes narrowed toward the floor.

A white couple sat between me and my parents—probably Redhead's parents—but we did not speak. No one spoke for a long time. What do you say when all has been lost?

As we waited, Mama became one contracted painful muscle. Her moans came again and again like spasms as she leaned against Midway Man. At some point, he spoke.

"I don't understand what Keenan was thinking. It doesn't make sense," he said under his breath, head shaking and looking in the empty space in front of him. We all heard him.

I clenched my fists and ground my teeth. Lamar's grip tightened on the handles of his chair. Angel sat dazed, registering no reaction. "It wasn't Keenan's fault," I said loud enough for everyone to hear me.

Midway Man responded in an even tone. "Tawny, I know you're upset, but—"

My brother's life had been sacrificed for their ignorance. I stood up, and moved a step forward. I swung my hands into fists and shook my whole body. "It was your fault—both of you."

"Tawny, Tawny," Midway Man said, calm and in control.

I stood right in front of them. "You just want to blame Keenan but it's not his fault. It's yours," I stood over them, wagging my finger at them. "You took his choices away. He was a soccer star. That was the only thing he wanted, and you took that away."

Midway Man stood up. I stiffened, refusing to back down. The skin below his eye began to tremble.

"Get angry, good. You should be ashamed of yourself. You liar. You told him you'd pay for him to go to the National Soccer Tournament."

His angry tremble ceased and a stunned look began in his eyes and traveled into his skin as the blood drained.

"Didn't think all those broken promises mattered. Is that how your parents did you? They didn't care what you wanted? Didn't think you deserved to go after your goals? Is that why you did this to him?"

Mama bent over and slammed her fist into the table as she stood. "No! No! This is not our fault. We taught him—"

"You taught him to give up on himself, to hate himself, to fight physically instead of with his mind." I threw the words at her. The acid in my voice strained my throat.

"You disrespectful bitch," she said, the words hissed out of her, the last bit of fight inside of her clawing at me.

Her words no longer hurt me as I pointed at myself. "This bitch was the only person that was worth respecting. That's why I left. I left because you left first. See, that taught me a lot. I learned that I was the only one that I could depend on, that I had to do what was best for me. Be damned to whoever didn't agree with me. I learned to walk alone!"

Then I turned my pointed finger at her. "You made me the bitch that I am."

A wail started deep within my mother and her face crumpled. A sorrowful lament propelled out of her to the sky or to her god or to somebody. But it wasn't to me or for me. Midway Man opened his arms and she stumbled to him, falling on his chest. I left them there.

Learning to Heal

September of 12th Grade, Age 17

Now that Brother died, I knew that the legacy work rested on me, weighed on me. The teachers and my parents wanted me to talk to a counselor. I knew that they couldn't help me.

The morning after the funeral, I began waking at five in the morning to read and pray. At Sister Barner's house each day, I'd begin with verses and short chapters from the Bible. Then I sought the turn: the new mindset, the new moves to make.

So much family and purity at the church, but too much bound up in the legacy of slavery. In our church, the big mural of a white Jesus greeted us every time we entered the new sanctuary.

Reflecting on Pastor's myth about a perfect marriage of 50 years, I wondered how we could heal if we couldn't tell the truth about relationships. How would I be able to make better decisions unless I got to the root cause? I told myself, *wasn't no counselor going to do that for me. I was the only someone who could do that for me.*

I decided to search bookstores for answers—for books with answers.

Last Church

September of Twelfth Grade, Age 17

On the fourth Sunday since Keenan's funeral, Sister Barner woke me up, real gentle. Gray morning light already filled the room. At 7 a.m., the sun had been up for over an hour.

She almost whispered my name, "Tawny, it's time."

The furnishings surrounded me quietly, stable and ever present — too normal when the world had shifted. Death didn't stop the world when Keenan's ever presence ceased.

The school bell still rang on weekdays and the Sundays kept coming, cycling through the weeks. My chest of drawers, the closet full of clothes, and the queen size bed felt lucky a few months ago. Now, I felt cruel and selfish for being here, and Keenan being…

I followed the steps for getting ready: showering, brushing teeth, and dressing in my church clothes.

Outside of First Church, the cold air bit through my clothes. Even the cold couldn't convince me to go inside.

The last time I'd been inside the church was the funeral itself, three weeks ago. I'd tried to attend service the very next Sunday, but couldn't make my body cross the threshold.

The second Sunday, I got dressed and rode in the car with Sister Barner. The panic attack came: crying, hyperventilating. I dwelled just outside of the double doors—just outside.

The prophecy predicting my death haunted me, yet fate snatched my brother's life away instead. Was this justice?

I heard myself screaming, "You all wanted me to die!"

Sister Barner held me and rocked me like a baby girl. She whispered a correction, "From the prophecy, some people thought it was you who would pass away!"

Where is my life? What is happening? How could I go back to church knowing that the devil dealt more harshly with church kids?

After a while, Denise came. She walked me to the car, rubbing my back.

On the third Sunday, Aunt Denise met us in the church parking lot. Sister Barner had called ahead. Every time I got close to the church, my mind spun into question after question: Who else would die? Did the prophecy cause Keenan's death or did his choices? Would someone else have died if Keenan had just waited for me instead of kicking it with friends? What if I had stayed at home instead of moving away?

This morning—the fourth Sunday—I called Aunt Denise before we even left. When Sister Barner drove Day-ja and me to First Church, Auntie waited for me in the parking lot. She understood.

If I went inside, I could trigger the rest of the curse. If I went inside, something would get hold of me. Kids who didn't go to church didn't get burned like us—like Keenan.

Brother's Dreams

October of Twelfth Grade, Age 17

In my nightmares, I could see Brother. I couldn't speak to him. He wouldn't speak to me. Keenan would be living a normal life, running on a soccer field with the sun shining exclusively on him.

In another dream, he sat in the cafeteria laughing with a group of faceless friends. A smile lit up his face, and something unknown highlighted his presence in the room. He only acknowledged me with a side glance.

I felt a churning, a sinking inside of the pit of my stomach. What if Keenan was mad at me? Did he blame me?

A deep sob awakened me. I could not breathe in the whole breath. Tears overflowed my eyes. Ready to take action, I jumped out of bed. Instinctively, I wanted to rush to Keenan. I could apologize and find out what I had done. My bare feet slipped on the thick carpet. The sensation made me grit my teeth and brought me back. Then I remembered. Keenan was gone, and I did not have any more opportunities to mend it. Keenan was murdered. Keenan was dead. Keenan was gone.

PART IV:
RECONCILIATION

Literacy for Healing

October of 12th Grade, Age 17

In my book quest, I started with *Breaking the Chains of Psychological Slavery* by Dr. Na'im Akbar. I kept reading every morning and journaling every night, whenever a thought demanded release.

Dr. Akbar wrote about personal inferiority. Many black people carry negative views of their natural hair, straightening it or adding extensions to enhance what God gave us naturally. As children, we internalize this as not being as good as white people. This has its roots in slavery, Dr. Akbar explained, because internalized racism means we've bought into the idea of our lower status. When we accept our lower status, it becomes easier to enslave us, easier to continue oppressing us.

I wore braided hair extensions most of the time. Teenage black girls didn't wear their natural hair. We slicked back our hair into buns, and added socks or hair to make it look bigger. A lot of us straightened our hair. If we wore braids, it had extra hair added.

Journal Entry, October 3rd

When I look in the mirror, what do I see? Do I alter myself to look less black? Dr. Akbar says when we don't have pride in ourselves, we carry shame instead. We help dehumanize ourselves by adopting practices that elevate white people and oppress us.

Dr. Akbar wrote that our diminished view of ourselves translates into the type of jobs we choose. Most black people remain in low level positions or continue to work as laborers because we don't view ourselves as managers and entrepreneurs. We're more comfortable being led than being the leader.

I thought of Midway Man starting his business, watching it fail. Did he get any help improving it? Did he even know any other black business owners? Did he internalize that failure as proof he wasn't meant to succeed?

Journal Entry, October 8th

Dr. Akbar says slavery taught us we couldn't provide for ourselves, couldn't protect what was ours. That mentality gets passed down like DNA. Midway Man tried to break that chain, but maybe he didn't have the tools. Maybe nobody taught him how.

Keenan tried so hard to protect me. But as a child, he shouldn't have to carry that weight. Is that another chain—putting grown-up burdens on kids?

The most pivotal information in *Breaking the Chains* focused on the family. Slavery destroyed black families because it didn't allow marriage, love, or unity. Masters reinforced this by not allowing men to protect their women or provide for them. Men were viewed as studs and workhorses—not husbands or fathers.

I thought of our biological father, Pete. He had a bunch of children scattered around. I didn't know any of them, but Keenan remembered some. All through my life, I'd been connecting the psychological effects of slavery to our problems without even knowing what I was doing.

When slave owners sold family members away from one another, black people remained divided and alone. Bearing children benefitted slave owners. Babies became equated with burdens for many black women: losing a baby to infant mortality, losing their own lives during childbirth, or losing the child to profit the owner in a sale.

Journal Entry, October 12th

I thought of Mama. Keenan and I became her burden. For so many years, I thought we caused the problems that made Mama mad. But Dr. Akbar says that's part of the mental chains. Viewing children as burdens instead of blessings comes from slavery. Did Mama's mama feel that way about her? Did it go back even further?

Pete left us like we were nothing, as if family was disposable. That's a chain too—men not knowing how to stay, not knowing how to be fathers. The system broke that in many of them generations ago.

I read, and I wrote.

Journal Entry, October 15th
What part of the rock is our heart? What part of the rock protects our heart? I don't even know what I'm asking, but the question won't leave me alone.

Sometimes I jotted whimsical words that didn't make sense even to me. Other days, I'd be contemplative, wrestling with bigger questions.

Journal Entry, October 19th
What does a kid owe the world? When do the roles change from us taking to us giving? I mean real giving, not just the joy from baby dribble or the precious newborn finger grip.

Many of us give sooner—helping a younger brother, sister, or other citizen of the world. Keenan gave when he took beatings meant for both of us. But when is it our turn, our duty, to make our contribution? And when does it end?

Should we be giving to the last breath, or only a limited time-span in our lives? Do we retire from giving like we do a job or a career?

It's different for everyone. That rent comes due for some of us much sooner than for others. Keenan's rent came due too early. Way too early.

Daily journal writing gave me a place to untangle all the anger. I had a place to put all the wounds pulsing inside of me: out of my head and onto the page. The questions I couldn't ask anyone else, I could ask the blank page. The rage I couldn't scream aloud, I could bleed onto paper.

Journal Entry, October 24th

Dr. Akbar says we need to develop Knowledge of Self by learning about ourselves, our history, and becoming aware of these generational and systematic attacks against us. We need celebrations that value black culture by commemorating our leaders, our traditions, and our accomplishments. That's how we build self-worth and gain the desire to improve ourselves.

But what if you don't know your traditions? What if your leaders are gone? What if your family broke so many generations ago that you don't even know what wholeness looks like?

Can you celebrate what you've never had?

What could I do with all this new knowledge? Dr. Akbar offered answers on how to remove the chains on our minds, but reading about freedom and living it were two different things. Maybe I did need to see a counselor eventually.

Still, I kept reading. I kept writing. Because somewhere between the pages of his book and the pages of my journal, I was beginning to understand that Keenan's death wasn't random violence. It was another link in a chain that stretched back centuries, young black men viewed as threats, as disposable, as workhorses instead of sons and brothers.

And maybe understanding the psychological remnants of slavery was the first step toward breaking it.

When the Test is Error Proof

November of 12th Grade, Age 17

A month later, I sat squatting above a toilet, while Harold waited outside the door. We met at his place again. Evening darkness pressed against the small bathroom window. Looking down between my legs, I caught it mid-stream on a plastic stick. The urine gathered, working its magic on the cotton padding, soaking into the indicator and deciding my fortune.

Minutes clicked by on the clock as I prayed for negative results, foolishly asking God's protection from motherhood, a consequence that I could have prevented. After a while, we saw the blue forming a plus sign—positive.

I looked at Harold. I could feel his excitement, but I could also see his boxer shorts where his belt and jeans ought to have been.

I needed to split our lives apart—permanently. The EPT test guaranteed 99% accuracy.

Looking in his eyes, I knew that he wouldn't breathe the breaths of ardor needed to support a child, consistently, reliably.

If I had this baby, I would become my mother—a teenage mom. But I wasn't her. I left home to be better, do better than live in poverty.

I thought of Eve who would become a mother any day. I thought I was so different from both of them.

"I've got to go," I announced.

I shifted my weight to another foot.

"No—what do you mean?" His eyes swam with confusion.

"It's just not working."

Saddened by the sound of the truth, Harold reached out to hug me. His voice broke, head shaking.

"Naw, you can't—we're about to have a baby."

Recoiling, I pushed away from him. I couldn't stand how those words floated in the air.

"That test isn't 100%!" I reminded him. I wished that I could be that 1% of error.

The feelings between him and me were too deep to wade through. I began to move away from him. He caught up, holding my shoulder.

"Wait. Where are you going?"

I sank my back into the wall, giving him a moment to accept the situation.

"Where?" Harold searched my eyes.

I shrugged my shoulders.

"I don't know. I have to go."

Killing Myself

November of 12th Grade, Age 17

Giving up my future child for adoption wasn't a real option for me. That required bravery and courage—qualities that I didn't have. I knew that I wouldn't be able to go through with it.

One look into his or her eyes and I'd want to keep my child forever. With just one look, I'd be trapped and the baby would be trapped, looping around and circling the drain in the same cycle that had ruined my great grandmother, my grandma, and my mother. Because I'd be looking in my own eyes—like when my mother looks at me, she is looking at herself. I knew that we were all the same now.

Caught up in my ego, I had made myself believe that I was better than all of my predecessors. I had convinced myself that the love between a boy and a girl in 1994 was so different from the love between my mother and father in 1976. My rebellion had set the mold and my mother's refusal to communicate had solidified it. Her anger had become my anger. I had become her; we had always been the same.

I lay on the table at the clinic.

To make sure that I wouldn't change my mind, I requested to be put under. I lay on the table and felt my energy drop and blackness take over.

I awakened from my dream crying, "No, no."

Dreams seem so real when they are happening. The terror of an abortion stopped me. On the news, the bombings of abortion clinics warned me. Was it fair to run from your destiny? If my mother was a teen mom, and her mother was a teen mom, and her mother before her was a teen mom... What did I expect myself to be?

Fully awake, I rubbed my stomach that still held my baby inside of it.

What would I do with a child? I didn't know, but I couldn't have an abortion. I wouldn't be able to go through with it.

Another Phone Call

January of 12th Grade, Age 18

The weak afternoon sun filtered through Sister Barner's sheer curtains. Almost 2:30 p.m., but Fairbanks only got about five hours of daylight in January. We lived in perpetual twilight—not quite day, not quite night, just this blue-gray existence that made us forget what real sunshine felt like.

Sister Barner sat across from me in her armchair, patient but persistent. She could wait all day for me to speak, but she wasn't letting me leave without saying something real.

"Tawny, you need to talk to your mama."

I shook my head, eyes still on my hands. *Here we go again.* I'd been staying with the Barners for over a year now, and Sister Barner had been circling this conversation for weeks. From the TV downstairs, *Martin* played. Cole, Gina, Tommy, and Pam solving their problems with laughter. Everything wrapped up in thirty minutes. Real life didn't work like that.

"I don't want to talk to her," I said quietly.

"That doesn't matter." Sister Barner leaned forward, and the movement shadowed her face. "What really matters is that she's your mom. She's always gonna be your mother, and that's not changing."

I stared at her for several seconds, refusing to budge.

She doesn't understand, I thought. *She doesn't know about the locked doors, the wine bottles lined up like soldiers, the way Mama would push me away when I reached for a hug. She doesn't know how it feels to live without Keenan.*

Keenan. Even thinking his name made my chest tighten. More than four months since the funeral, since I'd stood on 28th Street with a blanket, since I'd felt his blood soak through my shirt.

Sister Barner didn't give up. Instead she continued, "And you're gonna be a mom one day, and you've got to bridge the gap."

The words hung in the air between us. The light shifted again as clouds moved outside, and suddenly the room felt darker, more intimate. Sister Barner stood and crossed to the table, where the phone sat in its cradle. She picked it up, the spiral cord stretching across the space between us like a lifeline—or a noose.

"So we're going to call her, and I'll be here for the first couple of minutes. But I'm gonna leave so you can say what you need to say." Sister Barner's eyes locked onto mine, unblinking. "But you're not gonna hang up. You're not gonna curse. You're becoming a young woman, and you need to handle yourself like one by talking out disagreements. Because silence is not going to get you heard, and it's not going to change anything."

She held the phone steady with an unwavering hand. The lamp behind her created a halo effect, making her seem almost biblical. I thought about cycles and generations, about sins visited upon children and children's children.

I blinked a few times and looked away from her. Finally, I took the phone from her hands.

"There's still a chance," Sister Barner said softly, "for you to mend your relationship. Make better decisions and have a brighter future."

With this last sentence, I dialed the number to where I used to live—not out of respect. Because she was right. How would things be different if I started and continued the same way? Even though I hadn't been talking to Mama, I ended up being like her. How could I break the chains, if I couldn't talk through issues? So I agreed to have a discussion for my baby and for the future generations.

My fingers found the numbers without thinking—I'd dialed them so many times before. The phone rang once, twice.

"Hello?" Mama's voice, cautious.

"It's me." My voice came out smaller than I intended.

Sister Barner gave me an encouraging nod and retreated to the kitchen, leaving me alone with the phone and the fading light.

"Tawny." Mama exhaled my name like a prayer. In the background, I could hear music—old Negro spirituals, moaning and such.

"Sister Barner said I should call." I twisted the phone cord around my finger, watching the tip turn purple from lost circulation.

Silence stretched between us. Through the phone, I heard her moving, the music getting softer, a door closing. She was going to her room, the same room she'd locked herself in all those years ago, closing the same door I'd knocked on begging her to come out.

"I'm glad you did," she finally said.

Are you? I wanted to ask. *Are you really?* But I'd promised Sister Barner I wouldn't start a fight.

I told her why I didn't want to talk to her, and why I didn't feel like it made any difference anyway. Mama listened without much to say in response. I spoke about how she treated me when I was a kid. Her rejection made it so special to feel some love from a boy—even if it wasn't really love. Surprisingly, she listened.

"Mama, I..." I stopped. Outside, the sky had deepened to indigo. "I need to tell you something."

"What is it, baby?"

The word "baby" almost undid me. When was the last time she'd called me that? I pressed my free hand against my stomach— not even round yet from the secret growing inside. I hadn't told anyone except Sister Barner, not Day-ja and not the school counselor who kept asking me how I was "coping with my loss."

"I've been thinking about Keenan." My voice cracked on his name.

I heard her breath catch, that sharp inhale of pain. "Me too."

"He died angry, Mama. He died thinking nobody cared."

"I know." Her voice was so quiet I had to press the phone harder against my ear. "I know. I carry that every day."

"Do you know why he was angry?" I asked. Inside myself, I wanted to tell her about how she raged at him, how she pushed him away when he only wanted hugs, but I let the question hang.

"I…" Mama started, then stopped. "We did the best we could."

"Your best wasn't enough!" The words exploded out of me before I could stop them. Sister Barner appeared in the kitchen doorway, her silhouette backlit by the bright chandelier. She gave me a warning look, and I took a breath. "I'm sorry. I didn't mean to yell."

"No," Mama said, and I heard something shift in her voice. "You're right. We weren't enough."

The admission stunned me into silence. From the radio downstairs, I could hear Day-ja playing Boyz II Men singing something slow and sad.

"When I was your age," Mama said slowly, "I already had you and Keenan. I was trying to figure out how to be an adult when I was still a kid myself."

I thought about that—Mama at seventeen, eighteen, with two babies. Grandma Mabel mourning Uncle Raynell—another casualty of gun violence. The cycles Grandma had warned about, the ones nobody seemed able to break.

"I pushed you away," I said quietly, "because you pushed me away first."

"I know." Her voice broke. "I didn't know how to show love the way you needed it. My father didn't show love to me either."

Through the window, I watched a car's headlights sweep across the darkening street. I felt caught between those two worlds—the warm light of possibility and the encroaching darkness of history repeating itself.

"I'm reading this book," I said, "I got it from the library. *Breaking the Chains*. It's about what slavery did to Black families, how we're still carrying that trauma. How we learned not to show love because love meant loss. How we learned to survive but forgot how to thrive."

"Tawny," Mama's voice was thick with tears now. "I'm sorry. I'm so sorry."

"Before you left us, you were gone—locked in your room whenever we were home. You drank. You got high. You left us long before you went to California."

The words poured out now, unstoppable. Sister Barner had returned to the kitchen, giving me privacy. The living room felt cavernous—just me and the phone and the truth finally spoken aloud.

I heard Mama crying openly now, those same sobs I'd heard through the bathroom door as a little girl.

Silence stretched between us again, but this time it felt different. Not empty, but full—heavy with all the unspoken truths finally given voice.

"There's something else," I said, my hand moving to my stomach again. "Something I need to tell you."

"What is it?"

The streetlight outside flickered, casting strange shadows across the wall.

"I'm pregnant."

The words hung in the air like smoke. Through the phone, I heard Mama's sharp intake of breath.

"Oh, Tawny."

"I know what you're thinking," I said quickly. "I know I'm just like you. A pregnant teenager, just like you were. The cycle continues, just like Grandma warned."

"No," Mama said firmly. "No. You're not like me."

"How am I different? I'm making the same mistakes."

"Because you're an excellent student." Mama's voice grew stronger. "Because you're not dropping out or giving up. Because you called me. Because you're trying to understand it, to break it."

I hadn't thought about it that way. I hadn't noticed the ways I was choosing differently.

"I'm scared, Mama."

Inside Sister Barner's house, the lamp burned warm and steady. At 3:45 p.m. the crushing January darkness would last until mid-morning tomorrow. Outside darkness held dominion, but in here light persisted.

"Okay," I said. "We can try."

Talking to Daddy

April of 12th Grade, Age 18

I didn't know the last time I spoke to Midway Man. Sister Barner had been pushing me to contact him since February.

I'd finally agreed to meet him at the shop, but only with Day-ja as my escape route. My best friend drove me and waited in the car because I didn't know how this would go—if he'd be angry or defensive. Maybe I would get upset and want to leave.

My belly was just starting to show that undeniable curve that made strangers' eyes linger.

At nearly 4 p.m., the spring afternoon shined aggressively. In Fairbanks, the spring melt uncovers everything hidden all winter. The yard around the shop looked like a disaster of mud, trash, and shattered dreams.

I heard Midway Man in the garage, working underneath a car propped up on jack stands. He didn't come out when I entered, just kept busy with wrenches and oil.

I looked intently at his boots and his legs in coveralls. After a minute of waiting I yelled, "Daddy!" His bunny boots bounced, a ripple running through him from surprise. I hadn't called him that since before I moved. With that, he slid out from beneath the car.

"Tawny." He wiped his hands on a rag, still not meeting my eyes. "Thanks for coming."

The garage smelled like it always did—diesel and metal and broken promises.

"I wanted to talk to you," I said, "about Keenan."

His shoulders tensed, but he looked at me straight in the eyes. "Okay! Let's talk about whatever you want."

I moved closer, stepping into his line of sight. The afternoon light coming through the garage door cast long shadows, making everything seem larger and more ominous.

"You told him you'd have the money," I said. "For the soccer tournament. You promised him."

"I thought I would," Midway Man said defensively. "Business was supposed to pick up. That big contract was supposed to come through."

"But it didn't. And instead of telling Keenan the truth, instead of helping him find another way, you just… Did you think he'd forget about it?"

"It wasn't like that."

"It seems like you didn't care enough to make it happen. The other kids' parents made it happen. They found the money, they drove to fundraisers, they showed up. But you didn't."

Midway Man held up his hands. "Listen! Don't tell me I don't care. When we met, I chose you and Keenan. You chose me too—right away."

He slumped against the workbench, suddenly looking decades older. I turned away from the pain in his eyes.

"My commitment to be your father has never wavered. Your mother was drinking and smoking and depressed. She wasn't treating you guys right. I told her to leave to get her act together. I stayed because I am your father—not your biological father. I'm your natural father. God gave both of you to me. I haven't been perfect. But I've been here."

I crossed my arms and frowned, staring at the concrete.

Damon continued. "I've been okay taking the blame. The blame is safe with me. I won't take it and throw it back in your face. I won't leave because you put the blame on me."

This declaration proved to be a bitter truth. The one who stays often feels the brunt of the blame. This man tried to build something and failed, tried to be something and fell short. We hadn't been fair or treated him right. Even his decision to take over this business was about staying close to the family.

All these years, I wasn't mad at Pete. I hadn't nicknamed Mama. But Daddy bore it all ⸱ not because he caused all the issues. It's because he carried all the responsibility by staying.

He was my Daddy, my parent as much as Mama, much more than Pete. I wasn't the only one who cursed out their father ⸱ biological or otherwise. But I had something extra to add to my spewed hatred: the fact that he was not my real dad.

I was a kid, a cruel and stupid kid. Despite all that, he was still here being my dad — not perfect, not magical. He was just an imperfect human who gave unconditional love, and he still offered it.

I felt wetness on my chin. Daddy pulled me to him, and we hugged. I finally let go of the sob inside of my chest, crowding my throat.

"I'm sorry," he said. "I'm sorry, Tawny. No matter what, I'm fated to be your father despite rebellion, despite rejection, and even through your clinginess as a little girl."

We laughed. He held me away from him to look at me. "Through the years, we been up and sometimes we been down. But you and me, we gonna be. We gonna be."

Finding Peace Together

April of 12th Grade, Age 18

A week later, I met both of my parents. Sister Barner had arranged this meeting, insisting we needed to talk together, not just separately. She sat in the corner, not participating but present, a reminder that we were being held accountable.

Mama, Daddy, and I sat together in the windowless church basement after Wednesday night service. I still didn't attend service, just sat in the car doing homework until Bible Study ended. I allowed myself this one time to enter, bravery granted by my growing belly. Now the baby stuck out the size of a soccer ball.

The basement smelled like pine cleaner. Folding tables lined up along the wall with stacks of chairs in one of the corners. Sister Barner sat in an empty corner—close enough to hear but far enough to give us space. Our brown skin had a greenish tint from the overhead fixtures.

"Maybe you shouldn't go away to college. Stay here," Daddy said.

"We'll help with the baby," Mama told me.

They meant well, but I still couldn't trust them—couldn't leave my seed in their hands. I needed a new place. After mailing my application in February, the largest HBCU chose me. Clark Atlanta University offered me a tuition scholarship. I accepted. Soon, the baby-to-be and I would be on our way to

Atlanta, Georgia. I read that brochure, and I knew I had found the right place. I already lived the motto of Clark Atlanta University: "Find a Way or Make One."

"I don't know how to start," Mama said, looking between Daddy and me.

"Start with the truth," Sister Barner called from her corner.

Mama took a breath. "The truth is, I was angry. Angry at Pete for leaving, angry at myself for choosing him, angry at the world for being so hard. And I took that anger out on you kids. On Damon. On everyone."

"I was scared, too!" Daddy added. "Scared of failing, scared of not being enough. And when you're scared, you make stupid decisions. You focus on the wrong things."

I listened to them, these two broken people who'd somehow found each other and somehow broken each other further in the finding. Above us, I could hear footsteps from the sanctuary—church members cleaning up, locking doors. The rhythm of routine, of people trying to maintain order in a chaotic world.

"I need you both to understand something," I said. "I'm going to be a mother. And I'm terrified. But I'm not going to let that terror turn into anger or neglect. I'm not going to push my baby away when it needs me. I'm not going to make promises I can't keep."

"We can help you," Mama said eagerly. "You don't have to do this alone."

"I know I don't have to. But I also know I can't depend on you the way I did when I was a kid. We need to build something new—a new relationship."

The three of us sat, trying to imagine what that something new might look like. It wouldn't erase the past. But maybe, just maybe, it could be enough to stop the cycle for which Grandma Mabel had warned.

"I forgive you," I said finally. "For me. For this baby. I forgive you, but I won't forget. And I won't let history repeat itself. And I'm sorry for disrespecting both of you. I'm sorry."

Mama reached for my hand, and I let her take it. Daddy placed his hand on top of ours—rough, scarred, still smelling of motor oil. We sat there, connected in that basement, broken people trying to make something whole.

We climbed the stairs, and they insisted on helping me, but I felt vigorous and strong despite my expanding stomach. As we exited the church, the spring sun still shone bright after eight. All that light left nowhere to hide. Maybe that was what we needed. Maybe we'd been hiding in darkness too long, and it was time to uncover everything so we could finally heal.

"We're going to be okay," Mama whispered.

I didn't know if that was true. But I knew we were going to try. And sometimes, trying is enough to break a cycle. Sometimes trying is where transformation begins.

A Promising Future

May of 12th Grade, Age 18

Over the next month, I focused on completing plans for how the baby and I would make it in Atlanta. I'd insisted on meeting Mama and Daddy at Jeffrey's every Sunday after they came from church, meeting on neutral ground at a public place. At today's meeting, I finally had something to show them.

Inside my backpack, I held a stack of letters, a mix of large white envelopes and business envelopes. Each envelope held papers offering new opportunities, award letters, and a new path forward.

The air hung thick with the smell of deep fryer oil and burnt coffee, that particular scent that clings to your clothes long after you leave.

This was our fourth Sunday meeting at Jeffrey's. The first three had been awkward, careful. Today would be different.

The two of them sat on one side of the booth, and I sat across from them. I had worried that my stomach may not fit. At five months along, my stomach had grown the size of a basketball.

The vinyl felt cold through my jeans. In Fairbanks, May still remembers winter. Outside, the sun would stay up until nearly midnight, but it would dip into the 40s at night and early morning.

This meeting started with the envelopes. As soon as I pulled the pile out of my backpack, a couple of nosy church folk passed our table—Sister Henderson in her purple outfit that she'd probably worn to see *Waiting to Exhale* at the Goldstream 6, and Brother Morris with his jheri curl still going strong despite it being 1995. Their eyes lingered on the letters.

Daddy finally spoke, his calloused fingers drumming against the table's surface. "What you got there, Tawny?"

Mama just stared expectantly.

For the first time, I revealed what I had been doing. Following the advice from Ms. Neil all those years ago, I collected the winnings from my studying and my fervor to learn. Altogether, I applied for over forty scholarships and got accepted to six colleges. I had won over $30,000 from local organizations— Delta Sigma Theta, Alpha Kappa Alpha, Jack and Jill, Southside Fairbanks Neighborhood Council, Tutoring for Educational Excellence, the Fairbanks Black Teachers Association, and much more.

The letters fanned across the table between us, white against the brown-speckled Formica. I could feel the baby moving inside me, a flutter like butterfly wings, like it knew something important was happening.

"Whoa, girl! You're something else!" Daddy said it with a wide smile and twinkling eyes that caught the dim light.

Mama shook her head in disbelief, her hand flying to her mouth. "I can't believe it!" Her voice cracked on the last word.

"Been proving 'em wrong since 1977!" I proclaimed in the voice of an old man with the confidence of a rock and roll star.

Daddy burst out laughing, the sound bright and sharp. Mama hit the table, making the silverware jump and the coffee slosh in their cups. Daddy slapped his knee. I got into a giggling spell that made my stomach hurt and my eyes water. I laughed at Daddy's high-pitched chuckle. Mama laughed at my low belly trickle of guffaws. We couldn't stop cracking up at Mama's wide-open-mouth exclamation of joy.

For that moment in the worn-down restaurant—we forgot. We forgot that Keenan's funeral had been nine months ago. We forgot about the permanent empty space at our family table. We forgot that my pregnancy had happened in the aftermath of his death, another consequence of my grief and rebellion. For two minutes, we just celebrated good news, the way we might have been if everything hadn't gone so wrong.

My Graduation

May of 12th Grade, Age 18

On the day of graduation, I had what I wanted: an academic scholarship and choices. At six a.m., the sun already shone crisp and clear, the kind of brightness that makes everything look sharp-edged and new.

Before I left the Barner house that morning, a sudden realization bloomed inside of me. An internal wall of emotion burst. I sobbed and cried and wailed, pressing my face into the pillow that smelled like Tide detergent and safety. This time I cried release tears, freedom tears, tears for the girl I'd been. The baby kicked, and I put my hand on my belly.

Through the window, I could see Fairbanks waking up. Under the endless spring sky lay my scrappy interior town. Fairbanks taught me to survive, to endure, to know that spring always comes, even after the longest winter.

In the North Pole High School gymnasium, I walked across the stage like a normal kid. Some corny song played through the sound system, although it should've been Boyz II Men's "End of the Road."

Before, I had wanted to stand out. I had thought of turning a flip or taking a slow boastful stride. With my due date a couple months away, I waddled across the stage.

After everything I had been through, I no longer wanted to be any different than the rest of the kids. Day-ja walked the stage right before me.

As Principal McKenzie handed me my diploma, I could see Mama, Daddy, and Sister Barner on their feet—the few Black people in that space, easily visible in the crowd. Mama held up her arms. Daddy clapped. Ms. Barner wiped her eyes.

I walked off that stage carrying my diploma, carrying my baby, carrying the weight of everyone who said I couldn't and the strength of everyone who believed I could.

Epilogue: The Cycle

I've been running from it for a long time. I was very young when I realized it threatened to take me over, killing my dreams, hurting my self-esteem, squeezing my joy like an orange sacrificed for the purpose of juice.

It's The Cycle. It has taken away the progress of innumerable generations of my family. It's giving birth to a child as a teenager. It's the inability to choose the right father for our children and passing the frustration of being alone as a legacy. It's giving hateful love while believing we're providing tough love. It's the loss of educational fulfillment, opportunity flushing itself down the toilet. It's giving more than we can afford to give, disguising ourselves for others.

The Cycle was set in place by the slave masters and reset by each succeeding owner. When our destiny became our own—to reckon with or wreck—we've often followed suit. Pushing reset, we bequeathed the cycle to another generation whenever given a choice or a chance to do otherwise.

As an African-American woman caught in The Cycle, there are many demands: raising Black children on our own and navigating the white-dominated world with our dark skin and our Black hair. We try to prove ourselves to ourselves all the time. We want to prove that we're just as pretty as other women or just as strong as any man since we've been placed in the man's role.

We're pitted against each other by our mothers and by our men. Navigating and balancing the burden, we force ourselves to be more than we were given, passed on, or handed. So our skin becomes thick as our waists and our mouths grow too big. We become each other's worst nightmare, so that one day we'll be able to deal full force with the brunt of the world against us.

Most of us don't make it. We stop caring and become expanded and puffed beyond our original forms by swallowing wave after wave of hurt as if it is normal and acceptable in the making of a Black woman in a corner of the world.

You'll find my kind embittered and depressed in the margins of America, unable to express the angst, unwilling to put in the work of unbending our backs under the weight of self-hatred. Although I've seen her in the mirror, I've also fought her on the playground and competed against her for a man I could barely stomach. I've been her best friend, then dumped her because she was too honest or upfront or emotionally charged. So I know that we're out there looking for a solution—a way to express and finally stop the ache of looking for love that never works or functions the way we think it should.